The River Knows Its Own

The River Knows
Its Own

Jay Lake

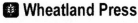 **Wheatland Press**
http://www.wheatlandpress.com

📖 Wheatland Press

http://www.wheatlandpress.com
P. O. Box 1818
Wilsonville, OR 97070

Library of Congress Cataloging-in-Publication data is available upon request.
ISBN 978-0-9755903-9-3
Printed in the United States of America
Cover photo by Joseph E. Lake. Jr..
Interior by Deborah Layne

Contents

Introduction

When you turn the page, in a minute or two, you're going on a journey. Jay Lake is your guide, and although there may be a few alarming moments, you're in good hands.

Jay lives in Portland, in the heart of the Pacific Northwest. He's not a native. He's not really *from* anywhere (he was born in Taiwan, raised in West Africa, went to school in Texas), but that's where he lives now, and where he's found his heart and his home.

Like any good guide, he knows this country like the back of his hand, like the inside of his own head—but knowing Jay, that includes some very strange territory. Because it's not just what's on the surface that he'll show you. It's what's underneath—what makes the trains run and people tick and the wind howl through the pines—and what's beneath *that* as well.

He's got a gift for details, for the texture of the forest and its creatures, as well as the grit of an old, neon-lined street and its denizens. He can hear the past singing in the steel lines of the railroads that run as straight and true as the river curves beside them, and he'll share those songs, if you care to listen.

Jay Lake

Jay's stories are deceptive. Clear, crisp prose that draws you immediately into the ebb and flow of ordinary lives. He has the skill to weave this word-spell so effortlessly that you don't realize, until it's too late to turn back, that he's led you into an unfamiliar landscape. Sometimes frightening, sometimes magic. Never ordinary.

Salmon can talk. Dragons soar over the Columbia. Rosebushes hide more than their roots, and brick walls may stalk your dreams.

It's not your mother's Oregon.

When you book a tour with Mr. Lake, you're in for an adventure.

Ellen Klages
San Francisco
January, 2006

Adagio for Flames and Jealousy

MAHONEY WAS HALF A DAY ahead of the fire. If he was lucky.

It had already taken forty thousand acres, including solid old growth timber. It had taken two fire trucks, a water trailer, and the lives of three college students working the summer fire lines for money and excitement. It was heading for Ranceville, an Oregon Cascades town populated only by ghosts and elk for most of a century. And one crazy old man nobody ever thought about.

Except Mahoney. Who'd run away at age eleven from his grandfather, swearing that he'd never return. Granddaddy had been living up there since God was a boy. School, then Vietnam, then thirty years of working in the Blue Mountains and eastern Cascades had kept Mahoney's promise for him.

"Weather ain't breaking before next week, Pog" he told his Australian shepherd.

Sitting on his raunchy old blanket, Pog had his nose out the window on the passenger side sniffing the breeze that reeked of engine oil and the death of forests. And whatever else the wind had to say to dogs. Pog thumped his tail once at the mention of his name, but didn't turn.

Mahoney kept the old yellow Dodge Power Wagon on the trail by brute force. Utility crews came up here once or twice a decade to service the high tension lines. Their chainsaws kept the big trees out of the track. Even so, the truck had to bull through thickets he couldn't have walked through without a machete. Sharp, bitter-scented greenery pulped under the tires sent the truck sliding toward the edge at every bend in the trail.

He swung the truck round a fractured outcropping to a steep vista of Douglas firs and lodgepole pines footed a thousand feet below by steep walls of glacial gravel and the icy white thread of a stream. Ranceville was nose-ahead of the Dodge, or would have been if the old truck could have flown. Mahoney figured on another hour of fighting his way along the last several miles of trail to reach the rotten mine head. Not to mention the town which spread below it like so many broken match boxes.

He sighed as something thumped too loud and hard beneath his feet. Half a day, God, Mahoney thought. Give me twelve more hours.

✢

May the second, 1863.

Jones and the second Chinee cook froze last month, but there weren't no more snow for a while after that and the diggings resumed. The first cook wailed and banged on pans until Mister Rance and I was forced to beat him to quiet him down.

We found a good seam of silver and lead here. All the white men drew straws for to see who would go down into the valley to fetch mule teams to haul out the goods. We all reckoned the man who went would have the emptiest pockets despite everybody's braying resolve to Christian sharing. As Mister Rance said silver fresh from the ground would tempt Christ himself to set aside a private share.

Mahoney took the short straw. He was in a temper ever since the Finney brothers signed up for soldiers. I reckon he misses Little Finney more than a man ought to miss another man. Mahoney offered me 8 oz. of coarse gold to switch with him, but I told him to go to the devil. After that he offered to send me to the devil in his place.

☦

It took two more hours to reach Ranceville, at the cost of both of Mahoney's spare tires and a broken shock. Mahoney would ordinarily have abandoned the Dodge and walked, but he needed the truck to get back out ahead of the fire. Of course, he was out of tires.

The old mine head — tower and winch above the number one adit — still stood. It was the last one, built in 1892 after the spur line was brought in. Rebuilt from the 1881 fire, Ranceville had already by then been sliding into mossy obscurity even though the seam would remain rich for two decades more.

Even now, perhaps, if anyone cared to work it.

The rotten wood served no more than barn owls now, but it still marked the town. Just past it on the downhill side were the chutes leading to the ruins of the stamp mill.

Then the town itself, buildings clustered along the hillside beyond the mine head like goslings after their mother. The water-stressed wood was long gone to mold, moss and dry rot, but many of the structures held their shape due to some alchemy of forest and flower. Roofs once dark with shingles were shaggy green brows frowning atop bow-walled buildings. Huckleberry and bear grass and a dozen other mountain flowers spread a knee-high carpet in Ranceville's street, their only traffic bees and butterflies.

Jay Lake

Mahoney pumped the old Dodge to a shuddering, squealing stop. His hands gripped the wheel tight, knuckles pale as the bear grass blooms, though Pog was already out the window in a joyous dance of release from the tyranny of seat and windshield. Other than the pinging of the engine and the dog's rustling and yips, it was quiet as a mineshaft here.

Only the smell of distant fire reminded Mahoney why he had come back.

He put his shoulder to the door and got out. Scanning the sky to the south, Mahoney could see the darkening smoke. The whole sky had a weird pearly light, like the bruise-yellow that came before a tornado. The smell was everywhere— that cindery, papery scent of woody distress. By tonight there'd be all kinds of wildlife moving through here, heading north.

Mahoney looked around the town. It was full of buildings from a time when an ornate storefront was a thing of pride. Between some of them were shacks, jack-built from timber country poverty and tall heartwood but outlasting their proud neighbors.

Ranceville Feed and Dry Goods. Silverlode Bank and Assay. Woolrich's Stable. Finney's Stable. Best Shanghai Laundry. The jail, though they'd never had a sheriff. First Methodist. Second Methodist facing it from across the street, near identical buildings separated by forty feet of right-of-way and some long forgotten middle-class schism.

Mahoney could name every building in town, and most of their histories. He'd heard the old man tell their stories enough damned times.

His grandfather could be dead, but Mahoney didn't think so. He would have known, even after forty years apart. For one, the endless stream of minié balls, uniform buttons, mining tools and arrowheads that Mahoney seemed to find everywhere he went had not abated. Sendings, he'd always thought, from his grandfather.

4

The old man was a crazy bastard, and mean as snake to boot, but no one deserved to die in a fire. His father had when their trailer burned in Bend, when Mahoney was nine. He be damned if he'd let his grandfather go the same way. Mahoney looked around then cupped his hands to bellow, "Granddaddy! Where are you, old man?"

✝

October, 1865.

I reckon the War Between the States is truly over. Just as well we was here, bringing silver and lead out by the pot full. Little Finney come back from the First Oregon last week without his brother. The boy told us he lost Big Finney somewhere in the Idaho territory but he couldn't say how. Mahoney was near to a quivering pet over the boy but Little Finney wouldn't hardly say his name.

Mister Rance allowed as seeing as how Little Finney had served with the cavalry he could tend our horses and mules. He set Little Finney up in the hay barn and had one of the lamp boys sleep there nights to keep Little Finney from doing himself a harm.

Three days later me and Mahoney and that pack of Willamette Valley farm boys Mister Rance brought up was shoveling out mine carts on account of the tip was busted again. Little Finney come up to us wearing the rags of his Union blues with a musket in his hand what had a bayonet upon it. He commenced to hollering about Nez Perce and some corporal named Jewitt or Dewitt or some such.

Mahoney damn near cried for Little Finney right there. He tried to grab hold of that rifle and damn us if Little Finney didn't stab Mahoney in the thigh. Them farm boys piled on and there was a lot more hollering and blood. Mister Rance locked Little Finney in the strong room at the mine office. Said if he could eat the silver he could have it.

Day after Big Finney come up the road with a white mule and pack full of dried beans. We all lined up to cheer which he for sure didn't cotton to. After thumping and yelling a while he explained that Little Finney had been killed in the Powder River country.

Mahoney run off to the strong room like as if his shoes was on fire. He was shouting for Little Finney. Mister Rance followed him with the key and opened it up. Weren't nothing in there but silver and the payroll chests. Weren't no sign of Little Finney nowhere except them ugly stitches Redbone Swenson put in Mahoney's leg.

Dead and buried in the War that boy was but he come back to stay a few days and stab a man. Some ghost I told Mahoney. Solid as a ham. He just swore to gut the little renegade if they ever met again in this life or the next. I don't know if Mahoney was more mad that Little Finney came back or that he left again.

☦

Mahoney trudged around Ranceville for the better part of an an hour. Pog chased butterflies and sniffed at old deer scat and was as generally unhelpful as a dog ever could be.

There were no signs of life. The old hotel where Mahoney had lived when he was boy now had blackberries growing in the front door and a rhododendron blocking the back. The ground-floor windows were sealed with years' worth of moss and cobwebs.

No one had been in there for a long time.

He checked both stables, and any of the buildings with enough roof left on them to keep the rain out of a room or two.

No one.

No where.

Had the old man died? Granddaddy had always lied about his age, claiming to have lived through the Civil War, but he had to be closing in on a hundred by now. Mahoney remembered his grandfather as being incredibly old back in the 1950s, but as a child even his father had seemed old.

Mahoney finally found his way back out to the middle of the road. The reek of smoke was stronger, a tang that nipped at the linings of his nose.

"I know you're here," he said, this time in a quiet voice. "You're never going to die, not without me knowing it."

Something clattered, but when he turned to look it was just a hawk landing on the roof of the jail.

"You're part of me," Mahoney went on. His voice was a little stronger. "I'm part of you. I won't let you burn with this town."

"Ain't nothing in this life gonna burn for certain but a man's soul."

Mahoney turned. His grandfather sat on the hood of the Power Wagon. The rust-speckled yellow set off the old man's blue pea coat like a postmodern flower. He had a moth-eaten Union army forage cap pulled down to keep his face in shadow. One liver-spotted hand clutched a home-rolled cigarette. The butt shook, sending stuttering wisps of smoke into the afternoon air like a prophecy of the flames to come. The other hand held a rusted bayonet propped across his knees.

Get to it, Mahoney thought. "You've got to come with me, sir."

"Ain't never done nothing I had to yet. Why you reckon I'm a'starting now?"

"The fire, Grandpa. There's a big fire coming for you."

"I seen fire before. I'm still here."

"I can't let you die."

"You don't get it boy." The old man hawked and spat, or tried to, though as always he seemed dry as an old well. "I ain't never gonna die."

✿

August 11, 1881.

Nine of us still alive. Fire swept across the mountain and took Ranceville in its grip like the hand of angry Providence. Mister Rance slapped Thom Woolrich to the floor to stop him screaming prayers. It got so hot here in the strong room that the lead sheets by the wall came soft. We lost four to that heat. Riddley Horan. Bobby Spotsworth. Bobby's sister Floriana that Mahoney had been courting at Mister Rance's say-so. Shanghai Wong's oldest boy.

They are all stacked in the corner together now. I reckon they're waiting to be set free just like the rest of us.

When the fire came I figured to hide down the mine shaft. Mahoney and Mister Rance argued against it. They said the fire would take all the air from inside there and we'd die like mice in a barrel.

Big Finney got angry this morning. Said he heard his brother crying outside. Little Finney been dead a long time but Mahoney was all for tearing the door open and heading out into the heat. Shanghai Wong and me held him back. Mahoney didn't much like being handled by a Chinaman but I reckon it beat breathing fire.

The heat fell today. We're going to open the strong when we reckon it's sundown outside. Dusk is lucky maybe. A time when the world changes and the eye don't see everything that walks.

I'm scared of seeing Little Finney. The fire might of made him into something worse.

◆

Mahoney's grandfather hopped down off the hood of the truck. "Come on," he said, then limped away, back toward the mine head. Mahoney whistled for Pog and followed, smelling the distant fire. The smoke over the ridges to the south was darker. He could hear muted rumble, more of a feeling that a sound. And dusk was coming. A bad night to be out in the wilderness.

Eight hours, maybe. Figure four or five to get back down the trail he'd broken open on the way up. They weren't dead yet, as long as they got on the road soon and the tires held up. "Grandpa, we've got to get moving."

"I am moving. Got something to show you."

They trudged through knee-high grass and flowers, Pog yipping and dodging. As his grandfather approached the mine head, the dog hung back, whining. Mahoney paused and stared up at the building.

Was it different? He'd played there as a boy. Nothing to upset the dog.

The wood was the same white-streaked pitch stained with moss. The brambles at the base weren't much different from when he'd last been here forty years before. There was a bare spot at the office door, where hand-chiseled slabs had been laid as flagstones. They still had scorch marks from the 1881 fire.

Pog began to back away. His eyes rolled to whites, pleading with Mahoney. Don't, said the dog. Please, said the dog. Come back with me, said the dog.

The animal was too dumb— or trusting— to fear a forest fire, but whatever the old man had inside the mine head scared the dog to death.

"Truck, Pog," said Mahoney. The dog slunk away.

The old man stopped at the strong room door set into the base of the tower. "Did you set it?"

Mahoney was brought up short. "What?"

"The fire. Did you set the fire?"

"What? I..." He didn't even know what to say to his grandfather. Mahoney would no more set a forest fire than he would drink gasoline.

"Mister Rance set the 1881 fire. Or put Little Finney up to it, which amounted to the same thing. Too many Chinamen up here, too many Catholics. Even a family of coloreds come to town. He burned them out. He had in-su-rance to rebuild the mine." The old man drew that word out of his mouth like candy. "I figured maybe you set this one. Finish the job here at Ranceville." He looked around the long-dead town. "Ain't no in-su-rance this time."

Mahoney was familiar with his grandfather's fixation on Little Finney. He'd heard the same stories. Hundreds of times. "They were all crazy from lead poisoning from the mine."

"Like Hell." The old man tapped his chest. "I was there. I ain't crazy."

"You weren't *here* then, Grandpa. No one lives that long. You'd have to be over a hundred and fifty years old."

The old man tugged open the door to the mine office. In the distance, Pog howled.

✢

June the 22nd, 1898

Mister Rance tried to shoot Mahoney last night.

No, I need to tell it like it come to me.

I woke on account of fighting in the street outside the hotel. I buttoned on my trousers and stepped outside. Mahoney's half-breed woman was on the porch with Mahoney's baby boy. The both of them was crying up a storm. And there was Mahoney rolling around on the street all set on killing the man he was fighting. I saw that it was Little Finney. He didn't look a day older than he ever had. For a ghost that boy does get around.

Mister Rance came out of Missus Loftus's house with his pistol cocked and his trousers uncocked. He yelled once at Mahoney then loosed a shot. One of them hollered like a pig but I couldn't tell you which. I saw a knife flash in the moonlight then there was blood like a mountain stream. Little Finney staggered off into the dark dragging Mahoney with him. I was all set to go after and help but Mister Rance pointed that gun at me next.

You didn't see nothing he said walking to me. I seen nothing I told him. Mahoney's woman just kept crying.

I don't know for sure what I really saw but this morning Mahoney was gone like he hadn't been here for the last thirty five years. No one said his name. No one made to look for him. His room at the hotel was empty. Every bit of cleaned out. Even his woman was gone though Janie the bar girl had care of the baby. She wouldn't say nothing about it.

I tried to follow the blood outside but it had been swept over.

Tonight when we was drinking and playing draw poker Big Finney commenced to talking about the Nez Perce and their spirit doctors and what he saw down some caves in the Powder River country. He ain't never talked about that since he come back from the War. Me and Thom Woolrich and Shanghai Wong just played our cards and for once in our lives shut up. I can't rightly write down here what was said but it ain't no wonder both of them Finneys are crazy as hares whether they be dead or alive.

And now Little Finney finally took Mahoney with him down to whatever hell pit that boy's been living in all this time. Or maybe dying in. I miss Mahoney already. I hate that crazy old bird for all he said and done but we've been shitting in the same pit most of our life.

Hate or no hate, some men love their wives less than I love Mahoney. Reckon I'll raise his boy for him.

⊕

"Come on, boy." The old man stood in the open door of the strong room, half hidden from view.

"No, Granddaddy." Mahoney could hear the distant fire roaring to itself. "Enough of this shit. This town's cinders in a few hours. I've already stayed too long."

Pog howled in the distance.

"Get in here."

Mahoney could smell something rank from where he stood, forty feet from the office door. A grave smell, or a spoiled freezer. God only knew what the old man had dug up.

"All right." Humor him, Mahoney thought. Do this one last thing, whatever the hell it is, and get Granddaddy out of here. He trudged toward the door, but Pog slammed into the back of Mahoney's legs, forcing him to stumble.

"What's the matter with you, dog?" Mahoney shouted.

Pog stood his ground, whining, then snapped at Mahoney's leg.

Mahoney shook Pog off and turned back to face his grandfather. The old man was pointing his bayonet at the dog, trembling with anger. "Get away from that beast and get up here."

Pog sank his teeth into the leg of Mahoney's jeans and tried to pull him backward.

Damned dog's smarter than I am, Mahoney thought. He reached down to gently touch Pog's head, then looked his grandfather in the eye. He could swear there were sparks there under the bill of the forage cap, tiny gleams echoing the holocaust to come.

The old man was too crazy to live. At least, too crazy for Mahoney to help. He turned to walk back to the truck, the dog slinking beside him

"History, boy," yelled his grandfather. "This country was built on what we pulled out of these mountains. What we pulled out of the west. It's *your* history."

Mahoney turned and yelled back, "It's going to burn!"

"This town burned before, it'll burn again. You want to be part of history or not?"

Mahoney walked away from history, back to his truck. Pog was a dancing bundle of nerves and muscle and fear. The fire smell was strong now, cinders on the air. Daylight dying in the west was matched by a false, mottled sunrise to the south. The air was electric, like before a storm.

He had stayed too long.

Mahoney started the truck, cut a circle among the flowers, and headed back out of town. He looked up the hill to the mine head and the strong room as he passed. Flames shot out of the open door, a little fire set to welcome to large.

History was burning ahead of schedule.

Inside the fire Mahoney could see two men dancing in each other's arms. It was a waltz, something slow, adagio for flames and jealousy. One was old, the other lithe and youthful. Granddaddy and...who?

The name came to Mahoney with the certainty of a landslide.

Little Finney.

He'd never separate the lies from the truth, but Mahoney knew that was Little Finney his grandfather danced with. Just like he knew he'd never find another minié ball or uniform button in his life.

"They can both just damn well burn and like it," he told Pog, finding second gear through the tears stinging his eyes. "Hell's coming for them anyway."

Pog pushed something toward Mahoney, something that been lodged under the dog's blanket.

It was the old journal his grandfather used to read aloud from when Mahoney was a boy. The history of Ranceville and the Finneys and some other man named Mahoney, that Granddaddy always claimed was him though he'd never pass the book over for inspection.

Mahoney drove into the fire, praying to make it to the distant blacktop before the fire jumped that road and came roaring toward him. Ash rained on his windshield like snow. He propped the diary on the dash so he could keep one eye on his history while watching the trail in the distant glow of the coming flames.

✚

Iron Heaven

BILLY HIGHPOCKETS CAME TO Portland looking for his grandfather's heart. Grandfather Highpockets, that everyone called Wallace though his Christian name was Frederick Fontaine de Luray, had been a railroad man in the Willamette Valley back when that meant something, before Mr. Ford and his automobiles leveled a tarmac death sentence on that most American way of life.

Wallace had been lost in the flood of '48, backing an old Union Pacific 4-4-2 down the trackage on Water Avenue in a futile effort to save the engine and the dying operations of his Portland, Oregon City & Eugene line. Billy had heard from his Daddy the story about how those muddy brown waters swirled around the locomotive, and Wallace hung on to that whistle cord until the boiler blew.

The Portland old timers in the Brown Hound Lounge still talk about that whistle scream tearing up into the rain-ravaged sky, rocketing Wallace Highpockets' soul straight to the iron heaven reserved for railroad men.

"Wallace died with a secret," Billy's father told him one day over a greasy cheeseburger in a little diner near Pyramid Lake, Nevada, three days before Daddy blew his brains out with a .410 shotgun over a thirty-dollar debt and an angry hooker.

Billy, who was young and foolish then, leaned his cheek on the sticky red naugahyde of the booth and stared out the window at two vultures fighting over half a dead cat. The heat off the parking lot made everything shimmer like some gigantic dry water aquarium. "Yeah?"

Billy's father, whose Christian name was Lucius Modine Elroy on account of Granddaddy Highpockets' irritation at his own given name, leaned across the table and grabbed Billy's wrist. Billy stared at his Daddy, who had a string of cheese on the left side of his mouth and little fragments of mustard-smeared onion on his chin.

"You listen, son. Wallace was a railroad man through and through. He had steam in his veins and an iron coupler where his dick ought to been. But he had a secret that even he didn't know about, it was so fucking secret.

"Wallace was an iron god. Metal bent to his command, and the rails sang when he rode over 'em. Billy, you go and find my Daddy's heart there where he died, it'll like to be a lump of coal the size of your fist, that was his power. My gift to you, son." Billy's Daddy pushed a crumpled little sepia photograph across the table, of a man with the beard of a Biblical patriarch and eyes like a locomotive's firebox.

"If it's so fucking secret," Billy said, wishing Daddy hadn't eaten quite so many onions, "how come you know about it?"

"My momma told me," Lucius Modine Elroy Highpockets said. "And there was a woman with a smile on her face every day of her life. You know what *that* means."

Billy didn't want to know what *that* meant, not with respect to his late grandmother, but he took his Daddy's drift. He took the photo, too.

Of course, he was seventeen at the time and didn't know his ass from bitterroot tea, but we all grow older and dumber, until we understand just how stupid we once were.

Which is how Billy Highpockets came to Portland in the forty-second year of his life, driving a 1973 Dodge Power Wagon with eighteen dollars in his pocket, looking for a lump of coal lost in a flood half a century earlier.

Only his grandfather's ghost could tell him where it was.

†

Billy drove real slow down Southeast Water Avenue, watching where the old rails appeared and disappeared beneath the paving. There were warehouses on both sides, their freight car loading docks long since converted to trucking use, or simply places where haggard women with frosted blonde hair took smoke breaks from their shitty paperwork jobs inside.

"There ain't been no train down this road in thirty years," Billy told his rear view mirror.

Billy's rear view mirror was his oracle, on account of it always showed him where he was coming from, and when he squinted past it, he could generally see where he was going to. Plus it had a familiar face, and never deserted him.

For an oracle, it was mighty silent, but Billy had learned to read the signs of the world. Having a god for your grandfather does that to a man.

One of the world's signs stumbled out in front of his Power Wagon, screaming over its shoulder and waving what looked like a dead monkey.

Billy slammed on the brakes (the old Dodge never was one to give up forward momentum without a fight) and managed not to flatten the girl to the steel-boned pavement beneath his wheels. She turned and set her mangy old sock monkey on the rusty blue hood and stared through the window at him with eyes that burned green.

He got that familiar tunnel feeling, like falling into the dark, and his sign swallowed Billy up into her heart and spit him out again. They had told him it was 'petty mall ep'lepsy,' but Billy knew it was a little piece of his Grandfather Highpockets inside him that led him to those visions.

He yanked on the bent coat hanger that opened the door,

jumped out of the truck, and confronted his green-eyed muse.

"You seen my coal, lady?"

"What the hell you talking about?"

She couldn't have been more than sixteen years old. He was probably older than her Daddy, wherever that lying skunk was. Her Daddy had to be a lying skunk, because she wouldn't be on the street this young otherwise.

"You're my sign, the oracle sent me," Billy Highpockets said. "On account of I'm looking for Granddaddy's ghost to tell me where his heart went."

"Oh," she said, and smiled a tiny sweet smile like his grandmother. "Excuse me. For a minute, I thought you were crazy or something."

"No, ma'am," said Billy. He took off his Peterbilt cap and twisted it in his hands. "I ain't crazy, though most people think I am." Including the states of Nevada and California. "I just got a purpose, a mission in life."

Her smile blossomed into a laugh as she hugged her monkey. "You're on a mission from God, right?"

"More like a mission for *a* god," Billy mumbled. This was where the conversation usually got difficult, in his experience.

Instead the girl put the monkey's mouth to her ear, listened for a while, nodding a few times. "Come on, then," she finally said. "Park your rig. I got someone you need to meet."

Billy couldn't believe his luck. He got back in the Power Wagon, and muscled it over to the kerb near a banner reading 'OFFICE FURNITURE 80%.' When he got out, he couldn't see his sign, but then he spotted the monkey waggling from a gap in a chain-link fence.

Billy followed the monkey through to a little junkyard, not something you'd normally see in the middle of a city. The girl was stepping on to a burned-out electric rail car, still in the colors of Portland's Tri-Met system. Billy figured the rail car was a sign from

Grandfather Highpockets, and silently thanking his oracle, he followed her in.

Inside was shadow dark. A red velvet curtain out of an old theater hung about halfway down the car, and there was an altar in front of it (an old refrigerator lying on its back) with lots of stubby little candles, and some books and papers, and some bottles of gin and scotch laid out before it on their sides. The whole place smelled of scorched garlic and sesame oil.

The green-eyed girl knelt in front of the refrigerator and stabbed her hand toward a spot to her right, that Billy should come over. He walked past bundles of newspapers and a dressmaker's dummy to kneel next to his sign.

"Now what?" Billy whispered.

"You got to make an offering," she said, her breath tickling his ear.

Billy took his last five-dollar bill out of his pocket, smoothed it out, kissed it, then laid it next to a picture of the Dalai Lama. Nothing left now but ones, and ones ain't lucky because they're so lonely.

He knew from lonely.

Her lips brushed his ear, almost a kiss, then she took his hand and led him around one end of the refrigerator altar and through a rip in the red velvet curtain to a place that was part of Grandfather Highpockets' iron heaven.

The world was huge, behind the curtain, bigger than that Tri-Met car, bigger than the office furniture warehouse. It was the marshalling yard for every piece of rolling stock that ever hit the rails, on the long side of a century of decay. Switchmen's towers stood skeletal in the distance, white crows nesting in the exposed beams of their roofing. Huge stacks of bogies and couplers blocked the tracks near Billy and the girl, while burned-out diesels lay in a jumble ahead. It reeked of coal and rust and that dusty odor of things too long unused, along with more garlic and sesame oil.

Everything was lit by a brassy glow from some invisible sun that Billy thought must be the firebox of biggest steam locomotive ever imagined. Work gangs called in the distance, rhythmic chants punctuated by swinging hammers.

"We got to find China Po," whispered the girl after consulting her sock monkey again. Tugging on Billy's hand, she led him through the stacks of parts and equipment and, well, he had to admit it, junk.

Grandfather Highpockets' iron heaven was the junkyard of the world.

It seemed to take forever to follow her, but every time Billy looked over his shoulder, the velvet curtain was just a few steps behind. Like it was following him.

Then she pulled Billy around the corner of an old engine house. In the shelter of a steam locomotive cab, a little man crouched before a fire, stir frying something in a wok. Sesame oil, ginger and garlic drove the old iron smell from Billy's nose.

China Po was a Chinaman all right, in the loose blue trousers and coolie hat of them who had really built the western railroads. Though he was small, China Po's arms and bare back were roped with muscles that could only come from a lifetime of swinging a nine-pound hammer.

"China," said the girl, dropping Billy's hand to hug her monkey. "I brought you someone."

The little man waddled in a half circle, so he could see Billy's face and watch the fire at the same time. Billy gasped to meet his eyes — for a moment, he thought he saw Grandfather Highpockets glaring out from China Po's sunburned Asian face.

"White man come, white man go, steel last forever," said China Po. "What you want, neh?"

Billy pulled the sepia photo his Daddy gave him from his pocket, where it had nested with the lonely one dollar bills. "Here," he said, giving the picture to China Po. "I'm looking for him.

Grandfather Highpockets. I got to know where he left his heart."

China Po looked at the photo for a while, then studied Billy's face, then he looked at the photo some more. Without saying anything, he turned back to his wok, stirring the food within with a very long pair of chopsticks. He didn't give the photo back.

"You hungry?" he asked, still not looking at Billy.

The girl tugged his shoulder and shook her head, an emphatic no. Billy was hungry, Billy was *always* hungry, but he had to trust his guide. "No, thanks."

China Po tilted the wok and used the chopsticks to shovel his food into a cracked bowl, an old soup tureen from the days of Union Pacific passenger service. He set the bowl aside, reached into the fire beneath the wok, and raised up in his fist a burning lump of coal, which he stood to hold in front of Billy Highpockets.

"You want your grandfather's heart? This here, his heart burn for iron. You, little man, what you do for iron? What you do for your Grandfather?" China Po's eyes were blazing to match the coal in his hand, though his skin remained unburnt. "You want to be iron god? Take it!" He shoved the coal right into Billy's face. "Take it!"

This was it. What he'd been looking for since he'd realized life didn't have much else to offer him. The secret of Grandfather Highpockets' power, the burning heart of iron that had beat in the old man's chest.

The green-eyed girl took his hand, kissed his ear, pressed her body close to his. Why *had* his grandmother smiled every day of her life? Was she married to an iron god, or was it just a man she loved?

Billy reached out for the coal, felt the heat blistering the tips of his fingers.

He couldn't do it. Couldn't take the coal.

He wasn't his Grandfather Highpockets, fighting for steel and steam in an age of rubber and plastic.

He wasn't his Daddy, brains splattered across two lanes of Nevada blacktop in drunken regret over cheap love and cheaper money.

He was himself, whoever the hell that was.

"Keep it," Billy Highpockets finally told China Po. "It's yours. You earned it, tying down the west with steel ribbons."

China Po grinned then, and set the coal back on the fire. "You good man, Billy Highpockets. Good man be he own man, no iron gods no more."

Billy nodded, then slid his thirteen one-dollar bills from his pocket and offered them to China Po.

China Po smiled some more, took the money, and tucked it in the waistband of his trousers. "Got to buy more garlic soon," he said, then sat down to eat his cooking. "Don't grow so good here."

The green-eyed girl led Billy back to the velvet curtain, which was still just a few steps behind them. Back in the burned out Tri-Met car, she kissed him, this time on the cheek, then pressed something warm into his hand.

He looked down. It was a garlic bulb, fresh from China Po's wok, smelling of ginger and sesame, powdered black with coal dust.

"It never hurts to have a little piece of god inside you," she said, then pressed his hand to his mouth until Billy ate the garlic.

"You want to come with?" he said, chewing. It was spicy and hot and charcoal-tasting, and the juice ran down his throat like a volcano in reverse, but he swallowed the magic.

She glanced at the monkey, then shrugged. "Sure. Why not?"

☥

Billy Highpockets left Portland, following the Union Pacific route south into the Willamette Valley. His oracle smiled at him from the rear view mirror, her green eyes flashing in the sunlight.

He didn't have any money, he didn't know where he was going, but Billy knew his luck had finally changed.

Maybe I'd always been lucky, Billy thought, and just never knew it before. After all, his Christian name was just "Billy," and his grandfather *had* been an iron god.

He could get used to the taste of garlic in his mouth. He hoped the green-eyed girl liked it, too.

☥

Heading West

The Sikh

Roy woke with the feeling that something large had passed him by. Like a shark in muddy waters, or an earthquake barely noticed aboard a rocking boat.

What had it been?

Then a distant siren began to wail. It howled a song of police and panic and someone in danger or fear, before being joined in chorus by a second, then a third, then quickly a dozen or more until he could not separate the voices.

Roy rubbed the crust of sleep from his eyes, sighed as he glanced at the clock — 3:42 a.m — then stumbled to the window of his hotel room and twitched back the curtain. Outside, downtown Boston rose in skyscrapers and neoclassical rooflines and the jittery orange glare of streetlights, just like always.

But above, where there should have been vague orange-tinted clouds, or perhaps a scattering of stars faded to irrelevance by urban light pollution, was...

What?

Gold, thought Roy. Or maybe marble. If metal and stone were translucent. The night sky had turned to glittering ice, threaded with veins of bright metal and odd, dark pockets like the gaping mouths of mineshafts.

A trio of police cars sped by below, even as gunshots echoed, audible through the glass of the hotel window.

Things were different now. Probably forever.

Roy grabbed his cell phone, tried to dial home to Oregon. Nothing. No ring of the phone in the old Victorian in southeast Portland. No voicemail. No signal or system message at all.

No Ellen with her exasperated sighs and loving silences on the phone. No Adrien with her newly-lost tooth he hadn't yet seen.

Almost frantic, but still too tired to be fully afraid, Roy tried the hotel phone.

It was just as dead.

Quickly he gathered a few clothes into his soft-sided briefcase. To hell with his wheelie and his suits. He had to get home, now.

Φ

People already roamed the streets in packs. Back Bay yuppies mixed with winos from the grates behind the public library. Bulky figures in hooded sweatshirts flashed guns and knives, but the early shooting had died down.

Somehow, Roy flagged a cab, an old Chevy Caprice in some dark color indistinguishable by streetlight. He wasn't sure why the driver had stopped. Maybe it was because Roy was by himself.

"This is not good," the driver said. He was a turbaned Sikh with sad eyes and an accent who stared through the plexiglas partition at Roy, his face distorted by the air holes drilled into the translucent surface. The cab stank of incense and spiced food. "Where do you hope to go?"

"Logan," said Roy. Not that he really expected to find a flight, not with the sky in such disarray. But there was a chance there. Plus a hell of a lot of rental cars. "I have to get home to my family," he added.

"I live in Revere." The driver's eyes narrowed. "I go home to my family, too, drop you off on the way."

Roy glanced at the meter. The Sikh had not yet started it running. That always meant a rip-off. "How much?"

The Sikh shrugged. "For you, nothing. I fear for you that it will not matter." He turned around, dropped the cab into gear. "Nothing will matter the same way any more."

☩

They rocketed through early morning Boston, down alleys and side streets, the driver avoiding places where people might be congregating. The Sikh had tuned into WBUR, which carried an NPR feed of a very strained Carl Kasell. "No one's talking right now, officially, not NASA or NOAA or the weather service. But I have, uh, spoken with a meteorologist, that would be Lieutenant Commander Berman Hackney of the Naval Observatory here in Washington. Lieutenant Commander Hackney reports that the moon does not appear to have progressed in its orbit since the, uh, event that occurred around 3:39 in the morning, Washington time."

Holy crap, thought Roy, as the cab ran a red light. What did that mean? What about the sun?

They rolled on through the gold-tinged night, the glowing sky drawing his eye over and over despite his efforts not to look up.

It had to be the end of the world.

☩

They made it through the Ted Williams tunnel, but the ramp to Logan Airport was blocked by cops and National Guard troops. The Sikh shook his head and kept driving. Roy didn't say anything as they exited onto a surface street he didn't catch the name of. The Sikh was muttering in some Asian language, prayers or imprecations. According to the dashboard clock, it was almost five in the morning, but the night didn't seem to be going anywhere.

27

Finally the cab lurched to a halt on a block of dilapidated row houses. The Sikh turned and stared through the plexiglass again.

Roy stared back. Neither of them said anything for a few moments, as if they were about to fight, or kiss. Then the Sikh smiled.

"Take the cab," he said. "I think I will not be needing it anymore now that I am home."

"I..." Roy stopped.

"Do good, be well."

Then the driver was gone, trotting between parked cars and up a well-swept set of steps. Roy shrugged, got out of the back and went around to the driver's door and sat behind the wheel. After a moment's thought he found the driver's city atlas. He realized that he would be better off heading north than trying to get back across the harbor and through downtown.

After checking his route, Highway 60 towards Malden, Roy dropped the cab into gear and set out. He fiddled with the stereo until he found a station that was on the air with music instead of commentary or static, and settled in to some big band music.

He tried not to think about gas. One thing at a time.

✢

The Student

Late morning, such as it was under that dark, gold-veined sky, found Roy approaching Williamstown and the New York state line on Highway 2. Traffic had been weird, alternating hellishly heavy and nonexistent, but he hadn't run into any full-scale roadblocks. He figured those were only a matter of time.

The gas gauge was low, but Roy had resisted stopping so far. He'd reasoned that he'd run out of gas all the same no matter when he stopped, if it wasn't there to buy, so he'd kept going.

He saw a dark Texaco logo ahead, one of those tall highway

signs. He slowed even though it was unlit. Lights were on inside the convenience store building. He pulled over, easing the Caprice up to a pump under the canopy. The old cab rode rough and steered loose, but he was already a hundred and some odd miles closer to Oregon, so he wasn't complaining.

Only three thousand more to go.

Getting out, he saw that the orange numbers on the pumps were lit. They were working, then. He tugged out the hose, flipped down the license plate to reach the filler cap, jammed the handle into place, then went inside to negotiate.

There was no one behind the counter, though the register hummed slightly amidst its honor guard of Slim Jims and cigarette lighters. The store was aisles of candy and crackers and automotive supplies, with a little deli corner featuring a flyspecked donut case and a skinny girl smoking a cigarette. She looked like she was about fifteen, face pale as cheese. She wasn't wearing a Texaco uniform, just blue jeans and a flower print sleeveless blouse a size too small for her.

"Where's the gas guy?" Roy asked her from his position at the counter.

She blew smoke upward, then shrugged. "Said he'd be back in a minute."

"How long ago?"

Another shrug. "Couple of hours."

Roy stepped around the counter to look at the cash register. He knew there would be a control panel for the pumps there.

"It's that tan thing with the square buttons," she said, startling him.

"I'm not—" A thief, Roy had started to say, but he didn't see the point.

"Sure."

He turned his pump on and trudged back outside. The old Caprice would have a damned big tank, so he had time to stop and

29

try the payphones. Dead of course. No chance to call Ellen or Adrien.

After a while, the car had taken slightly over eighteen gallons of premium. He hung the pump handle back in place, wiped the spill off the bumper, then went back in to leave some cash by the register.

He really wasn't a thief. Not yet, at any rate.

The smoking girl was leaning against the counter when Roy pushed open the station doors. "You taking fares, cab man?"

He leaned past her, set twenty-five dollars next to the register and weighted the two bills down with the penny cup. "No fares," he said.

"It's a *cab*." She jabbed with the cigarette, a sunset-orange firefly streaking across his vision to point toward the car. "You should ought to take fares."

Something in her moved him — her lack of panic, perhaps, in the face of the end of the world. "No fares," he repeated, "but I'm headed west. I can give you a ride."

"I'd really like to reach Buffalo." She sounded wistful. "Mom and Dad, they'd need me...now."

"*Now*," he said by way of agreement. It was as good as word as any for what had befallen the world.

As they walked back out to the car, he added, "No smoking in the cab."

She smiled like a beatific junkie and tossed the butt over her shoulder.

☥

Shortly after they'd crossed into New York state, she leaned against the back seat and began talking through the plexiglass partition. Her voice was a mumble at first, and he had trouble catching the first few phrases. He felt like a priest at confessional.

"...then they told me to go to Hell, and I told them I was already living there. I...I...I was real mad, but they weren't really wrong."

She took a deep, shuddering breath, but Roy didn't think he was meant to respond. Not yet, any way.

"He brought me out here," she went on. "Another state, another life." Then she laughed, a short, bitter bark. "Well, *there*, Massachusetts. Where we just were. Six months later, he's in holding on statutory and dealing within a thousand feet of a school and the cops are crawling all over me for an accessory. I didn't know nothing, but they never believe that shit. Not from the girlfriend."

Another shuddering breath.

"So I rolled, told them what they wanted to hear. It was lies, they knew it, I knew it, *he* knew it, but what the fuck was I going to do? No way Mom and Dad were going to take me back.

"Sick part was, I even got paid off by the district attorney's office. Some War on Drugs thing. Tell lies, make money. Kind of like politics, I guess.

"I'd had enough of that shit, his shit, my shit. They got this cow college out here, community college for the farm kids and stuff, with ag courses and dental hygienist and whatever. I been taking health tech, studying up to do lab work. God forbid I ever get anywhere in this life, maybe someday I'll go to med school. Be a doctor. Save people from themselves."

Her voice lapsed then, trailing off into another series of those shuddering breaths that eventually collapsed into a sigh.

Would Adrien be like this someday?

Roy watched a couple of more miles roll on the odometer. They were winding through hilly country now, farmhouses and little town centers gleaming under the gold-shot sky. A few people out on the road, not many. He was glad he'd stayed off the Interstates.

As for the girl, he wasn't sure what to say, but it seemed to be his turn. "You really want to help people, doctor's not bad."

"Doctor." She laid her cheek on the seat back, her head pressed up against the plexi. "Shit dream for a shit town girl like me."

That touched him. "No dream is shit," he said. "Especially not one about helping people."

"Pretty fucking deep for a cabbie."

"I'm not—" He stopped, again.

What was he? A marketing director, helping sell people software they didn't need. *Now*, as she'd called the new order of things, probably meant no more marketing directors.

He was just a guy who wanted to get home, a guy behind the wheel of a cab. That was kind of a neat idea, he decided.

"Not what?" she finally asked.

"Not one to piss on your dreams," he said.

After a while, he tried the cell phone again, but it was still unable to pick up a signal.

☥

Somewhere close to Albany, as Roy was looking for routes north around the metro area, she shouted for him to stop. "Let me out here!"

He pulled to the curb in a squeal of brakes. They were in a small town business district. "This isn't Buffalo," he told her.

"I *know*." She smiled. "Just wait. Give me fifteen minutes, and trust me."

Why the hell not, he thought? He nodded and killed the engine. She jumped out of the back of the cab, ran across the street and into a hardware store that had its lights on.

A few minutes later, she came out with an armload of cylinders—spray cans? he wondered—followed by a skinny kid in a red vest, carrying another armload. They both knelt down outside his door, and she got to work with the spray cans.

Roy couldn't decide whether to be angry or amused, but when he peered up through the windshield at the permanent, gold-veined twilight, he decided it didn't matter.

After a while she tapped on the glass, yelling, "Come look!"

He got out, pushed the driver door shut with his fingertips.

The cab company's name on the door had been painted over with a white cloud, a rather inexpertly rendered unicorn curled up on it. The words 'DREAMS FOR HIRE' curlicued above the image in silver and blue. The whole effect was reminiscent of one of those late 70's custom vans, only not as tasteful.

"Thanks," he said, suddenly wishing he smoked.

Her smile was shy. "I been taking art."

The kid in the red vest giggled. "Good luck, you guys," he said, then gathered up the paint cans and went back inside his store.

⚜

The Cop

Roy got stopped at his first real roadblock in Rome, Ohio, a day later. Day, at least, in the sense that more than twenty-four hours had passed by the Caprice's dash clock. He'd bought gas twice more, slept at an Interstate rest stop, and tried every payphone he saw.

There were two police cruisers pulled across the road nose-to-nose, though they didn't have their lights on. A cop with a flashlight and a shotgun stood in front of the cars, while a few more people stood in shadows off the road, smoking cigarettes.

Roy didn't like the look of it, but he didn't see much choice except to pull over. He cranked down the driver's window as the old cab eased to a stop.

The cop checked his front plate with the flashlight, then walked around to the driver's side window. All Roy could see was the glare of the bulb.

"Where you from, son?" The cop sounded like he was from a lot further south than Rome, Ohio.

Roy tried for polite. "Oregon, sir."

"This here's Massachusetts plates on this car."

"That's right, sir."

"Strange times we're living in."

"Strange times," Roy agreed.

The cop studied him for a minute, then lowered the flashlight. Roy looked back, really seeing the man for the first time by the golden glow of the sky. This was an old cop, with a hangdog face dripping wrinkles and skin that would have been chapped and red in a normal light.

It looked like the face of a man who might understand.

"I'm just trying to go home," Roy said.

"Ain't we all?" The cop leaned on the window frame, folding his arms into his elbows, flashlight wavering in his grip. "Governor's declared a state of emergency, son. Can't rightly be out on the Ohio roads right now except on official business."

Inspiration struck, or at least fizzled, in Roy. He smiled. "I *am* on official business."

"Official for who?"

He felt like an idiot even as he said it. "Dreams. I'm carrying dreams through the night."

The cop started laughing, stepped back from the door to double over, so that smokers in the shadows all turned to look. Roy sat, hands on the wheel, and wondered how dumb he really was.

After a couple of minutes, the cop got his breath back. He turned to shout into the shadows, "I'll ride with him to the county line, Brattain," then walked around the Caprice and got in the passenger side. "Best line I've heard since this stuff started," he said to Roy. "Just pull her around the tail of that right hand car. I'll see you through."

Roy dropped the cab into gear and did what he was told.

✿

The cop bought them donuts in downtown Rome, such as that was. The whole village would have fit into the block Roy lived on in Portland. He didn't much care for donuts in general, but he ate his glazed yeast in silence.

"I served in Vietnam, real early," the cop told him. "There was still some old French officers around then. They liked to sit in those little open-air bars down by the river drinking cognac with the hookers and talking about Dien Bien Phu. Must have brought their own cognac, 'cause I never got nothing there but local beer. Tiger Piss, we called it, for the angry tiger on the label."

Roy licked glaze off his fingers and kept driving.

"Anyway, to hear them tell it, Dien Bien Phu was the end of civilization. Everything since was just the corpse twitching. They were already dead, they figured, those old Frogs, and were just making the most of every day they woke up with breath in their bodies."

Was it the cab, Roy wondered? No one had ever felt the need to confess to him before. He'd liked things better that way.

The old cop continued. "So I figure these last couple of days, what with the sun gone from the sky, this is the end of civilization. The real end. We don't have no battle to look back on. The Earth just stopped turning. You know, over in Asia, they got sunlight all the time now. Whole countries are cooking. It's just chilly here. And there's weather coming like nobody's ever seen before."

Roy hadn't really thought of it that way, but the cop had a point. Other than the Earth stopping in place, the rest of physics seemed to still be working. Atmospheric dynamics would be catching up soon.

The cop cleared his throat. "So, dream boy, what do you think it all means?"

"I don't know," Roy said slowly. "It means a lot of things. It means I'm a long way from home. It means you're thinking back on the past like it was real all over again. It means this student I gave a ride to back in Massachusetts won't ever get to be a doctor. It means anything and everything." He thought for a moment. What did it mean to Ellen and Adrien? Or him? "Maybe it means we're supposed to consider our lives and what we stand for."

The cop chuckled. "Maybe it means you're a damned liar, or at least your car door is."

"There is that."

⊕

The cop, who was actually a deputy sheriff named Jasper Greggs, rode with him all the way to the Indiana state line. His badge got Roy past at least a dozen roadblocks. Along the way they talked about kids and families and arthritis and basketball and everything but the permanent night sky above them.

At the state line, Roy pulled over. "You sure you want to get out?"

Greggs rubbed his thumb across the badge in his hand. "Reckon I'm like those old Frogs drinking down by the Mekong. This here's my pond. I'm sworn to the State of Ohio and the people of Adams County. Indiana can take care of itself, and so can you, son."

"It's been a pleasure, Deputy Greggs," said Roy, offering his hand.

They shook, then the old cop got out and started walking east.

⊕

The River Knows Its Own

The Preacher

Indiana was a hassle, but Illinois was a nightmare. Chicago burned, the fire visible from fifty miles south, and what radio reports he could pick up said there was looting. The only thing that saved Roy was the coming of the storms Greggs had spoken of. Hail like bullets swept a lot of people off the roads. He was reduced to begging for gas at a truck stop, then driving away with the hose still in his tank when shooting started there. He didn't even get a chance to try to call home.

Time spent studying a map persuaded Roy to head for the Quad Cities. There were only so many bridges across the Mississippi, and he was hoping for a crossing that might be open, with minimal official scrutiny. He might have to abandon the cab, but at least he'd be halfway home.

Almost halfway, at any rate.

Somewhere in Whiteside County, Illinois, not too far east of Moline, his luck ran out. A thin man with wild eyes and pale hair, visible in stuttering strokes of lightning, dashed in front of the cab waving a spear. Roy locked up the brakes trying not to hit him and lurched into a ditch along Highway 2. As he tried to fight his way free of the seatbelt, the thin man began banging on the driver's side window.

"Get the hell away from my car!" Roy shouted.

The attacker shouted back, his voice lost in the rolls of thunder. He banged on the window again, this time with the butt of his spear. It seemed to be made of a shovel handle topped with a pair of flattened-out malt liquor tall boy cans bound by baling wire.

Roy got himself untangled from the belt and slammed the door open into the other man's knees. The stranger tumbled over backward on the gravel, then popped up again spear in hand as Roy got out to face him.

"The Lord's after you!" shouted the attacker. "Better take cover!"

37

"*You're* after me," Roy shouted back. His temper, frayed by two days of driving and very little sleep, snapped. He yanked the spear out of the man's hands and clubbed him over the head with it. When the attacker dropped to his knees moaning, Roy swung it again into his temple. The other man dropped all the way to the ground.

Roy got back into the Caprice as a new wave of hail arrived. He needed to be out of the ditch before he bogged his tires. He dropped the gearshift into reverse and eased ever so gently on the accelerator. The old car lurched, one wheel whining with a familiar spinning noise, but the other bit and the cab jumped backward onto the road.

By the time he got sorted out which direction he needed to be going, the hail was drumming on the roof and windshield like a rain of gravel. Roy glanced through the gleaming dark at his former assailant. "Oh, hell," he told the cab. "Help those who can't help themselves. Don't be a dead Frog. Believe in dreams."

It was the end of the world. What was he supposed to do?

He hopped out again and dragged the crazy man into the back of the cab, leaving the spear behind. Still unconscious, his erstwhile assailant was already bleeding from dozens of hail cuts, and bruised in twice as many more places. "Moron," muttered Roy, and got back in front.

✟

"You can't escape Him," whispered the crazy man in the back seat, his lips pressed against the plexiglass divider.

Roy yelped. He'd been focusing on how to get through Moline in the increasingly thick hail. The cab's windshield was cracking, and what he could see of the hood had developed a sort of inverse acne. He was damned glad he wasn't outside, and suddenly damned sorry the crazy man was inside.

"What I can't escape, shithead," Roy said, "is this hail and the fact that the Mississippi's out there somewhere."

"One of His biggest rivers." The guy sounded as proud as if he'd laid the Mississippi course himself.

Roy grunted. He hunched over the wheel, peering through the pale curtains of hail. "You can get out any time now," he finally said.

"No. I've got witnessing business further west. The Lord moves in mysterious ways. You're just His latest movement."

Roy glanced over his shoulder. The preacher's face was pressed against the plexi, flattening it so that he looked like someone found dead after three days face-down on a kitchen floor. His breath fogged the partition.

"Look," Roy said. "It's a cab. I'll give you a ride. But none of that spear shit, don't be preaching to me, and quit drooling on the back of my seat."

The preacher pushed himself away from the divider and settled in, looking almost normal for a moment, except for the wild glint in his eyes that was a maybe-mirror of the lightning outside. Thin as he was, the preacher was a big guy, dark skinned with a nose that wouldn't quit and hair that looked the color of ash in what little light Roy could see by.

"I'm sorry I hit you so hard," Roy added.

"No you're not, son." The preacher smiled. "You needed to do that. Turn left here, by the way."

"What?" Without really thinking it through, Roy swung the wheel left. Odd, the preacher calling him son. The guy was younger than Roy by at least a decade.

"You don't want the Interstate 74 bridge," said the preacher. "They're arresting people up there."

"You from here?"

"No, but I pay attention."

Like hell, Roy thought, recalling the spear, but he kept his mouth shut. It was the first time he'd been glad of the plexiglass divider.

"I'd try the railroad bridge," the preacher said after a few blocks. "It's at about 30th Street. Watch the signs."

Roy watched the signs. It felt like he'd been doing nothing but watching signs for three days now.

☥

The hail slacked off as they reached the rail yards, changing to sheets of rain. Roy was glad to be shut of worrying about his windshield.

The rail yards were unfenced, so he found a culvert spanning the overflowing drainage ditch dividing the rail yards from 5th Avenue, the street he was now on. Roy stopped the car and thought it over for a moment.

"If they're arresting people on the Interstate," he said, "they're going to take a dim view of me driving over the railroad bridge."

The preacher leaned back up against the plexiglass. "Whole world's a dim view now, son, except in the light of God's eyes. I need to get over the river, too. This here's the best way to go."

"God told you that?"

The preacher's voice had an infuriating smugness. "Of course."

Roy sighed again. It made a certain kind of sense. He'd already gotten a lot further than he honestly would have expected to. He killed the headlights and put the cab into low gear before turning into the rail yards.

The old Caprice bounced over the track, making for the long graded ramp that led up to the railroad bridge. Except when riven in stark blue-white by lightning strikes, his goal was barely visible gleaming in stray light from buildings along the riverfront. Roy concentrated on his driving. The railroad ties tended to yank the cab in unexpected directions.

"Behold," the preacher intoned from his perch in the back seat, "tomorrow about this time I will cause it to rain a very grievous hail, such as hath not been in Egypt since the foundation thereof even until now."

Despite himself, Roy grinned. This guy wouldn't give up. "Grievous rain is everywhere."

"Continuous daylight in Egypt right now, from what I heard on the radio." The preacher laughed, sharp and bitter. "Cooking their narrow brown asses. I think I'll take the rain. It is written that the Lord shall open unto thee His good treasure, the heaven to give the rain unto thy land in His season, and to bless all the work of thine hand."

The old cab began to strain up the grade, wheels slipping on the mixed hail and gravel that lay on the ties. So far Roy hadn't seen any evidence of a roadblock. "Could your Lord bring the sunlight back?"

"And He made darkness pavilions round about him, dark waters, and thick clouds of the skies."

"You got that right."

They crested onto the bridge deck just as bright white lights came on, shining into Roy's eyes to the flicker of red, blue and yellow flashers.

✟

Roy and the preacher were out of the cab, soaking wet as they leaned against the roof with their arms and legs spread wide. A cop—Roy wasn't sure what kind of cop exactly, but he seemed to be a railroad employee—patted down first him, then the preacher while two others had pistols out.

Roy didn't feel tempted to move.

"You're crazy to try this bridge," said one of the cops with a weapon drawn. They'd been waiting back on the bridge deck, hidden from Roy's approach. "What if a train caught you?"

"Ain't been a train in two days," the preacher said. "Ain't going to be no trains no more."

"You don't know that."

Roy heard the waver in the cop's voice. "We were just trying to get over the river," he said, hoping to speak to the man's uncertainty. "I've got to get home to Oregon, to my family."

"This is a stupid place to try it, friend."

"They're arresting on the Interstate bridges," the preacher said. "And the angel of the Lord said unto Manoah, though thou detain me, I will not eat of thy bread."

Lightning struck nearby, the thunder rolling over them all like a slap. Roy became very conscious of the fact that he was standing on an iron bridge in the worst storm in the history of the world. He could see the waters rushing through a gap in the ties at his feet, carrying dark lumps of debris he couldn't make out the details of in the eternal twilight.

Floodwaters.

"Just get out of here," said the railroad cop. "I don't even want to know your names. Go home."

"That's what I was trying to do," Roy grumbled.

"Come," said the preacher, "let us take our fill of love until the morning: let us solace ourselves with loves. For the goodman is not at home, he is gone a long journey: He hath taken a bag of money with him, and will come home at the day appointed."

"Does he do that all the time?" the cop asked Roy, holstering his gun.

"Hell if I know. I think he makes it up. I only met him an hour ago when he attacked me with a spear."

The cop pulled his gun back out again. "Then what are you doing with him?"

Roy shrugged, which made his hands slip on the rain-slicked roof of the car. "He needed a ride, I'm driving a cab."

"With Massachusetts plates and some mediocre gang tagging on the door." The cop actually laughed. "You don't have a taxi permit to operate in Illinois or Iowa."

"And this will we do, if God permit," said the preacher.

Comprehension dawned on Roy. "That was a joke, wasn't it?"

"Look," said the cop to Roy, "he's crazy. You're half-crazy for putting up with him. But I still can't allow you to drive across the bridge."

"It is written that He shall scatter them beyond the river," the Preacher intoned. "God can't do that if we can't pass beyond the river. Can't go over the road bridges 'cause they're up there arresting everyone who's not from the Quad Cities."

"Jesus Christ," Roy shouted, "you make a virtue out of persistence, don't you?"

"All right," said the cop. "You're both totally bat shit. But you know what? I don't believe the sun's coming back anyway. Throwing you in our truck in cuffs isn't going to change that. Go on over the river and get the hell out of here."

The preacher smiled. "And he made in Jerusalem engines, invented by cunning men. That's about all the Bible has to say about railroads, I'm afraid, but I offer you my blessings as well."

Roy smiled too, tentative. In the glare of their lights all three of the railroad cops looked tense and sad. He opened the door, got back into the cab, then rolled the window down. "Any of you need a ride west?"

"We got a job to do," said the cop who had patted him down. Their questioner just shook his head.

"Suit yourselves." He started the car. "And thanks."

The first cop, their questioner, leaned in the window. "You need a weapon?" he asked quietly.

Roy actually thought about that for a moment. "No, I don't think so. But thanks."

Then they were off, bouncing over the bridge. Roy didn't realize how much he'd been sweating until the heater started to dry him off and he could smell himself.

"Where you actually going?" he finally asked the preacher.

"West. I've got witnessing to do."

"Well, thank you for your help back there."

"You really want to thank the Lord."

Roy glanced up through the windshield into the rain clouds. He didn't feel very thankful in that direction.

"You can't escape Him," whispered the preacher.

☦

The Cab Driver

The preacher got out on a lonely roadside mile in the middle of Iowa, to a swirl of the smell of hogs and damp corn and a final blessing. Roy gave the man his cell phone—it hadn't worked since the end had come, and he figured maybe God would grant the preacher a miracle. There sure wasn't anyone else to talk to out there.

The miles went on and on after that.

Roy was surprised at how many people were glad to see him coming. The further west he got, the more rare news was. He could trade tales of the road for food and gas and a warm hour or two next to a wood stove or a fire. The rain had turned to sleet, then to snow, but the wind kept it from banking up too badly on the roads at first.

He gave rides to at least a dozen more people past Iowa City, finally driving the Interstates because the side roads were too few, and too clogged with the rising snow that even the wind, after a time, could not overcome. Every day he made fewer and fewer miles.

"You're never going to get through Wyoming," said an architect he'd picked up just outside of Grand Island, Nebraska. The architect was an older woman, so wrapped in coats Roy couldn't tell how big she was, sitting in front with him. A couple of teenagers trying to get to Julesburg, Colorado, boy and girl that were either in love or terrified out of their wits, were wedged in the back with a terrier he'd found shivering in an empty gas station restroom.

Roy had already figured he wasn't going to make it. Wyoming was a bit of a tough drive even when times were good and gas was plentiful. He just wished he could have talked to Ellen and Adrien one more time. "I'm going to try."

She put a hand on his, her puffy ski glove rasping on his skin. "I've got people in Cheyenne. Lay up with us until this either passes or ends."

"I'm not going to be a dead Frog," he said. "I've learned more in the past week, driving this old taxi into Hell, than I ever did in my life." Roy reached across the wheel with his other hand and patted hers. "I owe it to my family to keep going as far as I can. I owe it to you, and them," he nodded toward the back seat, "and God, if He exists."

"You're a good man," said the architect.

They didn't speak again for miles, simply listening to the sheet metal of the car groan in the cold, and the heavy breathing of the kids in the back seat.

✤

The windshield cracked badly coming in to Cheyenne, from the hail damage and the extreme cold, so that it hung in a loose web of tiny blocks. He would almost have preferred it shatter completely, but at least it still kept some of the air out. The last couple of times they'd found gas, he'd been afraid to shut the engine off. Pumps weren't working any more, not without power, which meant he had to find gas cans or siphon fuel from abandoned vehicles. At least people had shifted from fear and suspicion to a sort of pleasant resignation. Some had been downright helpful.

He hadn't seen another vehicle on the highway for over a day, not even a police cruiser or a National Guard truck.

The architect was stretched out in the back, sleeping curled up with the dog. A parka-clad Japanese tourist, a young guy with a bad haircut and earnest eyes, slumped in the front seat, playing with the settings on his digital camera and smiling at Roy from time to time. Roy couldn't figure out if he spoke English or not. They'd found him trudging down the highway in Nebraska close to the Wyoming border.

When the windshield snapped, with a noise like a foot the size of a house walking on snow, the Japanese tourist shouted something in his own language, then covered his mouth. In the back, the architect moaned. Even with the heat full on, the car was cold enough that Roy could see his breath. Outside air leaked in around the broken windshield.

He slowed down, leaned forward a little, and peered through the crazed glass. It was something like what spiders saw, he thought, if there were any spiders left. The air was so cold, even in the car, that his lungs burned with each breath, and his ribs ached. His sense of smell had deserted him completely, leaving him with the taste of brass in his mouth.

Drifts towered on both sides of the road. A lot of buildings were completely hidden. It was like driving through a soft-bottomed, pale white canyon. The architect woke up and whispered directions to him, many of which were useless in the piled snow, though he eventually found the part of town she wanted. Cheyenne wasn't very big, really.

"You coming in?" she asked from the back.

"No." He stared at the dashboard. "I'm going to keep going."

"You're not going to last out the day."

Roy met her eyes. "How much longer do you have wherever you're going?"

"Something might happen in time."

"Something might. But I've got to get home. And somebody might need a ride a little further down the road."

She nodded, then poked her finger through one of the holes drilled in the plexi, nudging the Japanese kid. "Come on. Warm inside. Food."

He looked at Roy, who nodded and made shooing motions. The kid got out while Roy thought about the architect's offer. Warm sounded good. So did food. He hadn't eaten in a couple of days. None of them had, not even the dog.

"The grace of God and the gift of a taxicab got me this far," he said, thinking of the French officers drinking by the Mekong. "All I can do is keep going." His words were sharp and frozen in the air inside the car.

The dog hopped in the front as the Japanese kid closed the door, and laid its head on Roy's lap. He turned on the roof sign, in case someone needed a ride, dropped it into gear, and eased away from the two dark figures already burrowing through a snow bank toward some hidden door. The tires slid on the ice, and he was colder than he had ever thought possible, but Roy kept heading west, talking to his wife and child as he drove.

☦

Hard Times in the State of Nature

TOMMY "LEVIATHAN" HOBBES was nasty, short and reeked of Brut. That morning he had used a pool cue to beat senseless a man who made fun of his name, then urinated between the man's broken teeth. A good fight always made his bladder tense, and he hadn't wanted to stain the floor of his second-favorite bar.

God walked into the diner where Leviathan was eating a late breakfast. He had possessed the elderly Mrs. Muriel Meeks as His earthly avatar, but neglected to reduce His divine effulgence. Muriel's eyes glared like the heart of the sun.

Leviathan looked up from his egg white omelet and stared unblinking into the radiant eyes of God. "You need something, pops?"

"I want to retain your services."

Leviathan occasionally worked as a freelance troubleshooter. He was accustomed to odd approaches. He continued to eat his omelet, waiting for the Rock of Ages to spill His story. The chumps always did.

"Someone's taken out a contract on Me," God finally said over the clinking of Leviathan's fork. "I would like you to arrange for the contract to be withdrawn."

Leviathan studied his plate for a moment, then cleaned his fork on his napkin. He took a sip of water. He glanced at God's shoes. Usually you could tell a lot about a chump from their shoes, but as

God was possessing an avatar, Leviathan mostly learned that Mrs. Meeks was tight with a dollar, sensible, and probably had flat feet. Finally he said, "I don't believe anyone would take that contract. You're what some would call a very hard target, pops."

God laughed. Every drinking glass in the diner shattered. "It's a *social* contract. Jackie Rousseau is recruiting atheists to return to a state of nature. That's how you kill God. Secular agrarianism."

Leviathan shrugged, ignoring the water pooling onto his lap. Everyone else in the diner had already fled through the kitchen. "So smite the unbelievers."

The Supreme Being and Creator of the Universe dragged a tip of one of Mrs. Meeks' sensible shoes on the linoleum, staring at His feet. "Can't," He muttered. "Against My own rules. Free will and all that."

"Huh." Leviathan tapped his fork against his teeth. "I suppose I could go see what Jackie's got up his shorts. What's my take?"

God buffed Mrs. Meeks' acrylic nails. "Oh... salvation, eternal life. Maybe a quick hack on your criminal record."

"Immaterial," said Leviathan, who was quite capable of hacking his own criminal record at need. "I live in the real world. You can do better."

"Uh...one hundred thousand simoleons and two first class tickets to Atlantic City?"

"I'd shake on it," said Leviathan, "but you know how it is. Germs and all that. My normal terms are fifty percent up front."

"Unmarked, small bills, out of sequence, I assume?" asked God. Leviathan noticed His teeth glowed as brightly as His eyes.

☦

"Jackie, Jackie, my friend. This would be a good time to be reasonable. It's what you're known for, after all." Leviathan leaned against the railing of the Broadway Bridge, his back to the traffic.

Jackie Rousseau was somewhat disadvantaged in their conversation as Leviathan had dangled him over the railing upside down, held seventy feet above the Willamette River by an orange outdoor extension cord. The knots were slipping.

"Tommy," gasped Jackie. "I don't...have...any idea ...what...the hell...you...are talking...*about*!"

"God. Without Whose divine favor we would all struggle in pain forever."

"I *know*...who...God...is..." Jackie began to curse in a monotonous voice, slipping into French after the first few bars.

Leviathan jerked on the extension cord, leaning over the railing to give it a heave. Rousseau began to describe an arc of about twenty degrees, swinging like Foucault's pendulum after a night of strong drink. "Social contract, friend," Leviathan reminded him.

Rousseau twisted around to face up at Leviathan for a moment. "God's a moron!" He gasped, then choked, as his body dropped again. The knots around the railing slipped. "Atheism...my ass. I...was talking...about...the... natural state of...free society." He groaned. "Consent of the governed...impulse control...everything the church isn't. I got nothing against God...long as He keeps..." Grunt. "His...place."

"You don't say." Leviathan considered that God might have been wrong. It wasn't like He was the Pope or something. And the Supreme Being's choice of avatars was a pretty good clue that the divine wiring had developed a short. Leviathan warped the cord in a bit, slowing Rousseau's swing. "So you ain't aiming for Himself?"

Rousseau sounded exasperated. "What kind of idiot...do you think I am? I'm trying to change the conscience of man...not God."

With a series of sharp tugs, Leviathan yanked Rousseau back up onto the sidewalk. "Maybe it was a mistake," he told the Swiss philosopher, "and maybe it wasn't. We square for now?"

Rousseau's face was puffy from hanging upside down too long. Regardless, he made a commendable effort at Francophone insouciance. "But of course. May I stand you a cognac?"

"Yeah. Then you can help me work out how to tell God He was wrong."

They walked along the bridge toward Portland's Pearl District. Rousseau looked at the skyline as he spoke. "People find and lose faith on their own. The social contract is about a better way to live with government and society, not with God."

"You want to whack the government, fine with me. I'm only looking out for His interests right now," said Leviathan. "Seems God owes me two tickets to Atlantic City. Lots of praying going on there. Maybe I should take Him to Pascal's and encourage Him place a wager."

☦

At Pascal's, God bet on Himself. He covered the spread to win, place and show. Leviathan invested the money in biotech after buying Jackie a new pair of jeans.

Muriel Meeks came to her senses in a skybox at a Portland Trailblazers game. She didn't need her reading glasses any more, and later found that she almost always won at bingo. Every year thereafter Leviathan anonymously sent her a pair of Manolo Blahnik shoes, with a note saying, "Life doesn't have to be so hard."

☦

The Philosopher Clown

"IN A PERFECT WORLD," said the clown as he peered up at the cop from his seat on a park bench, "man would never need to laugh. The epicycles of time and space betray us all into misery."

White greasepaint smeared across the coarse and vasty pores of the clown's skin in a trail of fingerprints, loops and whorls deposited by forensic transference. The clown's lips were painted baby shit orange. The extended borders of his mouth were ill-defined. One eye was filmed with cataract, the multi-colored pupil of the other bisected by a dark bar so the clown seemed to view life through a tiny pair of stained glass doors. Patchy stubble marred his peeling scalp where the greasepaint petered out to a filmy many-fingered residue. The clown reeked of stale sweat, cigarettes and the dusty rubber scent of old balloons.

"Epicycles my ass," said the cop. He was a one-time Latin Kings gang-banger who'd gone straight and joined Portland's Police Bureau because he wanted to do good in the world—whatever the hell that had meant. "In a perfect world you'd be in county lock-up instead of hanging around downtown bothering the tourists." The cop glanced at his wristwatch, a snappy Tag-Heuer he'd removed from the arm of a yuppie possession-with-intent collar who'd been too busy pissing his pants to notice. "But it's your lucky day, *pendejo*, 'cause I'm going off-shift in less than an hour and I ain't got time to process paper on a vagrancy rap. Get it in gear and I'll forget

53

I ever saw your sorry ass."

The Oregon winter wind splayed newspapers around the wrought iron leg of the clown's bench, followed by a rapid burst of chilly rain clearing the brick sidewalks of downtown so thoroughly that the clown and the cop might have been experiencing their own private Rapture-in-reverse, all the tourists and lawyers and bike messengers suddenly called up to Heaven *en masse*, or at least slid off to a bitching rave at some musty warehouse over in southeast Portland. The frigid drops made a lunar ruin of the clown's whiteface while spattering the cop's sunglasses until he saw the same rainbows the clown did. Dark-edged clouds raced above the narrow channels of the building-scraped sky in pursuit of their own annihilation against the distant Cascades.

"Laughter," said the clown in a diminishing voice so the cop leaned unthinking ever closer to hear him, "is born from pain. Pain is the ratchet on the gears of life. And without *pain...*" The clown's nicotine-stained hands grabbed the cop's collar as he head-butted the officer in the face. "...*nothing's fucking funny!*"

Chips of polycarbonate lens glittered on the rain-streaked pavement. The cop collapsed, whimpering through a smashed nose and tight-clenched eyes. Blood-stained greasepaint smeared his face in an inept echo of the clown's own handiwork. The clown delivered a sharp kick to the cop's ribs, stripped off the Tag-Heuer and walked away. His red size thirties slapped the wet brick in time to the clattering music of the spheres.

✦

"Martinez," says the sergeant with a patient sigh. He's on light duty — the only assignments he gets these days — guarding a fellow officer in distress and looking for information. "You gotta listen to me." Hospital smells overwhelm any sense of familiarity, those smells and Martinez' heavily-bandaged face.

The River Knows Its Own

The sergeant is a patient man. He was a sergeant of a different sort during the Tet Offensive. Soon he's scheduled to be a sergeant of the retired sort, then eventually a sergeant of the dead. This does not bother him—the sergeant has long since learned to listen to the rhythms of life. For the most part he gets by in life by not pissing into the wind. And Martinez shows all the signs of someone who unzipped to piss in the face of a truly heroic headwind.

"Doc says you're awake in there." He pats Martinez's knee under the rough-textured hospital blanket, an oddly familial gesture for a man who couldn't ever keep a wife long enough to have children. Lost Alicia to a DUI, Rose to cancer, Wei-Ling to suicidal depression. After the third funeral the sergeant had realized he wasn't a man meant for woman born. Sometimes the younger cops stood in for absent sons until they tired of him and moved on to their own familial distresses.

"Look, kid, you didn't lose nothing but that nice German watch. Kept your weapon, badge and wallet—that's a weird takedown. Doc says you had makeup on your face. You get beat up by a hooker? Should we be shaking down the drag queens? Give me something here." The sergeant's wet cough was a long-ignored harbinger of his own limited future. "This is embarrassing. The EMTs who transported you are telling everybody you gone done by a clown. A God damned *clown*, Martinez. Somebody over at the Fire Bureau sent a spray can of that silly string to our Lieutenant this morning."

Only the clicking of Martinez's monitors and the hissing of his oxygen feed answer. The sergeant is struck by how much those noises resemble the noises of a night patrol in the Asian jungle— boots clicking on rocks, smacking free of the mud, the wind hissing. The noises of the world, thinks the sergeant. The clattering music of life.

His awareness narrows with his vision. Some loose piece of the sergeant's lung has finally made its journey to his cerebellum.

"Martinez," gasps the sergeant, who sits a few feet away from monitoring equipment that could have summoned help.

Big red shoes squeak on the linoleum floor of the corridor just outside the door.

"Nothing's funny any more," whispers Martinez as the old sergeant steps away on the rhythms of his life, guided by three different partners, each glad to see him and already bickering for a piece of his soul.

✢

You will go to the funeral in your dress blues with the white gloves and the shoes you will carry in a bowling bag in the car so as not to scuff the shine. The honor guard will fire rifles over the grave to the wheeze of bagpipes in a stereotyped ceremony.

You will stand with two-dozen other cadets, solemn in your duty as an almost-sworn officer. You will endure the chilly rain and the fitful wind and the quiet weeping of his best friend's wife. Or you would if he had a best friend. The old sergeant was kind to the new fish, helping them evade the worst of the hazing. You won't benefit from his experience now.

After the funeral you will linger wondering who else will have come to mourn the friendless man. A younger cop with a Hispanic name and a bandaged face, a handful of bitter old men with tasseled VFW caps, a few of the sergeant's squad mates, a PR flack from the mayor's office, the cadet detail—including yourself—and the honor guard, along with an inoffensive Episcopal priest because even the Police Bureau chaplain won't have a clue what the old man might have believed in.

Finally it will be you standing alone next to the tarp-covered grave with its temporary marker in the rain, ruining your careful shoes and thinking about what it means to be a cop, to be human, to live in this universe. You will hear a faint clicking noise from the grave like the grinding of gears, or perhaps the chime of a distant music box.

Not quite frightened you will turn away only to notice a pale streak on the temporary marker. The streak will be white and greasy. In the mud right behind the marker you will find a very nice German watch also covered with pale flecks.

You will lift a corner of the tarp and toss the watch into the grave. It is the only funerary offering you can give the old man. You will walk away, ignoring the impossible clattering rhythms that echo ever louder from the old sergeant's last foxhole. Sometime soon a bad cop will go straight for the second time in his life and do some good. Somewhere else an old man will be loved, not once, not twice, but three times over, forever and ever amen. You will imagine a miracle worker walking this Earth, teaching hard lessons—an exhausted man, half-blind, with a pale, rain-blurred face wearing improbable red shoes.

Then you will laugh and remember the old sergeant fondly all the days of your life even as the clicking music of the universe never again quite leaves your ears.

☦

Green Grass Blues

THERE WASN'T MUCH IN THE world stupider than sheep. Except more sheep, perhaps. T.R. wasn't inclined to test the theory. In any case, the summer was warm, the meadow was green enough to hurt his eyes, and the chimney swifts that lived in the ruined mill were writing omens in the Oregon sky.

He sat in a deck chair with a Little Oscar full of Mountain Dew propped next to him and an air rifle on his lap. T.R. had found that potting the ewes with the air rifle was good way to get them to pay attention. This deep into the summer, their wool had regrown enough that the pellets didn't hurt them.

Something was bothering the sheep, though. The same thing that made the swifts write glyphs of warning in the air, presumably. Sighing, T.R. put down his copy of *The Chymical Wedding of Christian Rosenkreutz* and picked up the rifle.

With luck it would be a coyote, or a stray dog off the Interstate. Without luck...well, there was a reason the grassland wizards liked good, solid basalt beneath their soil.

He popped open the chamber of the air rifle and dumped out the orange plastic pellets. T.R. then reached into his pocket for an old Red Man tobacco pouch filled with an entirely different sort of pellet.

It always paid to be prepared.

Of course, now his rifle stank of myrrh and old blood.

Jay Lake

The Chymical Wedding fluttered to the grass as T.R. left his chair behind and walked his field, following the restless tracks of the stupid sheep, guided by the swirling calls of the swifts.

⚧

"A.P.!" T.R. shouted as he slammed through the aluminum door of his master's trailer. "There were footprints in the grass."

His master was stretched on the fraying plaid couch. Snoring, as usual, with mustard stains on the old man's wife-beater undershirt, while the fishing channel played in Spanish on the television.

At least he's wearing pants, T.R. thought.

Distracted from his excitement and fear, T.R. took a deep breath. When A.P. was meditating—at least that's what the old man called it—he didn't like to be woken up. The working to summon him back was simple enough, but they had an iron rule out here on the grasslands.

No magic in the trailer.

You never brought the stink of work into your home.

Without the working, there wasn't much T.R. could do. He knew from experience that even firing a starter's pistol next to A.P.'s ear wouldn't have much effect. Not til his master was done.

T.R. stepped back out onto the little pine deck. The afternoon was wearing on. Exurban commuters from the government agencies in Salem were filtering down the county road in ones and twos. A thin finger of clouds was working its way over the Coastals from the west. There wasn't any scent of trouble in the air here, not at all.

No footprints in the yard, either.

He stepped off the porch to gather the three identical grass blades he'd need.

"Who's watchin' them sheep, boy? You're early."

He jumped slightly, before hiding his grimace as he turned to face A.P. Some days the old man just wasn't worth it. Most days,

60

lately. "Bobbie Krausner is penning them for me, sir."

"And so you come runnin' back, drivin' like to draw somethin' down out of the mountains just to see what the hurry was."

"Sir." T.R. took a deep breath. "Footprints, sir. In the sheep grass."

A.P. locked stares with him a moment. His master was looking...thin. "Not your'n, I reckon."

"Big footprints, sir. *Big* footprints."

They both glanced east, to where the foothills of the Cascades dropped into the flat Willamette Valley floor.

"But nothin' there?" A.P.'s voice was soft as a shadow now.

"No sir. No feet at all."

"Walkin' backwards, they are. Well, we can't be havin' that. *Basta*." He stretched. "Here boy, get on with that grass. I'm projectin' right now. I reckon you need to wake me up."

"No magic in the trailer, sir."

A.P. gave him a look of profound irritation as he began to fade away. "Then open the damned door first and do it from the porch."

✢

They headed back out to the meadow in the evening dewfall. Grassland wizards mostly used pickup trucks for a variety of reasons, none of them esoteric. Vanished makes were strongly preferred, for reasons which *were* somewhat esoteric, so T.R. drove a rust-covered 1947 Hudson Big Boy with a redwood bed. A.P.'s vehicle was even stranger, a 1965 Mercury Econoline E100 with a spray-painted pattern of flowers and marijuana leaves all over.

Naturally they took A.P.'s Mercury, but T.R. still had to drive. He hated the old man's clutch. While he horsed the transmission and strained his knee, A.P. lit a twist of kind bud and stared out at the stars.

"You don't remember the last time, do you?" the old man asked.

T.R. clanked it down to second for a tight turn. The drive wasn't ten minutes, but still that was going to be too long in this monster. "Feet? No, sir. Before I got the call."

"Before you was old enough to know the difference, I'm thinkin'." A.P. laughed. "What'd you tell Bobbie K. when you asked her to bring in the sheep?"

"Told her there was a problem I had to hotfoot it out to take care of. I didn't figure something invisible was going to eat her just then. Besides, the sheep weren't that upset, and neither were the birds."

A.P. took a deep long drag. "Well, you'd be wrong about not being eaten by the invisible, but you was right about the signs." He stubbed the joint out in the Mercury's ash tray. "Probably."

They clanked to a halt along the west fence of the sheep meadow.

As promised, Bobbie had driven the sheep to their pen across the way. It was a smaller enclosure, fenced high to keep the coyotes out and with a shelter against the inevitable Oregon rain. A.P. got out, faced the pen with his arms spread wide, and just stood. T.R. stayed in the truck and listened to the ping of metal as the engine cooled. He knew his master didn't want to be interrupted while he read the flock.

Much more quickly than T.R. might have thought, A.P. dusted his hands together, then walked around the back of the truck. Never walk in front of a vehicle if you had the choice. Another grassland wizard rule, that was, one that made crossing city streets a significant challenge. But there were things which could see out of headlights which hadn't been properly treated. The front end of the Mercury stank the same as T.R.'s air rifle, when the air wasn't full of gas and burnt rubber.

T.R. slipped out the driver door and followed A.P. into the

sheep meadow.

The old man walked toward the foot prints as surely as if he had made them himself. He quartered around the track—three steps, two left and one right—staring at the ground in the moonlight. The dew had given texture to the shadows on the grass. The sheep had not stepped on the prints, either.

He wondered if that were a sign of intelligence or simply natural selection in action.

The footprints were roughly the same shape as a human print—as opposed to, for example, enormous chicken feet. Which was another possibility out here, depending on the season of the witch. T.R. estimated that the prints measured almost three feet from toe to heel.

A.P. bent down. "You look at these with any care, boy?"

"Came for you, sir," T.R. answered truthfully.

"Hmm." The old man fished a mechanical pencil from the pocket of the yellow Brake Specialists work shirt he'd donned on leaving the house. He reached down and touched the first of the footprints with it. "You ever ride in an early 1970s VW?"

"What?" That non-sequitur caught at T.R.'s wandering thoughts.

"Headliners were made of white vinyl. They had little pinholes in them. Don't know why, maybe kept the glue from coming loose from the heat. Who the hell knows why Germans do anything? If you stretched out in the back of an old VW and stared at the ceiling, after a while you couldn't tell if the pinholes were in the fabric, or floating above it."

"Did it help to be stoned?"

That earned him a sharp look. "Of course it helped to be stoned. It always helps to be stoned. There's more than one reason we call ourselves *grass*land wizards, boy."

"So..." T.R. tried to divine the point of A.P.'s ramble.

"So, look at these here prints, boy." He jabbed at the disturbed grass with the mechanical pencil. "See the grass? They's coming *up* out of the earth, not pounded down in."

T.R. bent down. Damned if the old man wasn't right. Despite himself, he shivered.

☥

A. What They Tell the Young Ones About Remembering the Balance

The thing you got to remember is we're not about fighting some battle between good and evil. The downtown wizards in Salem and Portland, they can balance the numbers and dance on the workings woven into GAAP and play games with the SEC and call it what they want. Down here in the valley, we're just living with the earth. Them volcanoes, them trees, them steams and rivers and elk and coyotes were all here long before any of us, and they'll be here long after we're gone.

But everything has an pattern. Actions that cause change in whatever's around them. And I don't just mean with feet or fingers or fins. Even a stone makes a dimple in the world. The thoughts of a squirrel or a trout mean something. Those purposes add up. Rock thinks slow, but there's a god damned *lot* of it on this planet. Salmon think in cycles, and if you don't think the river knows a fish's mind, then you're not paying any attention at all.

None of this has a purpose. Not in the way you and I do. It all balanced out, like cats in a sack too tired to fight in any more, til we came along. The ones before, the Indians, they weren't as bad as us. They didn't bind the rivers with iron and walls of stone. They didn't tear down the old forest and scar the land with roads and towns and cities. But they were like a fresh cat, stuck in that sack.

Us, with our cars and feedlots and silos, we're like a tiger stuck in that sack.

The land pushes back because that's all it knows how to do. It ain't evil, it ain't trying to hurt us any more than it's trying to help us. It's just seeking balance, like water seeking its own level.

Our purpose, us grassland wizards, is to help that balance along without giving away too much of what people need, nor taking away too much of what the land needs. Remember balance, and you'll never go completely wrong.

✦

The sat on the tailgate of A.P.'s Mercury and shared another joint. This one was a real spliff, fat as T.R.'s thumb, but they were on working time now. T.R. didn't toke on his own account, only when the magic called for it.

This was a night for magic.

The high-altitude cloud cover had moved in from the west, covering the sky and making a rainbow-dogged glow out of the moon. There was a will o' the wisp fog confusing the frogs and insects, though knee-high the air remained clear. The temperature was a bit more crisp than usual for July.

A.P. let a stream of smoke slip from his lips, staring upward. "We know some things it ain't."

"Not one of the Sisters," T.R. said. "That would be chicken feet."

"Right. You're thinkin', boy."

"Besides, it's the wrong season."

A.P. choked. It took T.R. a moment to realize his master was laughing. "You don't think a woman can't come out of her season? You got a lot to learn about girls." His voice trailed off into giggling.

"As may be, master, but there is a time for witches. This isn't it."

"Fair enough." He took another long drag, held it for a while, then let it slip away without ever releasing another stream. T.R. was

Jay Lake

impressed with the fact that A.P. never seemed to cough. "Ain't a witch. What else ain't it?" He passed the spliff back to T.R.

After a slow drag of his own, T.R. talked around the tingle in his throat. "Not a Skookum. Feet too big for bigfoot." That set him to giggling. He *hated* giggling. There was little enough dignity in being a wizard. This was just stupid.

Funny, but stupid.

A.P. seemed to agree without giggling. "No, no, not one of them. If it were, he'd have left a trail or not as he chose. 'Sides, they're polite. Whatever did this wasn't polite. Ain't neighborly to frighten the sheep. What else?"

"Nothing walked out of a river to do that. This meadow's too far from free-running water, and it would have left a trail."

"Right again." His master took another draw. "Damn, boy, who trained you up? They done a good job."

T.R. giggled again. He just couldn't seem to help it. "I wouldn't care to say, sir. Just a damned old fool."

"Reckon it was. Not one of the Sisters, not one of the brothers, not a water walker, no wise an air sign neither."

"Either the grass itself, or something of the earth." T.R.'s memory tingled. "You mentioned walking backwards, sir? I don't rightly know what that signifies."

"Walkin' backwards." A.P. hitched himself back on his elbows, despite the hard cold metal of the bed. "It ain't none of it magic, boy. You know that."

T.R. did know that. 'Wizard' was just a way of looking at things. "It's not magic, sir. You've taught me that time and again. Just nature by another path."

"Right. Well, some of them paths run backwards. Some things walk them."

☥

After that pronouncement, they passed the spliff back and forth in silence a while. T.R. reflected that silence had always been A.P.'s favorite teaching method. Or perhaps strongest weapon. Silence could just as easily signify support, questioning, disapproval or nap time. Sometimes all at once. It was almost always up to T.R. to break the quiet and fill the silence. If he didn't do that well, there were consequences. Usually starting with more silence.

The old man drove him crazy. But here he was, years into being an apprentice wizard. He could always go be a shepherd, he supposed, but that was basically what he did now. Still, all that grass could drive a man crazy.

T.R. turned his thoughts to the subject at hand.

Nature by another path. That was one of the catchphrases the grassland wizards used, when talking about the world. As with anything oft-repeated, the literal meaning was worn as a stone in a riverbed.

T.R. privately thought that words were another field waiting to be plowed, much as the transit wizards and the financial wizards did in the cities. Just as water flowed home to the sea, to be lifted into the air by the fire in the sun before returning to the soil and stone as it fell from the sky, so words flowed through the entire world of men. It wasn't that he disagreed with the balancing ethic of the grassland wizards—far from it—he just thought there were more ways to influence that balance.

It all came down to words, after all. Without words, the beacon fire of thought never bridged the gap from one consciousness to another. The world's purposes were powerful but wordless—no volcano ever wrote poetry, no forest ever told its children a tale of heroes rampaging amid quiet folk—and words were how the wizards tipped the balance back into place.

Even the little workings were no more than ways of making those words sensible to the land.

So T.R. turned the words over in his head.

Nature by another path.
Another path by nature.
Path by another nature.
Walking backwards. *Path another by nature.*
Passing by nature, passing in reverse.

Under the grass, of course. That was the key. That whatever had come had pushed *up* out of the grass. As if it walked beneath the earth, and for a moment stepped too deep, like a man treading more heavily than intended on mud.

He turned that thought around some more.

"It came from below," he finally said.

A.P.'s response was uncharacteristically quick. "Think so, do you?"

"How else could the prints be the way they were?"

"Our magic is almost always the art of the obvious, boy."

"So what would we find if we dug up the turf?"

A.P. took another long drag off the burnt-down nub of the spliff. "Shovel's in the toolbox. Knock yourself out."

⸙

T.R. spent some time carefully quartering the prints. The grassland wizards needed some money, after all, and often the sheep weren't right to sell. So they raised a lot of turf. The Willamette Valley was the leading source of both lawn grass seed and live turf in North America, so this was normal enough. It meant he'd had a lot of experience with turf cutters, rollers and little square shovels.

None of which A.P. seemed to carry in the toolbox behind the cab of his Mercury. Why would a grassland wizard carry grass tools, after all? T.R. made a note to add those to the collection of equipment rattling around in the bed of his Hudson, for future use.

So he chopped the turf with the round-point shovel A.P. did

have, the world's most generic utility shovel and not especially well-suited for the job. Lacking gloves, he accepted the blisters and splinters the old wooden handle gave him. At least the dark of the evening was cool.

There was even a kind of magic practiced around turf cutting—turbary, they called it. T.R. had spent his time studying sheep and birds and the movement of wind on grass, but he knew there was an entire clan of wizards that based their divination and power on the patterns of roots and tracks of worms.

He was no turbarist, that was clear enough, but still he'd worked the grass farms sufficiently to understand what he was about.

Eventually the first of the prints came up to only slightly bloodied palms. There was a strange clicking noise from the soil, as if someone had buried several dozen ticking clocks. He wasn't sure what he was looking for, so he didn't know what he'd found at first. Even with the veiled moon there was light enough to see by for his night-adjusted eyes. The lifted section of turf showed him churned soil writhing with large black beetles. A moment's gingerly inspection showed that they were concentrated in a rounded mass of loosened soil.

Where a leg might have extended downward from the upward-forced print.

It was the insects which were clicking, louder now that he was close. When T.R. tried to pick up one of the beetles to examine it, the insect bit him hard enough to make him bite off a shriek. He shook the beetle away and looked at the first knuckle of his middle finger. A drop of blood welled, black in the attenuated moonlight. The skin was already visibly pale in a ring around the wound site.

Even as he raced back toward the truck and A.P.'s assistance, T.R. wondered if the black beetles were really the color of blood.

☥

"Damn, boy, you really fucked that one up." A.P. had T.R.'s wrist in a grip so tight it hurt, while he probed the fingertip with the mechanical pencil.

T.R. held his breath behind his teeth, not trusting himself to scream. His finger was *cold*, which was almost worse than being numb. The ring of pale skin had already grown past the first knuckle joint, and he couldn't wiggle that finger any more.

He wanted to protest, to say that his master had sent him into danger, had allowed him to fuck up, but...so what? T.R. fell back on logic. "What about my finger?"

"I'll look to draw this out." A.P. gave him a quick, hard look. "Fire will be best, but you'll need to be ready for it."

"Ready how?"

A.P. pulled another spliff out of his shirt. "Light this, and don't watch what I do."

That was the first time since he'd been apprenticed to the old man that T.R. had heard his master tell him to look away. He lay down in the truck, stared at the sky and sucked on the joint. He ignored everything he could. The cold in his finger. The fear that the frigid cramping would extend to his entire hand, wither his arm, even stop his heart. The noises of A.P. rummaging in the tool box, metal clanging as the old man cursed quietly.

When a blow torch hissed to life, T.R. nearly swallowed the spliff whole.

When the cold in his finger was swallowed by a bright sun of heat-driven pain, he still didn't look. He just toked and stared at the veiled moon and tried to keep enough of his thoughts in order to wonder what walked beneath the soil and left deadly black beetles in its wake.

The last thing he heard before the combination of dope and pain put him to sleep was A.P. saying something about not letting the sheep back into the meadow.

✤

B. What They Tell the Young Ones About Why We Live Here

You ever wonder what's so special about the Willamette Valley? Why we live here, and not along the Truckee or the American River, or the Missouri back east? That's because here the thoughts of the lands are both hotter and simpler.

This is all volcanic rock here. Not marine rock, which is full of old slow life that's angry about being locked down for a hundred million years. Nor the stuff squeezed from the earth cold and hard with the complaints of gravity and geothermal stress. No, this here's scabs on the earth, simple stuff from a simple time.

Easier to do what we do without the ghosts of time groaning in the bedrock beneath the soil.

Likewise, this piece of North America has a mind of its own. The mother continent swallowed Okanagan completely, and has been chewing on California for long ages. All them volcanoes over there? Death cry of a land being swallowed back down into the fire far down below. This place remembers oceans and eons of life on its own. Kindly echoes, if land can ever be said to be kind.

So we live in a simple balance, compared to most. Water, soil, stock and stone, fish and bird and fur, we work with them without also contesting against older, stronger, slower wills out of the abyss of years.

Different places have different concerns. The land might as well be dead beneath the streets and rails of the old eastern cities. The Midwest sleeps beneath a deep blanket of soil, tickled by plows but not enough to wake from its windswept dreaming. The deserts of the southwest have their own thoughts, but when men enough go there to wrest the balance loose, they fence it in with watered lawns and a grid of streets. Here in the Northwest we can still live in the dynamic balance.

So here we live. We count the blades of grass that rise in the spring and watch the mindless sheep. It's not that we must. It's just that we can.

⚜

When T.R. woke up it was daylight. He was in his room at A.P.'s trailer, not much larger than a closet in a normal house, with a single louvered window, a tiny bed and several bits of cheap furniture. G.D., one of the few female grassland wizards, sat next to him on a wobbly dinette chair drinking coffee from a giant plastic Sapp Brothers mug.

At least he assumed it was coffee — that's what he smelled.

She was an old woman, old as most of the masters were. Where T.R. had the indefinable dissolution of a rummy who'd spent too many years on the couch, G.D. was still a head-turner. Her long hair flowed salt and pepper, the arch of her brows was dark and perfect over gleaming pale eyes, and she dressed like a Deadhead who'd gone into color divination. The flowing silks and South Asian prints suited her trim form well.

"Hello," he said.

She cocked an eyebrow. "Not good morning?"

"I doubt it, if what I remember from last night holds true." His right hand lay beneath the covers. It ached abominably. T.R. was in no hurry to tug it into the open air and count his fingers.

"So you are thinking clearly."

"Clearly as ever, I suppose."

She chuckled. "Not that he'd ever tell you any such thing, but I have it on good authority that A.P. thinks highly of you."

The words were out of T.R.'s mouth before he could stop them. "If he does, he does so in silence."

"That man does nearly everything in silence, T.R." The tone of G.D.'s voice made it clear what she thought of his disrespect toward his master.

"Well, yes..." He decided he wasn't sure he wanted to know the boundaries of 'everything' insofar as A.P. and G.D. were concerned. "I'm sorry." *Time for a change of subject*, he thought. "What was that last night?"

"The Western deathwatch beetle. *Xestobium rufovillosum maximum*. Not something we normally find here in the valley."

"I didn't think we had any poisonous insects in Oregon."

"We don't."

"But the deathwatch...?"

"Is not generally poisonous." She set her mug down and leaned forward, moving her hands to her knees. "That was imbalanced."

'Imbalanced' had a specific meaning among the grassland wizards. Things—animals, plants, weather, the land itself—acting out of character.

He tugged his right hand from beneath the covers. The entire hand was swathed in cotton, but there wasn't a familiar tenting finger at the middle. T.R. gently pinched the cotton there until his left thumb and forefinger met.

With that, he began to cry.

✦

A few minutes later as he settled down to a rattling, stressed breathing, G.D. stared over the rim of her mug. "Are you finished?" she asked.

It was more kindness than he would have gotten out of A.P. Though perhaps A.P.'s greatest kindness was to let T.R. come to terms with his missing finger without the old man having to watch his apprentice grieve.

"I'm..." T.R. stopped and took a deep breath. The sobs threatened to return. "It's missing."

"Sucks, doesn't it? Want some coffee?"

"I lose a finger and you offer me coffee. That's it?"

Her eyes narrowed. "If I had a finger to spare, I'd offer you that. What I *have* is coffee."

Chastened, he said, "Yes, ma'am. Please." T.R. turned his wrist back and forth, looking at his bandage hand from both vantages. It didn't hurt, really, except for a deep, dull ache which seemed to throb from somewhere down in his forearm all the way up to his hand and where the stump would be, if he could see the stump.

The stump itched horridly.

Carefully he poked at the bandage, almost wishing he had A.P.'s mechanical pencil. Nothing. Not even down past the point where he could swear the itch was coming from. T.R. sucked in another sudden breath.

"The nerves don't know the finger is gone," G.D. said as she poured some coffee from her mug into a Flintstone's jelly jar.

"I *do*." He tried not to let the horror into his voice. His revulsion was already mingling with a sense of mourning. Middle finger, at least. He could still push elevator buttons and point at people. He generally didn't do either one of those things very often, in point of fact.

Not a lot of elevators in the grasslands of the Willamette Valley, and wizards were trained early not to point. A lot of power could flow through a finger. In either direction.

At least he'd be more polite now, he thought. No more flipping the bird.

T.R. reached for the jelly glass. It was hot, of course, but he wanted the caffeine. More to the point, he wanted something to do.

The coffee within was as hot as the glass promised, and burned his tongue on the way down. Apparently G.D. took it black and unsweetened. He'd probably tasted better motor oil. Still, coffee was coffee, and the trembling he hadn't even noticed in himself seemed to subside.

"Where's A.P.?"

"Out with half a dozen others burning turf in your sheep meadow. Pretty much everyone else is looking for more prints."

"Burning turf?" Given the moisture content of both the grass and soil, T.R. found that difficult to credit.

"Pest extermination. You of all people should appreciate why."

He tried to make a fist of his right hand, but the fingers were bound tightly under the outer bandage. "Shouldn't we be out looking for more prints?"

She smiled sweetly at him, though T.R. could see the daggers hidden behind G.D.'s expression. "In point of fact, yes. Some of us, at any rate."

He rolled out of bed, wincing at the pain in his back. Of course, he'd been out shoveling last night as well. "Let's go."

"You might want to put some pants on first."

✝

T.R. drove his Hudson, slowly, and divided his attention between the little rural roads and the flocks of sheep, mixed occasionally with cattle, horses or even llamas. Cattle were too stolid to be useful for their work, horses too skittish, and llamas too smart, really. Of the three, he'd put his money on the South American bastards, but by preference it was sheep every time.

G.D. kept her head tilted out the window to stare at the sky. He knew she was watching where the birds flocked and wheeled, because every now and then she'd call a halt and point something out.

Working the gears turned out to be difficult with his wounded right hand, so T.R. kept it mostly in second. The stiff linkages in the three-on-the-tree shifter required more leverage than he could reasonably deliver with an open palm. The old six banger labored as he alternately lugged and raced it, but the truck kept on.

"Everyone in the valley's out today," she said after pulling her head in so they could cross a major junction with Highway 99. "Can't recall last time all the grasslanders came out on the same summoning."

"How dangerous is this...thing?"

"It's not the backward walkers they're worried about. It's the beetles. What they did to you? Imagine that happening to the sheep."

"Ah." He should have thought of that. T.R. drove on in silence, still watching the grazers. After a while he asked the next logical question. "What are we doing about the backward walkers?"

"You know the Trouble Rule." Her voice was too mild, a form of rebuke much as A.P.'s silences could be.

He did indeed know the Trouble Rule. Whoever the trouble found was the one to lay it down again. That was one of the basic commandments of the grassland wizards.

"Right. So why are we out looking at birds and cows?"

"It's what some of us should be doing," she said mildly.

He turned the truck around. "I'm heading back to my meadow. Can you watch the birds on the way there?"

"Surely as I can anywhere else."

<p>

There were half a dozen trucks parked along the road by his sheep meadow, including A.P.'s Mercury, along with two post-war Studebakers, a 1948 Diamond T and a 1930 REO Speedwagon. Unfortunately, one of the other vehicles was a late model Dodge belonging to the Marion County Sheriff's Department.

Grassland wizards and law enforcement didn't mix much. Other than the little matter of industrial-grade marijuana consumption, there was no reason to. The wizards were law abiding citizens, and their trailers and farmhouses tended to be in the center of a fair amount of peace and quiet. Rural crime was sufficiently irregular in its distribution that no sharp-eyed demographer had noticed this yet, but an occasional topic of conversation among the wizards was whether some genius with a computer model would some day notice them by that trail of peace.

Still, a lot of their activities didn't bear close examination. The haruspicators among the grassland wizards especially were at risk, for example.

T.R. pulled up behind the sheriff's truck and made his way out into the field where a group of people were gathered around a smoldering mess. As he got closer, he could hear the discussion.

"...care if it's wet...burn out here without a permit."

"...pest control..."

"...not much trouble, but..."

He stepped up into a circle of silence. T.R. didn't recognize the deputy, but the deputy apparently recognized him. "You're the one Bobbie told me about."

Kearns, his name tag read. He was a big man with a beefy face who was perspiring even though it wasn't seventy degrees out here.

"Deputy Kearns," T.R. said politely, nodding.

"Look, I don't care what kind of cult you fellows are running." Kearns glanced at G.D. "We got enough old hippies out here to start another revolution. I'd have to move to Malheur County to get away from your kind. I don't even care what you're smoking, long as I don't have to watch you and you're not selling meth to the kids. Which you aren't. But you *cannot* go setting fires in the summer." He hooked his thumbs in his belt. "People complain."

"I'm the one was hurt by the bugs here," T.R. said. He saw the wizards around Kearns tensing. "Dug 'em up without realizing what I was getting into."

The deputy scowled at T.R. "You couldn't call the extension agent like everybody else?" Out of the deputy's line of sight, A.P.

was working a Banishment with a hank of black wool and three dried clover flowers.

Stall, thought T.R. "Can't say I thought of it, sir. Little buggers hurt like fire. I was worried they might be like the fire ants down south, or those killer bees."

"I can see where a fellow might panic." He looked down at T.R.'s bandaged hand. "Hurt you bad, huh?"

T.R. winced. "Yeah. Bad enough."

"Let me guess. You folks don't believe in doctors, neither."

"We live in harmony with the land, sir." Utter bullshit, but it was what the deputy was expecting to hear. The wool in A.P.'s hands smoldered, then blew away to ash, just as the deputy's radio squawked an incomprehensible gabble of code.

Kearns looked around. "Alright fellows, that's my number. No more fires, though, or there will be more trouble. People looking into barns and things. Which I reckon you guys don't want too much of."

"No sir," said L.F., another of the senior wizards. He was a chubby man with a moon face pocked by old acne scars. "No trouble."

"Alright then. I'm not going to file a report, this time."

With that, Kearns lumbered back to his truck.

A.P. glared at T.R. "Come to fix it, boy? What took you so long?"

G.D. started to say something, then changed her mind.

"I've come to fix it, sir," T.R. said. "And I came as quick as I could think it through."

"We was a long time waiting," mumbled L.F. The senior wizards headed back toward their trucks.

✢

"It had been headed east," T.R. said. He stood behind where the last—or first?—of the footsteps had been, visualizing the line of travel. The area stank of kerosene, burning and turned soil.

"Into the Cascades," said G.D., still sipping her coffee. She and A.P. were the only wizards who'd stayed with T.R.

The Cascades indeed. Which was a bit odd, since when trouble did come, it usually came down out of the Cascades, from the east. Not toward the east.

T.R. turned and faced west, toward the line of the Coastals cropping up on the horizon a few miles that way. "How far are we from the river here? A thousand yards?"

"About right."

"So...say it came out of the Coastals, heading for the Cascades. The brothers live in both places. So do the Sisters. This...whatever it was...could do so too."

Silence this time. T.R. glanced at A.P. His master wasn't frowning, at least.

That meant continue.

"If it walks backwards..." he stopped, thinking about the paths of nature. "Not backwards. Not exactly. Inverted. Earth as air to it, our air as the rock beneath the soil. Like a..." Elemental was the only word he could think of, but that wasn't right, he was sure. "A pattern, a push from the soil. A sending. Carrying a purpose from the Coastals to the Cascades. It crossed the Willamette, from beneath, and came up here to do the equivalent of a man wiping his wet feet after wading a stream. It broke through."

A.P. grunted. "Is it dangerous?"

"No, not in and of itself. This is land business, the land talking to itself. I don't even think this is a push. Not like some of what passes. We just happened to be where it wanted to go. Like people in the path of a mudslide. But what the sending leaves behind is dangerous. Those deathwatch beetles. Not dangerous, in and of itself, but still trouble. Under the Trouble Rule."

A.P. turned to G.D. with exaggerated delight. "The boy does remember a thing or two."

"The boy does indeed," snapped T.R. "Now how do I keep this from being trouble?"

"How do you cross a river?" G.D. asked softly.

"Use a bridge," T.R. responded without thinking.

If he was right, if this made sense, if there was a way to get the sending to cross whatever arrangement they made.

Guide the land, set the balance, keep people safe and the land as whole as it could be while infected with humans.

☦

The only bridge which made sense was the crossing at Independence, Oregon. It was a concrete deck bridge, a very typical highway bridge. T.R. would have strongly preferred wood, but wooden bridges were long gone, except for a few creek crossings and the odd historical structure. Concrete wasn't his natural medium, not at all, but it would have to do.

The bridge was accessible from open fields, that was one strength. They couldn't have done much in the middle of Salem, for example. The bridge also ran almost directly along an east-west axis, each end pointing at one of the mountain chains. That meant if T.R. could set the proper wards and signs, it would be a path that the sendings would not resist.

He'd parked the Hudson in the woods below the eastern end of the bridge, where an odd little circular interchange linked Riverside Drive to the highway. Just north of that, no one would ever question the old truck. They walked west, picking their way through the riverbottom brush under the bridge itself. Traffic passed overhead in occasional hot, thumping whoosh.

"It walks beneath the soil," T.R. said. "We can't just direct it to the underside of the road deck."

"There are piers every few dozen yards," G.D. pointed out.

A.P. growled, muttering something that might have been "Trouble Rule."

T.R.'s finger itched. He massaged the palm and back of his hand, trying to distract himself from the sensation of what was missing. "The far side isn't built up, either. As long as we can get them to pass close to the town over there, this may well work. These piers extend below the soil to be stabilized. They can use them as stepping stones."

G.D. laughed lightly. "If you can get the land to pay attention."

"If not, I'm not very well going to solve the problem, am I?"

"How you going to do it, boy?" demanded A.P.

"Draw the sending in here with some kind of beacon, and set wards further out to keep it from trying another way."

"What kind of wards?"

T.R. noted that his master had abandoned silence. He felt obscurely vindicated. If A.P. felt the need to push, T.R. was going in the right direction. "This is a sending of soil or stone. We'll alternate fire and water wards. Smoldering Wool, I think, and Jar Water. One every quarter mile in a line opening out from here dozen miles in both directions." He grinned at A.P. "A lot of work, I know, but not any more than going out beating the meadows for deathwatch beetles."

G.D. snorted.

"Meanwhile, we'll set a beacon here. Something that will call to soil and stone." He paused, took a deep breath. "Bright Grave would work well."

"You planning to bury someone, boy?"

That was a flaw in his plan. T.R. didn't think this was worth a bit of grave-robbing. "I don't believe Bright Grave needs to be a person. It just needs to be bright."

A.P. pushed harder. "And if you make all this? What next?"

"I'll watch for another sending, and leave it in. The land learns, after all. The world was never stupid."

"So you're going to kill a sheep to fill that grave, and then go calling deathwatch beetles on yourself while the rest of us are out planting wards?"

Suddenly T.R. was very tired of A.P., the old man's cranky ways and damning with faint praise. "No, no sir. I'm going to help all of you plant wards, then send you home before I kill a sheep. Trouble Rule makes the bad part of this mine, surely enough."

✦

C. What They Tell the Young Ones About Our Names

When you were born, someone called you Tanner or Mary Lou or Enrique. Your parents gave you names. When you come to the wizards, whether you're a babe in arms or an old woman who's finally heeded the call, that changes.

We still carry driver's licenses, most of us. Only a few drop off the rolls completely. It's an advantage to be able to see a doctor or take a trip, after all. So we've got those names. But they're not ours any more. We gave them away.

Without those names, we're harder to find. More difficult to pin down. Neither the power of the land nor feuds of the hand have the same effect. Think about it. Trees don't give themselves names, and more than rivers or mountains do. A name is just a label.

So your master, or at least some master, will take your name away when you're read, and give you another one. We like them to have meanings, then we remove the meaning by only using the initials. Pro Bono, for example, becomes P.B. Used to have a wizard named A.V., for Ad Valorem.

You might think those kinds of names sound stupid. And if you're an Enrique or a Mary Lou, they do. But those names, they're real words with real power that still can hide in the chatter of the world around us. No one calls himself Geometricum Demonstratum except one of us, yet the words are out there.

And no one knows they're names. Not even the land. Especially not the land.

Sooner or later you'll be an H.O. or a B.B. Take that name with pride. No one but your master will ever know, except if you choose to tell them. It's all about hiding in plain sight.

✢

It took T.R. the better part of a week to organize the setting of the wards. At the same time he had to prepare the Bright Grave, a greater working than he'd ever done before. All of it was in service of turning nature to another path, which seemed fitting to him.

His finger ached, though. All the time. With everything he did. It was as if his hand were crying for its missing child. T.R. tried telling himself to be grateful that A.P. hadn't taken his thumb or forefinger. This was merely painful and inconvenient, as opposed to debilitating.

He couldn't work Bright Grave at the trailer, of course. No magic in the trailer. So he moved out to the sheep pen by the meadow. A.P. had done some sort of land swap with Bobbie to keep the sheep away from what they'd had to burn. That meant it was quiet and calm. The smell he didn't mind, save for the whiffs of kerosene and ash from the burnt spot.

The final part of Bright Grave would be worked under the west end of the Independence Bridge, of course. But he needed time to carve the ash poles, weave the grass ropes, and soak the dull knife in stale wine.

T.R. still wasn't sure about how to call another sending down toward the Bright Grave in the first place. He figured on spending some time camping over at the west edge of the Willamette Valley until another one of them came out of the Coastals.

If one didn't come, he wasn't sure how the wizards would determine the trouble had been settled. The Trouble Rule didn't address that. Whatever would come, would come, but the land's sense of time in no way corresponded to how human beings in general and the grassland wizards in particular saw things.

He smoked a lot of dope, too, to put him in the right headspace for Bright Grave. Killing a sheep would be difficult. He'd done slaughtering before — that was part of rural life, after all. But to bring one to the pit he'd dig and use that dull knife to cut its throat over the fir boughs and the grass ropes was another class of ritual entirely from the slow progress of the food chain.

Counting birds in the sky was one thing. This was another.

When he was waiting for the elements of his working to cure, to set up or set down, T.R. continued to read *The Chymical Wedding*. It made more sense when he was stoned, he realized. The air rifle was never far away either, with its blood load.

If he had to drive something away for which he had no working of Banishment, that silly little weapon would be his only friend.

Meanwhile the wizards came and went. Their old trucks wheezed up to his fence line, while they approached by ones and twos and, occasionally, threes, to give and take counsel. T.R. found himself exercising his proposed word wizardry through the medium of the old fashioned art of discussion. So much time spent in the laconic company of A.P had left him out of practice.

"You'll be setting your wards out along the rail line where it runs just west of south," he told F.Q., a woman wizard who was one of the youngest of the masters. "The steel will help drive the sendings along the wards."

"It will turn away from the metal bindings," she told him.

"The last one had to cross the rails somewhere. Several times. Find a culvert just south of Independence, leave some Openings there. That will help draw it to the Bright Grave."

And so it went, both the sympathetic mostly younger wizards, and the grumpy old men like L.F. who were friends of A.P.s and distrusted everyone under the age of 60. He talked, parried, crafted the workings, looked over maps of where the wards would be laid.

Somewhere in the process, his finger came to matter less and less.

⚛

The night of the Bright Grave working came. T.R. had already told Bobbie he'd be taking one of the ewes out of the herd to pass on to a buddy over in Lincoln County. G.D. drove up around sundown in her 1975 Plymouth Trailduster as he was checking the ties in the bed of his Hudson and loading the materials for his working.

"Bright Grave's a dead man working," she reminded him without any preamble of greeting.

"You know anyone planning to die tonight?"

"No. But L.F. put it around the working might go best if you cut your own throat."

T.R. jerked hard on a bungee, so that it snapped away and stung his left hand. His right he kept in a work glove, the middle finger stuffed with a scrap of wool. "*Why?* Why would he say that about me?"

G.D. shrugged. "You were here the day the sending came through. It was you the beetles bit. Some of the old guys are mad that you didn't stop it at the time, and convinced they could have done better."

"There was nothing to see that day, I assure you. Just circling birds and nervous sheep. I could have been standing on the spot and it wouldn't have made much of a difference."

"You're making a difference now," she said.

85

"Just following the Trouble Rule." He threw a satchel in the front of the Hudson. "Most of the grassland wizards are out watching tonight, aren't they?"

"It's a big working. The problem could be big, too. Especially if your plan doesn't work."

"Who gets the Trouble Rule if I fail?"

Her teeth flashed in an aggressive grin. "A.P."

"Then L.F.'s an idiot, making book against me. Those old men don't want to be creeping around under bridges at midnight. They should be doing everything they can to help me."

"Tell me," she said slowly. "Are you ever motivated by anger?"

He opened his mouth to answer, but G.D. just turned and walked away.

✦

The ewe, ear tag 24-017, wasn't happy about the truck ride in the dark. It was more difficult to find a discreet parking spot at west end of the Independence Bridge. A bawling sheep did little to improve that situation.

Still, he whispered a little Quiet in her ear and loaded up his duffel bag as she moaned softly. T.R. had bundled his shovel with his ash poles and his fir boughs. He shouldered his bag, grabbed the air rifle and the bundle and led the ewe down the embankment and along the west bank floodplain beneath the bridge. The combination was too heavy and too balky both, but he only had to drag all that junk a few dozen yards. Somehow he got the ewe out of sight without being blown out by passing headlights, and the attendant questions.

She was a soft-eyed, dark faced merino that he recalled having a pleasant enough disposition in the flock. 17 had never been a troublemaker, unlike some of the other ewes. He'd picked her for tonight's business due to her relatively tractable disposition.

Fighting a ram down here was almost beyond his imagination.

The river sulked nearby in the dark, burbling to itself. Some night hunting bird meeped and flew just outside the range of his vision. There were water and grass smells, and the stink of the frightened ewe. Other than occasional rumble of traffic on the bridge deck above him, it was an Oregon summer night.

T.R. tied her off to a pillar and set up a little electric lantern from his bag, then began digging the Bright Grave. He had brought A.P.'s shovel, the same one he'd used to cut the turf and find the beetles. Down here was an odd mixture of shifting sand and hard clay, the result of decades of intermittent flooding and occasional shifts in the river bank. He had gloves for both hands now, so while his back ached and his hands hurt, he wasn't collecting splinters and kept his blisters to a minimum.

By the time he was done with the hole, sweating and gasping, the ewe had settled into chewing her cud. The traffic above him seemed to have stopped passing somewhere in the process, so the night had fallen silent save for the river itself.

Even the birds were quiet.

Was it coming again? He wasn't ready. The Bright Grave was a beacon, not a protection, but it was meant to set the path.

T.R. pushed the fir boughs into the grave, then grabbed the ash poles. After a second of thought, he picked up the air rifle as well and jumped down into the grave to prepare the working.

As he arranged the boughs, the ewe bleated once, softly. T.R. looked up to see A.P. His master was between the lantern and the grave, but T.R. would recognize that stance anywhere.

The old man was carrying a weapon — rifle or shotgun, in silhouette, T.R. couldn't tell.

The real meaning of L.F.'s griping suddenly came clear as T.R.'s breath caught in his throat. His master intended T.R. to fill the Bright Grave. He grabbed at the air rifle, wondering what good the blood load would do when used against another grassland wizard.

Less than whatever his master had chambered in that other weapon. His only chance was that A.P. wouldn't want to kill T.R., for fear of ruining the working.

"You want some help there, boy?"

Just as T.R. brought the air rifle up, A.P. bent over and set down the shovel he'd been carrying. T.R. managed to jerk the barrel aside in time for the blood load to spang against the bridge deck above them.

A.P. grinned maniacally. "Damn, you are nervous." He extended a hand. "Come on out of there."

T.R. mostly wanted to throw up, but he climbed out instead, arms and legs shaking. "You bastard," he hissed.

"Take the damned sheep," said A.P. "I'll hold her, but its your working, boy."

"I am not a boy," T.R. snarled.

Together they wrestled the protesting 24-017 to the edge of the grave. He'd already laid the boughs and the ash poles. All he needed to do was cut the wool twists from each shoulder, say a few quiet words, and slash her throat.

The dull knife sawed slowly through one bit of wool as the ewe began to buck. The other bit followed. He was breathing heavy now, his gut like lead, not ready to kill an animal so uselessly.

His finger tingled, though, the phantom pain strong. How many would have died if the sheep had strayed into the deathwatch beetles?

The knife went in more easily than he'd expected. The ewe's warm blood spilled across him, but he wrenched her head back and let her bleed into the grave. The words came easily enough, a simple invocation to sky, water, stock and stone, then he shoved the body in.

So much easier this way than with one already dead, he thought. The working sealed itself.

He turned to say something to A.P., some angry denunciation, when the grave began clicking. T.R. whirled back to see a mass of deathwatch beetles squirming out of the sand and clay of the open grave, already almost covering the ewe.

"Fill it, quick," hissed A.P. For the first time in his life, T.R. heard fear in his master's voice.

As they spaded the spoil back into the grave, A.P. threw something in with the first few tosses. It was small and dark, and T.R. thought he knew what it was, but he said nothing. He just bent and lifted and thought about the power of anger.

✞

Later, after they'd washed themselves in the river, they wound up in A.P.'s Mercury. The old man produced two spliffs in an uncharacteristic show of generosity.

"You did well, boy," he said.

"How would you know?" T.R. asked bitterly. The hard words still crowded in his head, fighting for his tongue.

"You wanted me to be nice?" A.P. chuckled and took a long drag. "It was too easy for you. You knew how to do the little workin's just fine, and you liked sittin' with the sheep. Ain't too many come to the grasslands to loaf, but I do believe you did. So we threw you the goose, and made you work for it."

T.R. thought about the finger A.P. had thrown into the Bright Grave. "You called that sending?"

"No, not exactly. Let's just say I invited it your way. It was past time for you to grow up, boy."

"I am *not* a boy!"

"Not any more. That was kind of the point."

He thought about that for a little while. "What about the finger?"

"You were stupid. A stupid wizard doesn't live long. Think of it as tuition."

"Yeah?"

A.P. reached across T.R.'s lap and pushed open the passenger door. "One more thing. You can't keep living in that sheep pen. Time to get your own trailer, *wizard*." He gave T.R. a none-too-gentle push.

T.R. got out, torn between dazed amusement and smoldering anger. A.P.'s truck coughed to life and he headed into the night, east across the Independence Bridge.

Glove off, his hand looked odd. The missing finger was a shout. And it still hurt like crazy.

"I'm a wizard," he told the tiny ghost of part of himself. Whatever that meant. He hardly wanted it now.

Had the Bright Grave been worth the trouble? Had the price of the finger been worth what he'd bought?

Questions for another day, T.R. told himself. He went back to his own truck and headed home to the sheep pen. He could read the rest of his book by the light of the lantern, think about the power of words some more, and burn a little incense for the ewe's tiny, puzzled soul.

Tiny Flowers and Rotten Lace

THE BRICK MONSTER LEFT footprints where Timmy would see them. Mossy with red flecks, the prints were longer than his fifth grade math book and almost as wide—huge feet. Every day walking to and from school in the Oregon winter rain, he would see the tracks. Sometimes they were on the sidewalk, sometimes in the grass at the park. He hadn't seen the brick monster yet, but he knew it was around.

Was it following him home or leading him there? He didn't know which was scarier.

One day after school, Timmy stopped by the saggy old wall at the corner of Lafayette Street. It held up the bottom of the steep yard of the house that had once belonged to his grandmother, the bricks keeping the garden from sliding over the sidewalk and into the street. His grandmother had died before he was born, but Dad had told him this was where Mom had grown up. The red bricks were stained black with mold and grime, covered with moss. They were exactly like the brick monster's footprints.

"Hey," Timmy whispered to his grandmother's wall. Maybe the brick monster could hear him here, through his family's old bricks. That idea felt stupid, but the footprints were real. "Stop following me. You're scary."

"Help," the wall whispered back in a great, slow voice that creaked like his house in a windstorm. "Help me."

Timmy dropped his book bag and sprinted all the way home, screaming.

That night in bed, Timmy's butt stung from Dad's whipping for losing the book bag. Upstairs his mother shrieked at the walls to shut up and leave her alone. For the first time in his life, Timmy knew what she was talking about.

Unable to sleep, Timmy stared at his window. It was old-fashioned, narrow and tall. The streetlight outside made weird shadows on the shade as it shone through the lilac bush. The house was wood, but the basement walls were brick. Could the monster come through them?

The window rattled. Timmy jumped, drawing the sheet to his chin. Something tapped on the glass, then the window gave a grinding squeak as if it were being tugged upward. It sounded like the glass was about to break. The orange shadows of the streetlight shifted as the lilac bush shook.

"Go away!" he shouted, pulling the covers over his head. A bus roared by outside. Then all Timmy could hear was his mother yelling again. She finally stopped for breath. The sudden silence echoed with the creaking of the old house.

After a while Timmy stuck his head out again and watched the shadows on the window shade. They were back to normal. He waited a bit more, then got the flashlight from his secret box of R.L. Stine books and slowly raised the shade to look at the window.

A huge handprint filled the center of the glass. It was hard to tell for sure in the flashlight's glare, but he was certain it was made of moss and brick dust. The brick monster *had* come for him.

⊕

The next day at school he got beat up for bringing his lunch in a Fred Meyer grocery sack. When Timmy had been a dorky fourth grader, fifth graders were cool. Now he was a fifth grader, and he was still dorky as ever. Things never seemed to get better. Dumb stuff like carrying a paper sack or wearing cheap blue canvas shoes just made it worse. The brick monster was scary, but it hadn't tried to hurt him, which was more than he could say for the cool kids.

During lunch Timmy hid between the rusted green dumpster and the outside wall of the cafeteria. He didn't have anything to eat, not after Ti-Shaun and his friends had stomped Timmy's jelly sandwich into the leaves that morning, so he wasn't missing much. At least in the damp, smelly shadows he was safe, and alone.

"Timmy," whispered the orange bricks of Rhone Elementary School.

He shrieked, jumped up to run, and banged his head on the dumpster. Timmy sat down with a thump, his ears ringing.

"Timmy..." This voice was drier than the garden wall on Lafayette Street, bricks mixed with rustling paper and squeaky chalk. Timmy realized it had a smell, too, old wood and a little bit of mold, like the attic at home.

"What?" Timmy rubbed the sore spot on his head.

"Help me."

Timmy scuffed at the wall with his canvas shoes. "Help you what?"

This time he saw the faint movement in the bricks, like gigantic lips pressed through the skin of a balloon. "Come to your grandmother's garden."

"I ain't talking to no walls," Timmy said fiercely. He didn't want to be like his Mom, not now, not ever. He got up, more carefully this time, and fled to the doubtful safety of the cafeteria.

Walking home from school that afternoon, he saw that the brick monster had been busy. Grass was trampled along the curbs. Mucky red footprints spread on the damp sidewalks. When he looked real close, twigs were snapped in the bushes of some yards. Had it been dancing? Or fighting?

At Lafayette Street, Timmy almost crossed to the other side of

Milwaukie Avenue to avoid his grandmother's wall, but that would be sissy. He stayed on the sidewalk, as far from the old bricks as he could get. He glanced over as he walked past the wall. One of the bricks wiggled.

Timmy stopped. A hairy root sprouted in the crack between the loose brick and its neighbors, twisting like a worm. The brick slid outward slightly, paused, then leaped at him.

Timmy leapt into the street, only to dash back onto the sidewalk as a UPS truck honked. The jumping brick lay shattered. He nudged it with the toe of his shoe. The brick's rectangular shape collapsed to dust. A bright, shiny bullet rolled out from what had been a little space in the middle of the brick.

He looked back at the garden wall. The hole where the brick had just been was filled with tiny blood-red flowers, as if the brick had vanished years before. Timmy slipped the bullet in his pocket and followed the brick monster's tracks all the way home.

<p>

That night Mom thought she was a bird, and kept jumping down the stairs to crash into the steamer trunk on the bottom landing. After she sprained her ankle, Dad finally padlocked their bedroom door from the outside.

"Timmy," Dad said with tears in his eyes when he came back downstairs. "You can't tell no one about this. They'll take her away from us."

When Dad hugged him, Timmy kept the bullet clenched tight in his fist. Then Dad asked him what had happened to the Fred Meyer grocery bag and the hugging stopped.

Later, the brick monster tapped on his window for hours, but Timmy put a pillow over his head and told himself he was in faraway Araby with a magic lamp and a genie for a friend and no parents but his mother wit and the luck of a widow's son.

The River Knows Its Own

✚

In the morning, someone had used a scrap of brick to scratch "HELP ME" on the sidewalk in front of their house. Timmy found it when he stepped outside to go to school, and spent five minutes scuffing it with his shoe so Dad wouldn't see.

All the way to class, walls whispered and cried, but he ignored them. Timmy got detention for being late. He didn't care. Detention meant he didn't have to go home. He forgot his lunch, too.

When he finally left school around four, some of the cool kids were outside — Ti-Shaun, Jason and Zachary. They straddled really nice eighteen-speed mountain bikes, not like the rusty old one-speed banana bike Timmy had in the garage at home.

"Hey, Timmy," said Ti-Shaun. "Where's your book bag?"

Timmy tucked his chin down and tried to step around them. Jason walked his bike to the left to block Timmy. "Don't want to talk to your friends?"

"Don't got no friends," Timmy told his feet. He stuck one hand in his pocket, clutching the bullet.

"Sure you do," said Zachary. "Timmy talks to the walls, 'cause he ain't got no balls. Been taking lessons from your Momma?"

Timmy looked up at them, his eyes clouded with tears. He squeezed his face tight, holding his anger and shame and hurt inside until he felt like he'd burst. "My mother ain't none of your business."

All three of the boys laughed. "She ain't none of no one's business anymore," said Zachary. "Least of all her own. She crazy enough to try to put diapers on you, crybaby?"

Timmy thrust his hand out, with the bullet in his fist, then opened it. "This is for you guys if you don't leave me alone."

"Ooh," said Zachary, glancing at the other two boys. "Timmy's got a gun." He leered at Timmy. "Ever hear of zero tolerance, loser? We've got your ass now. You ever say a word about us, we'll turn

95

you in. Never come back to school, go to juvenile hall. You are *so* screwed, shithead."

They rode off laughing.

When he got to his grandmother's garden wall, Timmy leaned against it and whispered to the blood-red flowers. They glistened like raw liver as he brought his lips close to them. He could smell dirt and old metal.

"I'll help you," he said, "Whatever you want. But you have to help me."

"Good," said the wall. Its voice was stronger now, more confident, as if Timmy had fed it just by being there. "Bring a shovel. Come back tonight."

Timmy bolted his way through the cold beanie-weenies Dad slapped down for dinner. Mom was upstairs, singing at the top of her lungs about stars in the sky.

"Don't bother her, son," Dad said with a growl. "At least she's peaceable."

Not trusting himself to speak, Timmy nodded. "Uh-huh," he grunted as Dad continued to glare.

"I'm going out. Do your homework, go to bed by nine."

Timmy hadn't done homework in weeks, not since he first saw the brick monster's footprints, but he hadn't brought home any of Mrs. Williams' notes, either. He just nodded.

Dad cuffed Timmy in the side of the head, smiled one of his rare smiles, and walked out the back door, padlocking it from the outside like he always did when he went out at night.

Timmy waited ten minutes, then climbed through the living room window by the gas meter, the garage key in his hand. He got a short garden shovel and pair of gloves and laid them behind the meter, then scrambled back into the house. He figured going to the wall tonight meant after Dad got home, around two in the morning. That would be safest.

☦

Timmy woke to the sound of giggling. He was still fully dressed, but had fallen asleep despite his best efforts.

"Shhh!" his Dad whispered, except way too loud.

"Why?" It was a woman's voice, not Mom. She giggled again.

"My mother's asleep upstairs," said Dad. "We have to do it down here."

Even more giggling. "Oh, Roger," said the woman.

His Dad's name was Warren.

Timmy heard the couch springs creak. How was he going to get out? He crept over to his bedroom window. It was nailed shut, like most of the windows in the house. Could he slip through the hall to the bathroom, and wait for Dad and his friend to fall asleep or something?

Timmy hung his shoes around his neck, strings tied together, and snuck into the hall. One end opened into the kitchen and the bathroom, the other end opened to his room and living room. The lower stair landing was in the middle. He peeked around the corner into the kitchen.

The back door was cracked open.

Timmy waited until the giggling got real loud, then dodged through the kitchen and out the door. On the back steps, he struggled into his shoes. He was free.

The shovel clanked against the gas meter when he pulled it out.

"What the hell was that?" Dad asked, his voice coming through the glass of the window just above Timmy's head.

"Come on, Roger," whined the woman.

Just then Mom started singing real loud about angels on high. Timmy sprinted toward the street as the shouting began.

The wall greeted him when he got there, in a voice that echoed with the secrets of the night. "Timmy. Follow the flowers. Dig. Set me free and I will set you free."

He pushed his fingers into the soil where the brick had jumped out. The blood-red flowers around his hand looked black in the moonlight. He carefully uprooted them, set them near the curb on the damp grass, then put on the gloves and began prying away more bricks with the shovel.

There was a sigh, relief and sadness, as he pulled at the wall. Roots and soil tumbled onto the sidewalk. He heard a rattle, and bent to pick up the next bullet.

It wasn't a bullet, it was a tiny bone, spotted and damp. Timmy gasped and dropped it. Then he poked at the soil with his shovel. Dirt slipped toward him, a miniature landslide, and a skeleton hand stuck out. It was small, no bigger than his.

Timmy whimpered, but the wall had said it would help him. Help him with the boys at school, stop Dad from hitting him and Mom, make his life be good like other kids'. Hesitant to touch the bones even through his gloves, Timmy tugged gently at the hand. It popped free with a snap, collapsing to pieces in his grip. There was a longer arm bone still hanging from the soil, with little flecks of dirt and brick stuck to it, wrapped in a few scraps of rotten lace.

Timmy retched, holding his stomach down with tears in his eyes, then continued digging. He found a skull, hollow-eyed with a hole in the temple, staring from the dirt. The rotten ruins of a lace-trimmed dress circled the bones of the neck. Tucked under a shoulder of the skeleton was a rusted old flour tin.

He stopped digging and pulled the tin out, trying not to touch the bones any more than he had to. The lid was stuck, but Timmy banged at against the bricks until he could pop it loose. Inside he found a wooden-handled revolver wrapped in a dishtowel, and two more bullets loose on the bottom of the tin. Timmy fiddled with the revolver until the cylinder popped open, then slipped the bullets in.

It worked just like in the movies. And just like the movies, the gun would make him a hero, make Dad be nice to him and Mom, make the bullies leave him alone.

The skull stared at the street, blood-red flowers already creeping like snakes from its eye sockets and the bullet hole in the temple. Timmy realized he was done here. The girl behind the bricks was set free, out where others would find her and take care of her, and he had the gun to help him as promised. Taking his gloves and shovel along with the gun, Timmy left. Walls whispered and cried as he walked home, but Timmy didn't care about their voices anymore.

Clutching the revolver, he hid in the rhododendron next to the back steps of the house, where his Dad would come out in the morning. The bricks of the foundation whispered sweet lullabies to him until Timmy dreamed of faraway Araby and the sunny sands of freedom.

⚭

He woke to the sound of sirens going by in the street out front. Even as he blinked his eyes, Timmy realized the police were heading for Lafayette Street and garden wall he'd torn apart last night. It was raining again. He sneezed.

The gun lay in his lap, warm to the touch. Timmy used the corner of his shirt to wipe the water off the old revolver and carefully cocked back the hammer. Moments later, the door above him creaked open. Timmy raised the gun, his hands quivering. Mom stuck her head out, looked around, then smiled down at him.

"Good morning, Timothy."

It was the first time in months she'd even said his name. Somehow, the way she said it sounded a little bit like the voice of the wall.

The gun shook wildly. "Mom?"

"My sister is finally happy." She leaned down and held out her hand. "Give me the gun, Timothy. It doesn't belong to you."

He wasn't quite ready to hand it over yet. "Where's Dad?"

99

She glanced toward a muddy bare spot in the back garden. Timmy could see his shovel leaning against the fence. Even from where he sat, it was obvious that the soil had been churned in a long, narrow patch, then pounded down by someone with large, heavy feet. The brick monster had been here while he slept.

"Dad ran off last night with some woman he met in a bar," Mom said.

Timothy stood up and handed his mother the gun. "Be careful."

"It's not loaded," she replied. Her smile drew tight. "I'm going to visit your grandmother's grave. You coming?"

"It's a school day, Mom," he protested, sneezing. "But I'll come," he added when he saw her face collapse toward tears.

"Good." Mom smiled. "We can return her gun together." She glanced down at the weapon in her hand. "Your father borrowed it many years ago. He never gave it back."

On the bus on the way to the cemetery, she let him look at his grandmother's gun again. Timmy peered into her purse, careful not to pull the gun out where people would see it. The bullets really were gone.

"Mom."

She brushed a damp curl of hair from her cheek. "Hmm?"

"Who was she?"

His mother sighed. "My sister."

"I don't have an aunt."

"You did. Years ago."

Timmy's hand rested inside her purse, touching the gun. It was like handling a metal snake. "But Dad..."

"We dated in high school." She leaned her head against the glass of the bus window. "Things happened."

✝

His mother still sang in the night, but during the day she was mostly okay. Dad never came back, but a few days after he found the gun, Timmy saw the brick monster from a distance, early in the morning as he walked to school. It was huge, a rough and rotten statue covered with moss and grime, and it had Ti-Shaun dangling from one giant hand and Zachary from the other. Jason grabbed at Ti-Shaun's leg, screaming and crying. Timmy heard his own name booming on the wind, and he smiled down at his feet. When he looked up again, all three boys sprawled on the ground, their mountain bikes crushed. Timmy never saw its footprints again.

Tiny blood-red flowers grew in the back garden for years after. Sometimes in the winter, Timmy would find scraps of rotten lace twisted among them, little messages from his aunt. He figured she was happy, that the lace was just a reminder of the things that could happen in a person's life.

After a while, Timmy didn't really mind that Dad was gone, and he was glad to have Mom back, but sometimes he missed the brick monster.

♁

Those Boiled Bones

HOUSES DREAM, TOO. Mostly in the present progressive — the brush of snow upon the roof, the sensual massage of hard rain, the moon's progress across the arch of the sky. Some dreams are fast and hard, nightmares to make joists groan and wiring crackle blue within dust-filled walls. A man and woman argue, doors slam, the reedy wail of an infant goes on for hours, weakening until finally silence, like the mice in the basement, returns to its rightful place.

Then there are tiny bones to be boiled clean and pounded to dust and spread with fishmeal and compost among the rose bushes in an unending palimpsest of warm life within the wriggling soil.

☦

Starr came early, surprising us into an unplanned homebirth. Eloise went into labor late one evening with the suddenness of a lightning strike, water breaking into the sheets and shouting like a madwoman for hot chocolate and her mother's help.

I called Mother, put a kettle on the stove, called the doctor, remembered to turn on the gas, threw the overnight bag into the car, took the pinging-hot kettle off and filled it with water, and ran upstairs, turning back only to put the kettle on the burner once more.

"Walter!" Eloise screamed, shredding one of her Irish linen pillowcases. Her face was the same compressed red I imagined our emerging infant's would soon be. "You're too damned *slow*."

"I'm sorry, sweetie," I said, panting. "It'll be okay."

Her breath chuffed. "It...will...never...be...*okay*!"

The kettle screamed. I raced back downstairs ahead of her wrath as brakes squealed in the street. Metal crumpled with that weird, quiet thump. Outside, people shouted. The kettle continued to screech.

For a moment, the entire house shuddered as if it grieved.

♦

Faced with a choice between birth and death, the doctor treated Eloise's mother where she lay in the street. A severed femoral artery was only the most immediate of Mother's worries. The doctor sent a passing pizza boy into the house to help me until the ambulance no one thought to call arrived.

Hello-my-name-is-Thad and I stood gaping in the bedroom as Eloise screeched Starr into the world, cursing like a sailor and continuing to shred the bed linen. I held the baby while Hello-my-name-is-Thad cut the cord with Eloise's nail file to the ringing of his cell phone.

All the pizza boy had in his thermal bag was an anchovy special. I tipped Hello-my-name-is-Thad fifty dollars and we ate pizza and hot chocolate while Starr nursed and Eloise wept, until someone outside finally remembered we were in the house and sent three firemen in to get us.

The joists moaned their pain all night long though there was no wind.

♦

The spring after Starr was born, when she was a few months old, the rose bushes in the side yard bloomed with such astonishing vigor the *Oregonian* sent over a reporter and a photographer.

"Funny house you have here, Wally," said the reporter, a woman named Diana to whom I took an instant dislike. She was large and puffy-pale with hair far too big to be real and eyes like a vodka martini — clear, cold and bitter. "Pulled some stories from the morgue. Over the past century, there's been a suicide, a burning death and missing child."

"If houses dreamed, this one would have nightmares," the photographer added helpfully. He changed lenses and wormed in scratching-close to one of the fecund bushes.

"Thanks," I said, "but it's a happy place now. Pitter-patter of little feet and all that."

We both feigned amusement.

"So what's your secret?" she asked.

I shrugged. "Oregon weather? No cats pooping up the yard? I don't know. Eloise usually handles the garden, but it's been a busy spring with the baby and all."

"Roses grow everywhere in this town, but you've got blooms the size of Chinese chrysanthemums, thicker than daisies." Diana winked at me. "There's old women around here that would kill for your secret. So tell me, when did you purchase this property?"

✢

Eloise's mother came to stay, *to care for the baby* everyone said, but it was more for us to care for her. She'd nearly died just as Starr was born. That experience had driven her to a point somewhere between God's kind regard and a quiet, private madness. Mother limped around the house's polished oak floors with a dog-headed cane, eyes constantly flickering into corners.

"Walter," she said, thumping the walking stick. She seemed to have aged decades since the accident. "That baby cries all the time. Why do you leave her out in the yard?"

"Mother." I sighed my way to patience. "Starr almost never cries. She's sweet." The baby was oddly quiet, in fact. As quiet as a house. And we certainly didn't leave her outside, either.

"Keeps me awake nights, crying out there beneath those awful roses." Tears stood in her eyes. "Children shouldn't cry alone."

I went to boil some water. Doors slammed upstairs. I thought I heard yelling, but when I went to look, Eloise was sleeping, Starr was cooing in her bassinette, while Mother was still in the living room staring into corners like a cat.

✜

It all came out in the end, thanks to Diana's newspaper story. Someone recognized the rose bushes as a rare varietal. A breeder was called. The breeder had a cousin who had once lived in the house.

The missing child had never been found, the cousin's family a good one in the days when that counted for something with the then-deferential police. Still, witnesses emerged. Serious men with shovels and trowels dug up the side yard and sifted soil. The roses were taken away, fragments of shinbone were sent off for testing, Mother had a stroke and the baby said her first words at eight months of age.

"Wake up," Starr shouted from her bassinette. All the doors slammed at once while water ran down the insides of the windowpanes.

✜

Houses dream, too. Not just nightmares, but sometimes fantasies, for houses love those who live within. They nurture their families inside a cocoon of wood and glass and brick, swaying in the winter winds and warding off the worst of the summer heat. Wishes come true in dreams, for an hour or a season.

In the waking world the house sighs its regrets while blood roses bloom the size of Chinese chrysanthemums in the side garden, fed by those boiled bones.

⚘

Eye Teeth

TURNING ON TO S.E. BELMONT Street, I ran into Shark.

Literally.

He was a Ukrainian kid originally, but that was even before I met him. After a few too many swims in the retro vat, some wicked surgery and a whole lot of transposons Mother Nature never intended, he was...well...something else.

Shark wasn't much over one meter forty but he had to mass two hundred kilos. His head was bullet-shaped and it melted into his shoulders without benefit of neck or throat. I'd heard he had carbon fiber mesh woven into his muscles for scaffolding—true or not, he had arms bigger around than *my* fat head. Legs to match.

The weirdest thing, what got him on virteo every now and then on some extreme mod program, was his skin. Shark was armored head to toe with a mosaic of enamel fragments growing straight out of his epidermis. He was covered in human teeth, basically, on every part of his body except his jaws. There he had pointy freaking shark teeth, about four rows' worth.

And I do mean *everywhere* on that tooth skin thing, if you know what I mean.

The only thing human besides his general shape was his eyes. They were a pale, watery blue, like you expect on a librarian or a tax accountant. Which was weird because even a natural guy like me pops custom Eyes every chance I get—I was wearing gray market

109

StarEyes that day, supposed to help pick up chicks and charm the world — while Shark's peepers were original equipment.

Of course, he got groupies, which was more than anyone else I knew. They didn't last long, but they partied hearty until E.R. time.

Still and all, I wouldn't want to get up every morning and scour my happy ass from stem to stern with a toothbrush. The guy must buy Colgate by the case lot. I could only imagine what his hemorrhoids were like.

He was also perfectly capable of ripping my arms off by way of friendly greeting. Shark demonstrated this character trait by peeling back the hood of my Skoda Hybrid.

I hit the emergency flashers and fumbled open the gull wing door. "Hey, cut that shit out!"

Shark sort of patted the hood back down. The sheet metal looked like tinfoil after the baked potato has gone to its reward. "I lookin'k for ch'ou."

He didn't talk so good either. But that had been true years ago too, back when he still had lips.

"You finding'k ch'me," I said, ignoring the honking horns behind me. Shark would take care of them if they didn't quiet down quick. "What d'you want, Shark? I ain't done nothing to nobody."

Not true, strictly speaking, but I certainly hadn't done anything that should interest the sort of people that kept Shark in toothpaste money.

"Ch'ou got what belong'k to Big Ch'akov. He got respec'k for ch'ou, so ch'ou got til midnight to bring'k it in. Mary's on Broadway."

That was a long speech for Shark.

"Shark, I wouldn't know Big Yakov if he bit my ankle. He wouldn't know me either. What the hell are you talking about?"

"Don' ch'ou play dum'k." Shark gave my hood a punch that slammed the Skoda's front end to the pavement, then waddled off.

"Okay, I won't," I said as I got back in. Miracle of miracles, the damned car still ran.

✦

The Natural Ink on Belmont, just past 33rd, is a pretty good place to meet girls wearing tie-dyed tank tops, cut-off shorts and no underwear of any kind. On the down side they usually haven't shaved or bathed in a while and are waiting for their dope-dealing boyfriends. It's a place to start. Besides, getting a carrot-gazpacho smoothie dumped on my lap would be a change of pace. It's all part of Oregon's natural beauty.

My StarEyes glittered at the counter girl as I ordered a bowl of vegan chili and a big pot of chamomile tea. Once I had my food, I sat down at a little table decoupaged with pages out of old luxury car brochures and issues of *Architectural Digest* and wondered what the hell was I going to do about Shark and Big Yakov.

Despite my misgivings and his close resemblance to a natural disaster in progress, Shark I could handle. Sort of. He and I had been in junior high together for a while, before his phenotype got too weird for the school board. Plus that bit about ripping the arms off two Cambodian guys that had been giving him shit for three or four years.

Back then he'd been nubby and weird. I was pretty sure he remembered I was halfway nice to him while everyone else was beating the crap out of him. Ever since, we'd moved in different circles.

As for Big Yakov, he ran lots of action in the northwest industrial district. Got his picture in the paper every time he endowed a park or came to the mayor's swearing in. Last time a cop tried to collar him, one of the desk sergeants had thrown the punk off the bridge after Big Yakov made a few phone calls.

Law and order type, Big Yakov. I was a small time clerical worker. No more interesting to him than the rivets on the Steel

Jay Lake

Bridge. And I had no more influence over him than I did over Mount Hood.

I thought about messaging my friend Mellie the cab dispatcher through the comm hack in my StarEyes, but I couldn't see how much help she'd be. She could always send me a cab.

"Hey."

The woman in front of me was just my type. Or at least just Natural Ink's type. Frizzy blonde dreadlocks, one of those small faces like you see on daughters of old New England money, a purple macramé shirt that left nothing whatsoever to the imagination and pair of faded European hiking shorts that had been patched a dozen times with denim and old bandanas. Big knobby-ass boots too, with rolled down socks the color of the red peppers in my chili.

To hell with Melli.

"Hey yourself," I said. I looked at her with my StarEyes thinking happy sexy thoughts:

Pheromones, baby.

The rhythm of your pulse.

I look like Freedom Barrymore in Hawaii Helldive.

Damned things were supposed to guarantee seduction, but they blew chunks. What did I expect for fifteen cents on the dollar, gray market? At least I still had my CargoEyes for work.

"You're sitting on my jacket."

So much for StarEyes. I pushed the chair back, stood up and looked. Nothing there.

"I don't think so," I said, but when I met her eyes again the gun in her hand interfered with my full attention. Some sort of sleek, black pistol I couldn't identify, but then I'd never paid much attention to firearms before.

"We really have to talk," she said in a breathy voice.

I stood up slowly as the pistol slipped back into the cargo pockets of her shorts. "I don't think this relationship is working out so well."

"You'll love it." She smiled. Perfect teeth, like little pearls. "Trust me."

There were a lot of things about her I could love, for a few hours at least. That pistol was not one of them.

To add insult to injury, somehow even though I was the hostage I had to drive.

⸙

I'm a non-union dock clerk. Guns don't scare me much. I see drunk union apes with thirty-inch drop-forged wrenches going at it almost every day. One time Mike the Mouse chased me out of my little portable office by driving a forklift through the wall. I figured if nature girl was going to hurt me, she would have done it already.

All the same, I'm not in Shark's line of work. I'd been looking for cheap sex, not cheap violence. Hell, I wasn't even wearing the right Eyes for this.

My Skoda pulled up next to an old railroad car near the Ross Island cement plant, the one under the 99E viaduct. No one around, not even a delivery truck. The railroad car was a metal boxcar of the last century, dry docked on an old siding with a cement skirt around its base. Sort of the ultimate in mobile homes. I hadn't remembered seeing it down here before, but that didn't mean much.

My Portland hippie chick made me get out first. She came around the car behind me and set one hand on the small of my back. "The other side," she said. "There's a door."

There was, facing a blank warehouse wall. It looked like the storm door off my grandma's house when I was a kid. Someone had torched a rectangular cut in the side of the boxcar and welded this thing in. It was weird, like seeing a dorsal fin on a cat.

I tugged it open. The thing even *squeaked* like a screen door, with that faint scent of aluminum and vinyl. Behind it was cheap office type door. I pushed that one open too.

There was a little office inside, paneled with cork and whiteboard, which in turn was covered with scribbled notes, sheets of paper, photo printouts, maps, and probably half the deep dark secrets of the past couple of decades for all I could tell. A metal desk straight out of an old private eye movie dominated one corner, while fluorescent lights flickered in a drop ceiling overhead. A hat rack in the corner held a couple of light rain jackets. The only modern thing in the room was the monomer-pane data display on the jumbled desk, sticking up like a sheet of glass with a zoning variance from the law of gravity.

It was mighty cool for a boxcar. The air moved slightly, underlain with a stale smell.

"How come it's not hotter than July Fourth in here?" I asked.

Then the room lurched a little bit, my stomach dropped, and I thought, *uh-oh*.

I was wrong. There was no cheesy knockout gas or some such stupid crap. The office was an elevator, dropping downward.

After about forty-five seconds a tone sounded.

"Out," she said. She wasn't bothering to hide the gun any more.

The door seemed to be the only choice, so out I went.

The office had come down an i-beam shaft like a big old freight elevator, which was basically what it was. In front of me was a tunnel perhaps fifteen or twenty meters to the far well extending to darkness in either direction. An array of desks, cabinets, twen-cen cube walls and so forth spread out from the elevator like a stain from a spilled box of offices. Bare long-life bulbs dangled from the ceiling high above.

Two more women and a man waited for me. They were all dressed in puffy boots, bag-suits, loose breath masks and goggles around their necks. Ordinary office clothes, nothing to make them stand out, unlike my lovely captor.

"Mr. Daley Lorenz," said one of the women, a short brunette

with a pinched face. She reached out a hand. "Welcome."

"No thanks," I said. "Can I go home now?" I knew a few dockworkers I could sic on these people. Hell, Shark might even do it, once I got past the Big Yakov problem. Whatever that was. Doubtless my captors knew about it too.

I hoped someone would tell me soon.

"Adele, did you brief him?" she asked, looking over my shoulder.

"He's a prick," said Adele. "Didn't stop staring at my breasts the whole time."

"Hey!" I said.

The brunette shook her head. "I am sorry, Mr. Lorenz, for the theatrics and for the lack of information. Time is short. You have a rendezvous with Mr. Yakov tonight, am I not correct?"

"I have no idea what this is about." I stepped over to the nearest desk chair, sat down, put my feet on the desk, right over the papers. "I don't know what Big Yakov wants, I don't know what you want, and I don't really care. I just want to get out of your way."

"You wish me to believe that you are a simple dupe in these proceedings, Mr. Lorenz?"

"Yes! That's me. Dupe, simple dupe." I leaned over, rummaged around on the desk until I came up with a half-full bottle of water. "Happy to stay that way, too. Why don't *you* meet Big Yakov tonight and work it out amongst yourselves?"

"We are on..." She glanced at her companions. "Opposite sides of certain questions from Mr. Yakov."

I chugged water, then wiped my lips with a satisfied gasp. "I'm on no side of Mr. Yakov, nor you."

"Your Eyes, Mr. Lorenz. The StarEyes you recently acquired *sub rosa.*"

Oops. "What about them?"

"There was a mistake. They were--"

"Wait," I interrupted. "I've seen this movie. They were stolen,

115

there was a mix-up, the fence sold me the wrong set, you want them back, blah blah blah. And let me guess, Big Yakov wants them too."

"In a manner of speaking."

"Fine. You can have them back. Have Adele run me home, I'll swap them for my CargoEyes, we're done. Hell, I don't even need a refund."

"It's too late for that."

Double oops. "Too late for what?"

"By now they've...adapted to you."

"Adapted how?"

"You are their host. They will work for no one else."

That wasn't how it was supposed to be with Eyes. Interchangeable parts, hotswap technology. Blah blah blah. "Look, they don't work for *me*."

"Oh, yes they do," she said. She turned to the other woman to her left, a thin Chinese gal. "Doff your clothing, Mei-Wan. All of it."

Mei-Wan stepped out of her bag-suit and puffy boots to reveal tight, lacy bra and panty set in cobalt blue. Well, this was getting interesting. Or so I thought, as the bra and panties came off.

Until Mei-Wan unfastened the skin of her neck. Then it just got nasty. There were a lot of little whipping tentacles inside Mei-Wan, and a lot of them had tiny eyeballs, and a lot of *them* were looking at me.

Now was a real good time to panic. After a couple of minutes, Adele's gun to my temple brought me back from an extended hissy fit.

"Most people would have seen an attractive young woman Mr. Lorenz, rubbing her skin. You saw an attractive young woman removing her skin."

"The Eyes." *Never again*, I promised myself. "Is it ... she ... it ... real?"

"Ah, ah, that would be telling."

Oh, shit. "Now what?"

"We deliver the Eyes to Big Yakov. As originally promised. You are simply the carrier."

"For God's sake, I could have delivered *myself* myself."

The brunette smiled. "We desire the credit, Mr. Lorenz."

As she walked off into the darkness, I turned to Adele. Her perky pink aureoles were certainly convincing under that macramé top. "You too?"

Her tongue flicked out, licked her nose and lower eyelashes and went back way too fast for any normal girl. She just grinned before pulling up a chair to block to the door to the elevator-office.

⚚

I spent the rest of the day and evening making up scurrilous limericks about my captors and wondering what the hell I was going to do. Not to mention who the hell these horrible tentacle people really were.

Big Yakov would cut the Eyes out of my head as soon as look at me. I knew his rep. Shark could pop them out for the fun of hearing me squeal. I was a human Eye box to these...people.

And who were these *people*? Some ancient evil species from the cracks beneath the earth. Or the universe's lowest-budget alien invasion. I was losing my mind, pure and simple. The Eyes were taking me over. That's all there was to it.

I considered just popping the Eyes out, dropping them on the desk, and walking out of there blind. There were serious drawbacks to that plan. So instead I slammed my hand in a drawer twice, to see if I would wake up. That didn't help. I tried one of my limericks on Adele:

"There once was a snake named Adele

"Riding the express train to Hell

"She held up a guy

"Who did nothing but sigh

"And complain about how she did smell."

She pointed the gun at me and told me to shut the hell up or they'd deliver the Eyes in a body bag.

Were they real? Were the Eyes a scam? How could I tell the difference?

All Eyes were visual preprocessors, by definition. They managed images before sending them to brain's visual cortex. The military used SniperEyes, with enormously extended focal ranges and multiple grades of monatomic lasers to assess wind speed, air density and so forth. Firemen used SmokeEyes. Hell, I used CargoEyes at work, that let me read bar codes on containers and manifests without screwing around with a handheld.

So anyone could spoof an Eye, if they could hack into it. Normally Eyes were shielded, raw data flowing in from outside, processed neural signal flowing back. It wasn't like they had an IP address.

But the Eye could be prehacked. Could be built with some kind of access channel.

Or some dope like me could open an auxiliary channel to my presence server via my bonefone, and *give* a hacker access.

Melli. My friend the taxi dispatcher. She knew everyone, everything that was going on. I set about subvocalizing a message for her, hoping like hell Adele was too bored to realize what I was doing. I used the crawler squirt via my StarsEyes—low bandwidth text, more likelihood of getting out from down here underground.

:::MEL:::NEED SOMEONE ASAP 2 HACK MY EYES:::LIFE OR DEATH:::D::::

After a few minutes, her words came into my field of view.

:::SHARK GOT YR TONGUE?:::

So she didn't know everything.

:::I WISH:::CANT XPLAIN:::NEED 2 KNOW IF EYES ARE CLEAN:::

:::W8:::WILL DO:::L8R:::

Later? The direction my evening was headed in, I wasn't going to *have* a later.

☥

We went back up the office elevator around 11:30 that night. No word from Melli. No sign of Mei-Wan the snake woman since her little magic act with the skin. Just me, Adele, brunette and her boyfriend.

Or snakefriend.

Whatever.

At least there was no talk of using my Skoda. The snakefriend went off in the dark, returned a few minutes later with a safety orange Hummer H6—four axles of pure road-crumbling power on the rubber hoof. He got in to drive, Adele and I sat in the distant back seat, while brunette took a jump seat that could have hosted a family of starving Belgians. Adele's pistol came along for the ride too, out on her lap in her little right hand.

My message crawler jerked to life as the Hummer rumbled into the night.

:::DALEY:::WHERE U BEEN?:::BAD CARRIER:::MEL:::

So the snake people had started jamming me after my first round of messaging. I couldn't very well subvocalize now with Adele and her pistol sitting next to me. How was I going to do this?

"*I need help* knowing where we're going," I said to brunette.

:::EYE NEEDLE KELP:::

Shit. The parser wasn't going to cut me any slack.

"Shut up," Adele suggested.

:::D, RU DRUNK?:::ALEXI SAYS YR CARRIER IS STRANGE:::

"I'm *not drunk*," I said. "I'm worried."

:::KNOTTED RANK:::

"Shut *up*." This time she jammed the pistol into the soft skin of my lower jaw. I swear she bruised my tongue from the outside.

119

:::UR N TROUBLE ARNT U DALEY?:::

All right, Melli. I wasn't getting anything more out to her right now, though.

After a minute or two, as we rumbled across the New Morrison Bridge—New, New, New Morrison Bridge actually, but who counted that sort of thing anymore?—Melli came back on.

:::ALEXI SAYS YR EYES HAVE BN HACKED:::B CAREFUL:::

You're a freaking genius, Melli.

"Mr. Lorenz," said brunette, "I suggest you stop whatever it is you are doing before I change my mind about needing a live host for the Eyes."

"Yes, ma'am. Sometimes I can't *help* myself. I'll try to *help*."

:::HELP:::HELP:::

Adele jammed the gun into my jaw so hard she bruised my sinuses that time. So I shut up to finish out the ride and watch Melli's last message on my crawler. Somehow she'd looped it.

:::TAXI COMING:::TAXI COMING:::TAXI COMING:::TAXI COMING:::TAXI COMING:::TAXI COMING:::TAXI COMING:::

Great. A freaking taxi. I sure hoped that was good news. I'd had enough bad news for one day.

⊕

The H6 idled into a warehouse, overhead door rolling shut behind us. Given that we were ten miles or so from the airport the contents of the warehouse were a bit odd. There were huge tapered cylinders of jet engines on their rollaway stands, all piping and exhaust. Wings, tails, fuselages in various states of disassembly loomed in shadows surrounding a single pool of bright light where we had parked.

Me, I would have stopped near the door and avoided the light. These people were amateurs.

As if my captors were people.

Brunette shook her head at Adele then got out leaving the two of us alone. A whole bunch of guys stepped out of the shadows, guys in various stages of bulkiness. Big Yakov and Shark were at the head of the little army. At least I assumed it was Big Yakov. He didn't look much like his pictures in the paper.

If Shark had an opposite, Big Yakov was it. He wasn't even as tall as Shark, and his face was smooth like a baby's—no lines, almost slack. Puffy lips pursed around a lit cigar like it was a nipple or something. Just *owning* tobacco products was good for hard time downstate, let alone *smoking* them. His arms and legs were pudgy and bowed, something even the swanky twen-cen suit he was wearing couldn't cover up.

I would have sworn from the photos Big Yakov was a meter taller, but this little guy was smoking and leading Shark around. It had to be him.

Brunette and Big Yakov talked for a few minutes before she nodded at the H6. Adele opened the door, got out, and waved me out with the pistol.

:::GET READY:::

Word from Melli. Nice to hear from her before I died. Ready? For what?

"Mr. Lorenz," said Big Yakov. His voice was as squeaky as I might have guessed from his body. "Welcome."

Shark shifted a little. His toothed skin gleamed in the warehouse lights, the thousands of little crowns giving him a stippling of shadow. His blue eyes narrowed as Big Yakov looked me over.

That's right, Shark, I thought. Remember when I used to be nice to you. When you were a kid, Shark.

"Hello, Mr. Yakov sir," I said. "Sorry about the mix up."

"And have you seen the stars in your Eyes, Mr. Lorenz?"

Adele's pistol thumped into my kidneys. What the hell? All I'd seen so far was snakes. "Yes. They're beautiful."

"Tell me. Where is Cassiopeia right now?"

Having a drink down at the White Horse? How the hell should I know? "Who's Cass--"

The pistol thumped me again. Brunette glared at me. "Enough, Mr. Yakov. Here are your Eyes. I suggest you make the payment, try them on, and then we shall go."

Big Yakov held out his pudgy little hand. "My StarEyes, Mr. Lorenz."

Shark stirred again. There was something here he didn't like, something beyond all the obvious stuff I didn't like. Such as me going home blind, if I ever went home at all. Brunette had said the Eyes wouldn't work for anyone else. She hadn't said I couldn't take them out. Common sense suggested that.

Unfortunately I didn't have a bargaining position. My pinkie touched my right Eye, as if I were ready to dig in and pop it loose. I put on my best nonunion-goober-talking-to-angry-longshoreman smile. "Alright, sir, but I'm going to have to trus—"

Then all hell broke loose.

A taxi smashed through the rollup door. It was one of the red zone duty cabs with armor and slit windows. There were several more behind the first cab, all sliding to a stop inside the warehouse. Big Yakov's footsoldiers had guns and tasers out like the pros that they were, ready for a little merry murder.

My buddies from the dock came out of those cabs like water from a bilge. The same union pricks who rattled my teeth every day of my working life were here to save me. And they were impressive. These boys started out big and got bigger. They came equipped with pipes, chains, wrenches, zip guns, tasers. I even saw Mike the Mouse with a cutting torch in his hand, tanks strapped to his back.

"Jesus H. and the baker's dozen," I whispered.

Adele must have been impressed too, because she forgot to bruise more of my internal organs with the muzzle of her pistol.

For three or four seconds, everything was balanced. Like

watching one of those buildings they blow up—the explosives crackle, some dust shoots out, all the concrete and steel thinks about it for a just a moment, and you're wondering if maybe everything will just hang there unsupported for a while, before gravity body-checks the whole business.

The gravity of testosterone kicked in amid a roar of bullets, tasers and very angry men.

I dropped to the floor and tried help out by tangling Adele's ankles. Pistol or not, I'd have rather duked it out with her than one of Big Yakov's trolls. She was already moving though, her skin rippling like a cheap special effect.

Holy fright! For one minute I'd actually forgotten about the eyeball-tipped snakes inside these people.

Shark had Big Yakov over one shoulder and was making a dash through his friendlies to the shadows beyond. I sort of assumed he'd be back. Me, I was getting the hell away from the gunplay. The underside of the H6 looked good, so I scooted between the tires to find snakefriend there shooting out from under the back bumper.

I didn't have anything to fight with. Instead I reached up, slipped my hand under his belt and gave him a magnum wedgie. He yelped and dropped his pistol. I dragged him back a little, away from the weapon, and we wrestled. Which isn't easy to do under a car. Not even a big SUV.

I did manage to bang his head against the suspension a few times. This made him woozy. I snagged the pistol and slid out the other side.

A lot fewer bullets there, so I scuttled for the shadows. I tossed the gun as soon as I was safe—I didn't know how to shoot it, I just hadn't wanted snakefriend coming to his senses and shooting me.

The firing was dying down, replaced by shouting and screaming and promising meaty thumps. I had no more interest in returning to the fight than I did in performing major surgery on myself. Hanging back was just, well...the right thing to do.

I looked around anyway. There was a tractor parked nearby, a little thing like one of those airport luggage tugs. It had a roll cage and a front attachment with a big rotary brush. Maybe something for cleaning pavement.

Okay, I thought.

I wrestled a metal fuselage skin segment onto the front of the roll cage, got in the driver's seat, and studied the controls. It had obviously been designed for operation by trained monkeys like my union buddies out on the warehouse floor.

Start the engine, a compressed hydrogen rig that was eerily quiet. Engage the auxiliary power. The brush was plenty noisy to make up for the engine. Put it in gear, roll out of the shadows peering around my shield and look for some trouble. "Party time!" I shouted, then whooped.

Snakefriend was in full tentacle mode now, duking it out with two of my boys just on my side of the H6. His back was to me. I rolled forward, rammed the brush into him as the boys stepped aside. I kept going until the brush was throwing off bits of orange H6 paint along with snakefriend goo.

"Good job, Dolty!" shouted Majid, one of the longshoremen. He was bleeding from cuts that looked like they'd been laid down with a wire whip, but grinning like a fool at the same time. Then Majid and his buddy scuttled around the back of the car.

I reversed and drove around the front. The hiss of the brush on pavement sounded different now, lubricated with snakefriend.

Here was the main action. Most of Big Yakov's guys were down. Longshoremen were sitting on some of them. I didn't see little big man himself anywhere, but Shark was back in it, tangling with two of the snake people—had to be brunette and Adele. There wasn't anyone else.

They were all over him, crawling and twisting, but something about his tooth enamel defeated their grip. All they could do was chip away. Shark was snapping with his mouth teeth, spitting out purpley brown bits. It was a fight of attrition.

My boys were obviously happy to stand aside and let it happen. They weren't rooting for anyone in this fight, and probably figured on rumbling the winner. I should have felt the same way.

But this was *Shark*. He was a freak, but he was our freak. Or at least my freak. Not like those snake things.

I could still remember that scared little Ukrainian kid in school, whimpering through black eyes and a busted lip. I mean, I also remembered him yanking Billy di Paulo's arm off at the shoulder and beating Billy over the head with it, but that was after three years of Billy slapping Shark on the back of neck every time they passed in the hall.

Everybody has a limit.

Brush at the ready, I moved in to clean some teeth. Adele and brunette never saw me coming. Shark did.

He just smiled.

✤

Turned out Melli had been driving the first cab. She'd stayed within the armored cockpit, waiting for the fight to finish one way or the other. Now we stood in the moonlight as the longshoremen loaded up their wounded and took care of business inside. The three snake people were history, but no one was dead on our side. A couple of Big Yakov's people had bought it.

There were going to be a lot of folks in the hospital on Pill Hill for a while.

Shark had stopped fighting as soon as I'd cleaned up the snake women, just stood there staring at the longshoremen. Nobody had felt terribly motivated to take him on.

"How'd you do it?" I asked Melli. "Those longshoremen don't like me any more than they like broccoli. They think I'm a punk."

"Yeah, but you're their punk." She smiled. "That's how Mike

the Mouse put it. Plus Big Yakov's been smuggling aircraft parts out of the country. They're not getting any of that action. They were happy to show him the value of good union labor."

"What about the Eyes?" Nobody else had seen what I had seen, I knew that already. Majid had thought he was fighting a guy in a suit, a guy with real good training but no more. Same for brunette and Adele. I wasn't sure what Shark thought he'd seen, but everyone else saw me mow down two women who were giving Shark holy hell.

"Alexi's not sure, except that they've been well and truly hacked. What do you think?"

"I didn't see what anyone else saw." Except maybe Shark, but I wasn't willing to say that even to Melli. "I saw...something terrible."

"You want to get rid of them? Alexi would love to have those Eyes."

I thought about that. Would I rather see snake people around me? Or just know they were there, and never be able to tell? Besides, I had decided that I believed brunette when she said the Eyes wouldn't work for anyone else.

"No," I said. "Not right now."

"Want a ride home?"

"No thanks. I'll take the Hummer."

When I went back inside the warehouse, Shark was still standing there, covered in Adele and brunette goop, watching the longshoreman trash the place and spatter kerosene around. The tractor's brush had scarred him up pretty good.

"Big Ch'akov no' happy," Shark said. "But I t'ink he forgive."

"Next time, have the dock boys smuggle it for you," I suggested. "You always get quality with union labor." Then, in an unaccustomed bloom of fellow feeling, "You want a ride somewhere?"

"Nye. I walk." Shark looked at me for while, his watery eyes almost blank in the warehouse lights. "T'ank ch'ou."

I nodded at floor, at the goop covering his enamel. "Did you...see them?"

He didn't answer that. We stared each other down for minute then I got in the Hummer and backed out carefully, weaving around the cabs.

By the time I got over the New Morrison Bridge there was a column of smoke visible in the morning twilight over northwest Portland. I went by the railroad car, just to see, but it was gone. No big surprise there. Scuffing around on the siding where it had been, I couldn't find any sign of the elevator shaft, either.

I left the Hummer there with the keys in it and went home. My CargoEyes were there, but I thought I'd stick with the StarEyes for while.

Maybe I'd see Cassiopeia one of these days. Besides, I had to keep an eye out for snakes.

✢

Fading Away

AARON WAS SENT TO THE PARK while the visiting nurse helped Momma. Momma coughed a lot more lately, but quieter, while Daddy prayed harder and harder over her. There was nothing Aaron could do but be in the way. Outside it was easier not to think about Momma—Aaron liked the hot Nevada summer days. Sometimes the other moms at the park were nice to him, too.

He saw the fat man sitting on the swing. The stranger had dark glasses, shaggy dark hair down over his ears, a white suit with spangles all over it, and a big cape like Superman's. Except the cape was white, and shorter. Aaron could see the park right through the fat man's white suit, kind of the same way he could see things when he walked around with his t-shirt over his head.

Aaron was a little afraid and a little curious all mixed together, so he went over to the swings. "Hey, mister, you gonna sit there all day?"

The fat man looked at Aaron, his eyes hidden behind the big dark glasses. He seemed surprised. "You can see me? Sorry, son. I'll move on." He gathered his weight and stood. The bottoms of his boots floated slightly above the ground. The fat man looked lost and lonely.

Aaron knew how that felt.

"You don't need to leave," Aaron said. "I don't mind you being here."

"That's mighty nice of you, son." The fat man had a rich voice, like listening to chocolate cake talk. He settled back on to the swing. "Is there anything I can do for you?"

Aaron knew the fat man was a ghost. He'd never seen one, but everyone knew you could see right through ghosts. He wasn't scared now—his Momma had become more of a ghost than this fat man. Aaron tried to remember what he'd heard about ghosts. "You're supposed to help someone before you can go to Heaven, right?"

The fat man looked disappointed, as if he'd expected Aaron to say something else. "That's not quite it, but near enough, I reckon."

Aaron imagined money, candy, Disneyland. "Cool. What can you do for me?"

"Not much, son. Show myself, sometimes. Talk." The fat man tried to smile, which made him look even sadder than before. "Sing."

That sounded so stupid to Aaron. "Sing? What good is that?"

The ghost glanced away from Aaron for a few moments before meeting his eye again. "Some folks love music, son. It lifts up their hearts."

"Momma loves music," Aaron said. She had, before she got sick.

The fat man smiled. "Who does she like?"

Aaron couldn't remember the names, but Momma had had albums everywhere. "Lots of people," he said, scuffing his shoe. "But she can't listen no more."

The ghost frowned. "Why not?"

"She's real sick." He scuffed his shoe again. "I'm not supposed to talk about it."

The fat man squatted down in front of Aaron, looking him face to face. "What's the matter with her, son?" He sounded like he really cared about Aaron and Momma.

Aaron's voice caught in his throat. "Got the cancer. In her belly.

She can't get out of bed, she can't eat, she can't do nothing." His chest shuddered. "Nurse Simmons says Momma's lost her heart."

"Son..." The fat man's voice sounded like he was going to cry. He started to pat Aaron's shoulder, then pulled his hand back to smooth a wrinkle out of his white suit. "Let's go see her."

Aaron cut off his sob. The fat man seemed to mean it. Aaron figured Nurse Simmons was gone by now. "I ain't allowed visitors at the house. But if Daddy's out, I can get you in. Maybe your music can help Momma find her heart." Aaron didn't know how to help her, and it seemed no one else would.

✝

They came in through the kitchen, past the old round-shouldered refrigerator. The house was quiet.

"Here," Aaron whispered to the fat man as he eased open the door to Momma's sick room. The nurse was gone. Everything smelled like pee and mold, not fresh and warm like Momma used to. Followed by the ghost, Aaron moved to the foot of the bed, clasping his hands behind his back so he wouldn't bother her. Aaron's eyes had that peppery about-to-cry sting they always got around Momma. The fat man touched him lightly on the shoulder, like the brush of a bird flying by in the woods, then moved to stand alongside the bed, where Daddy always sat.

In the dark room the fat man glowed, each little sparkle on his suit flashing like a star in the sky. He took off the glasses, which showed his glowing brown eyes. The fat man reached out and brushed Momma's lips with his fingertips.

"Frank?" Momma's voice was more of a gasp than a whisper.

"No, darlin'." The fat man's teeth glowed as he smiled in the dark. His chocolate cake voice was stronger. "It's me. You know who I am."

"The King." Momma sounded relieved, almost happy. "But

you're gone..." She sighed. "It's really you, isn't it?"

The fat man looked down the bed at Aaron. "You sure you want me to do this? She needs to go on."

Aaron was so pleased Momma sounded happy, so pleased he had done something to help, that he couldn't bring himself to stop the fat man.

"No sir, go on. Sing to her. Please."

The fat man took Momma's hand and starting singing in a low, rich voice. He sang a song Aaron had never heard before, about how the fat man couldn't help falling in love with Momma. Momma cried—real small, quiet tears. Aaron wasn't sure why, but it made him happy to see Momma cry like that. It meant she forgot about hurting long enough to care about something.

After a while, Aaron realized the fat man wasn't singing any more. Aaron wiped his eyes. He could see Momma smiling in the glow from the fat man's suit.

"Why'd you stop, mister? You were helping her."

The fat man stared at Momma, and brushed his fingers over her lips one more time. "She's found her heart, son. Your Momma just needed someone to tell her it was okay to go on."

"Momma?" Aaron ran to the other side of the bed and picked up her hand. It felt like a bundle of sticks wrapped in tissue. He looked at her mouth real close, put his fingers near her lips. She wasn't breathing, not even a little bit. His heart seemed to fill his throat, so he couldn't breathe either. Aaron wanted to scream. He'd told the fat man to sing, and the fat man had killed her. "No, Momma..." he gasped.

Aaron felt a bird brush on his shoulder once again. But the fat man was still across the bed from him, now growing fainter. Aaron could see the dresser real clear right through the fat man, even in the dark, like he was less and less there.

"I'll watch over my boy for a spell now," said Momma from behind Aaron, her voice strong again.

Aaron's fear drained away like dishwater from the sink. He'd done Momma right by bringing the ghost to her. "Thank you," he whispered as the fat man faded away.

Then: "I love you, Momma."

✝

Eggs For Dinner

COURTNEY'S LIFE HAD CHANGED over the years, though never for the better. Her father left for overseas when she was eight. "Oil," Mom always said in the years since, but oil came from the earth everywhere — Alaska, the Middle East, Texas — sucked up by pumps like giant mantises praying to the sun-burned grass. Dad left, and only his postcards came back from foreign parts.

After a while even the postcards stopped.

Much later, as Courtney was starting high school, her Grandmother McCandless came to stay. Mom needed to go spend a long time in a cuckoo hospital, talking to doctors about oil and Courtney's father. Grams didn't hold with doctors, or much else, but Courtney had nowhere to go. So she ate the same burnt-edged eggs every morning, rode the same bus to school every day, and came home to the same homework and prayers every night, wondering if life would ever get better.

Or when she could run away, too. She would escape, but like her father — free — not like her mother, wandering into crazy. Like him, Courtney would go over the seas, live her life on the water she'd never yet seen.

When Mom finally did return, she was different. Like a postcard of herself, sent in reminder from a distant country.

"Hey, sweetie," said the woman standing on the second step of the front porch.

The house hadn't been painted since Dad left for overseas. Seven summers had flaked the color away to silvered wood with long-grained cracks like the lines on Grams' face.

The woman on the porch had lines on her face, too, that ran from the corners of her eyes and mouth. She looked like Mom but was twice too thin to be Courtney's big, comfortable mother. She had on a crisp blue sundress that didn't seem like it could be hugged.

"Hi, Mom," Courtney said as she stopped in front of the porch. She knew what was expected of her.

"It's been a while." The woman's smile already looked brittle, sharp as the creases in her dress.

"Grams is inside, I expect."

"I wanted to see you first, sweetie. I...I..." The woman sat down on the old porch rocker. The chair creaked like the backyard larch in a windstorm, and Courtney could hear the baling wire that held it together popping free. "I got some things to explain."

"No." Courtney leaned forward and dropped her book bag on the porch. Loud. That was an extra ten minutes at evening prayer right there, but she didn't care. "You don't have nothing to explain."

The woman's lined face ran with tiny rivers of tears, but Courtney ran harder, faster, further than even her mother's sobs could carry.

✦

Courtney hid under some cottonwoods in a place by the river that had been her secret even when Dad was still around. Maybe it was dumb, having a secret place now that she was a sophomore, but no one had ever known to call her stupid. Sometimes she needed the quiet.

The spot had grown with her, mud hardening to clay with the passage of years, rocks brought in one by to one to make an almost-floor. It always smelled of moss and mud and that faint whiff of river-rot. From here she could watch the herons stalk their way toward the death of fish, and hear the little frogs peep when they thought no one was around.

Only the mosquitoes were indifferent to her secrecy, rising up off the water to find Courtney whether she was hidden or exposed.

It was almost sundown. The riverbed was cloaked in deep, warm shadows, and summer pollen glittered in the air like fairy gold. The far bank rose in runneled lines of graveled clay to a drunk-walking barbed wire fence behind which Old Man Elliot ran his cattle. This bank was bottom land, as overgrown as anything in eastern Oregon ever got, with her at the bottom-most of the land, hiding in the shadows.

Something plopped in the water.

Big.

A footstep?

She peered out through the bushes. Grams never followed her down to the river. The old woman couldn't make the trip, really, not without fear of falling and losing her dignity. Grams stood on dignity the way some people stood upon the earth. That and fear of the Lord were her twin anchors.

Could it be Mom?

Not walking in the river.

Plop.

Courtney scanned some more, but there was still nothing, just mosquitoes and the failing light of day.

Plop.

"I see you," said a voice.

Male, female, Courtney couldn't tell. She spun, looking for an intruder in her secret place. She saw nothing but rocks and the cottonwood trunk that always watched her back.

"I see you."

This time she was sure the voice came from the river. Courtney grabbed a stone that fit well within her fist and stepped out into the open.

"Where are you?"

"Right here."

And there, in the water, was a salmon long as she was tall. The water was so shallow that half its body was out in the air. It was ugly in the way of all salmon, with an upside-down mouth and fish-staring eyes and too long for its width.

"You?" A thousand stories leapt to mind—Indian lore, Grimm's fairy tales, that book of Chinese myths she'd read in the library—but somehow a talking salmon had never been among them.

"Me," said the salmon. "I see you, Courtney Summers Laing. You should see yourself."

With a flip of its tail, the salmon was gone, disappearing in water too shallow and fast to hide a football in, let alone a fish five feet long or more.

✦

When she came back to the house, all the lights were on. Grams never left the lights on at night—for the waste—which meant Mom was really home.

Or the woman who looked like Mom, Courtney told herself.

She banged through the back door. The woman was in the kitchen, one of Grams' cardigan sweaters covering the shoulders of her sundress, cooking eggs on the stove. The burnt-butter smell of frying filled the little room.

"Eggs? At this time of the night?" Courtney didn't try to hide the scorn.

"Henfruit," her mother said. "Always a treat." She looked up from the pan. Her eyes were red with crying, and the tears had left faint tracks on her cheeks. "I've missed fried eggs. All we ever had was scrambled."

"Could have stayed here and fried eggs every night." Courtney opened the fridge and grabbed the milk carton. Then she went to the drainer for a glass. No drinking from the cardboard.

What had the fish meant, that she should see herself?

Courtney sat down with her milk, perching on the edge of the chair, and stared at her mother. Was that who she was supposed to be?

It was a scary idea.

"Grams worries," Mom said.

"Grams always worries."

Another red-eyed glance. "Some day you'll worry about a girl too. Then you'll understand."

Courtney already knew she'd never have kids. Not ever. Not with what people did to kids and kids did to people. She was going to have her tubes tied as soon as she was old enough to sign the forms herself.

Just in case.

Mom slid the eggs onto one of the chipped china plates leftover from Grandma Laing's wedding set, then sat down opposite Courtney. Courtney stared. There were six eggs on the plate, cooked so far past hard they made Grams' rubbery eggs seem delicious.

Her mother laughed nervously. "Out of practice, I guess."

Courtney sneered. "Six? What a pig."

Mom stared at the plate. From the way her shoulders moved, Courtney figured her mother was wringing her hands under the table. Mom had done that a lot, before Grams came to stay and Mom had gone off to talk to the doctors for a year and more.

"It was supposed to be better now," her mother said in a small voice.

"Better than what? Prayers all the time? Better than rubber eggs every day of my life?"

Jay Lake

When her mother burst into tears, Courtney fled to her room. It felt good to run away from the sting in her own eyes.

✦

Later, she said her prayers in case Grams was listening at the door. Sure as shooting God hadn't listened much lately. Then Courtney turned off the light and sat on the foot of her bed to watch the silver-bellied moon rise outside her window.

Something in the color reminded her of the salmon's scales. The longer she thought about it, the less Courtney believed in that talking fish. She'd been tired, sad, worn out — whatever. Imagination was a powerful thing. They kept telling her that in school.

"I imagine myself on the moon," she whispered to the window screen and the insects buzzing beyond it. "In a land of silver cities with a watery sky, where everyone is cool and no one leaves until they're ready for their journey, and the river always carries them home."

That night she dreamed of fish, tiny little fry lurking among the algae-fringed gravel while skinny dark bird's feet stalked past, death on tall sticks.

✦

Grams made eggs the next morning. There was no sign of Mom. Courtney sat down at the table. Her book bag waited on the floor.

"Gave you your head yesterday, girl," Grams said. "Even though you showed no respect." She set the plate down in front of Courtney. Two rubber-whited eggs, two glistening, limp pieces of bacon and a slice of whole wheat toast, dry.

Just like every day.

"Eat up." Grams flicked her towel. "Don't get used to having things your way, neither."

"Thank you, ma'am," Courtney said, though Grammy was already running the faucet to wash up. Then she folded her hands and prayed grace over her food. "Dear God who is in Heaven, watch over me as I consume this food, bless the hands that made it and the hens that laid it, and forget not the little fishies in the sea. In Jesus' name we pray, Amen."

Her grandmother rattled dishes in the sink—a warning in their little household code—but did not turn with a hard rebuke. Courtney ate and watched Grams clean.

She supposed her mother's mother wasn't old, not really, not like Mrs. Andersen down the street with the walker and the Pekinese. Grams' hair was still mostly black, and Grams was small and slender like a girl. The woman whom her mother had become looked a lot more like Grams, in fact, than like her Mom from before.

Courtney turned this over in her head. Everybody got fat. That was life, and a trip to the Wal-Mart showed the truth of it. You just tried to find a nice boy before your boobs swelled out and fell down.

But Grams wasn't fat. Grams was the opposite of fat. She wondered what it had been like for Grams as a girl. Had her grandmother's mother gotten lost in words, pining for someone who never came home?

"Get on to school, girl," Grams said over the rush of more hot water from the faucet.

Courtney headed out the front door with nothing more than a mumbled, "God Bless."

There was no sign of Mom, the old or new version, that morning. Like the salmon, her mother could have been a dream.

✟

141

School was school, same as ever. Math was more fun than Courtney would admit, and physical education was torture just like always. Fifth period was her study break and she found her way to the little frog pond behind the science gardens. A few nerdy kids were tending their radishes or whatever, but other than them Courtney had the place to herself. Everyone else was playing basketball out in the bus park or, God forbid, actually studying in the library.

"What did you see?" asked the salmon from the scummy surface of the pond.

Courtney shrieked, dropping her book bag to spill a small riot of pens, pencils and paper across the muddy grass.

"You okay?" asked Carleton Smoot from over in the radish patch. He was a skinny kid with pimples like an ape's butt and dorky black glasses. Courtney actually felt more sorry for Carleton than she did for herself, but she wouldn't ever tell him that.

"None of your business, monkeyface."

"Okay." He smiled anyway and went back to work.

Courtney stared at the pond. Now there was nothing there but algae and slimy rocks, though ripples ran back and forth through the green water as if something had just dove. Which was idiotic — the pond wasn't two feet deep, and it was fed by a hose most of the year.

"I know you're in there," she said, hunched forward.

A crooked silver mouth broke the surface, fishy eyes staring like dinner from just under the water. "I'm here," the salmon agreed. "Did you see yourself yet?"

"No." Courtney wanted to throw her bag at the fish, or her books, but something stopped her. Sheer improbability, for one. She was no better than Mom if she went around talking to fish that weren't there.

Couldn't be there.

"You're not real."

"Maybe not. Maybe I am. But that's my problem."

"No, it's my problem. There's enough crazy people in my family. Grams is crazy-sick for Jesus, Mom's crazy-sick for Dad and his oil. I don't want to be crazy-sick for a fish."

The salmon wriggled in a way that suggested a shrug. "Crazy is as crazy does. You just need to see yourself."

Courtney thought about watching Grams in the kitchen that morning. She hunched over even further and began to weep. "I did look. All I saw was crazy-sick."

"Then you're not looking close enough," said the salmon.

With another plop it was gone.

✢

Courtney skipped the bus and walked home. It was almost four miles, but she wanted to be alone in her head without Tom Reynolds grabbing her butt in the aisle on the bus, or having to listen to the cool kids from over on Ainsworth Street talk about *some* people's horrible taste in clothes.

She didn't believe in the fish, not really, but it was trying to tell her something. She wished she'd paid more attention in social sciences when they talked about Native American legends.

Were salmon supposed to be wise? Or were they just food, like trout?

The walk took some kinks out of her back and legs and cleared her head. When she got home, she decided to look more closely. She couldn't see the harm in following the salmon's advice.

She walked in quietly, like Grams wanted her to. Her grandmother sat knitting in an old wingback chair she'd brought with her when she'd first come to stay.

Grams knitted for the poor. God knew their household could barely afford the wool, but that's what Grams did. She didn't hold with television and she couldn't stand whatever was on the radio,

Jay Lake

so she knitted.

Courtney sat across the little living room from her grandmother, on the love seat with the bad spring. She set her book bag down and looked, really looked, at Grams and her work.

The wool was bright red.

Courtney had never thought about it before, but Grams always knitted in bright colors. The older woman never wore anything but blues, browns and blacks, mostly knee-length dresses or polyester pants suits from the Goodwill, but she knitted in colors that could frighten a hummingbird. Courtney watched the hands move with the needles. Grams wore two rings, on the ring finger of each hand. Her left was a simple gold band, her right was a silver ring with some chasing Courtney couldn't see from across the room, and a green chip of a jewel.

"What is it, child?" Grams finally asked, not looking up from her work.

What was there to see? Courtney knew she was the sum of this woman's hopes and fears, passed through her Mom like water through coffee grounds. Could she see herself in her grandmother? She reached for the thing she knew least about. "Grams...please tell me about Grandpa McCandless."

The needles clicked for a while without any answer to her question, but Grams didn't roll her eyes, or snort, or reprimand like she often did. Finally: "Child, why do you got call to ask that question?"

But her voice was soft.

Courtney tried again. "Because I...I don't know, ma'am. And I want to."

"Wanting to know has been the death of many." The needles clicked a while, then the older woman actually smiled. "It's your history, too."

She stopped then, staring into nothing. Then, "When I was a girl, William Roundtree McCandless was the most beautiful boy in

144

Malheur County." Grams' smile mellowed into a sort of ease Courtney had never seen on her grandmother's face. "He had hair the color of a chestnut horse, and eyes gray as a summer storm, and his shoulders could have carried a brace of carpenters at their work and never jogged the level."

Courtney held her breath, afraid to distract her grandmother. She'd never seen Grams smile like that. Besides, she knew nothing about her mother's father.

"He took a shine to me when he was nineteen and I was fourteen." Grams actually laughed. "Pawpaw was fit for a scandal and said he'd shoot Bill McCandless in the belly if he caught him sniffing around me." She glanced up at Courtney, their eyes meeting for the first time. "That was so Bill would die slow, you know."

"Uh huh," said Courtney. Who knew her Grams had lived such a life as this?

Then the smile clouded. "We wooed anyway, and when I was fifteen Bill and me run off to Idaho and got married. He never lost his beauty, I must say, but when President Johnson had his war there in the Vietnam, Bill signed up to go off. He was too young for Korea, and he'd grown up on stories of the big one. Your mother was born right before he shipped out to Fort Lewis for training."

The needles resumed their clicking. Courtney hadn't even realized they'd stopped. Grams was silent for a long time, sort of smiling, sort of frowning.

"He came home, didn't he?" Courtney finally asked.

"Yep. I reckon he did. Everything comes home in the end. Left the best part of him behind, though." The needles stopped again, her grandmother meeting Courtney's eye to stare intently. "Don't get me wrong, girl, I still loved him. I love him yet. But that beautiful boy came home with an anger in his heart that no amount of praying, no amount of drinking, no amount of fighting could close up or cast aside."

"Oh."

"Oh is right. When finally we laid him to his rest in 1976, it was time to have said good-bye. But I hadn't seen that beautiful boy of mine in ten years by then. Just the sad, sorry man he'd become. The good Lord didn't mean my Bill to have a happy life."

"How'd he die?"

The needles clicked once more. "Fishing in the river. Pulled in by something, big bull salmon maybe. Drunk off his head, drowned in a pool eight inches deep, wedged between two rocks."

"I'm sorry."

"It was the Lord's will, child, the Lord's will." Needles clattered as Grams slapped the arm of her chair. "Now go do some homework."

⊕

Later, over a language arts assignment on European folkways, Courtney stopped and stared out the window. It was near sundown and the Sheepshead Mountains glowered brown and gray in the distance, their ridgelines touched with a pinkish gold. The river wasn't visible from her room, but the tops of the cottonwoods were, poking up from where they grew down in the channel. Their unseen trunks would already be deep in shadow. A light breeze brought the stale water smell to her nose.

Had her grandfather died right here? Courtney's salmon had come up in impossibly shallow water to speak to her. She could imagine a handsome man, gone to age and drink, arguing with a big old fish.

The thought made her shiver.

⊕

After a while she heard the back door with that odd squeak from where the frame was out of true. Grams never went out at night. That had to be her mother.

Mom.

The thin woman, Courtney couldn't help thinking.

She closed her book on a picture of a smiling girl in a red dirndl carrying a tray of huge pretzels. Outside was dark, with just the yellow lights of town fighting with the stars.

Courtney liked taking her bike out into the country sometimes. It wasn't far to ride and she could lay down among the warm, stinky cattle for windbreaks and stare up. Away from the lights of town shooting stars were easy to count, and she could imagine sailing a sea that looked like the night sky. Being penned up just made her want to run. Her whole life was nothing but a pen, she a fish caught behind a dam.

"Mother," she whispered, then headed downstairs.

Grams' light was on under her bedroom door at the bottom of the stairs. The rest of the house was dark. Just the way Grams liked it.

Had she imagined the noise of the back door?

Courtney glanced into the kitchen, then turned to look in the living room.

Mom sat on the love seat, at the end with the busted spring. Courtney snorted. That figured. She walked over and sat down next to her mother, who smelled of butter and sweat.

There was silence between them for a while, broad and bright as the stars over a country field. Courtney didn't want to be there, didn't want to be talking to this woman who'd left and not really come back yet. But the fish had been right about her grandmother.

Maybe it was right about her mother.

Eventually, she cleared her throat. "Tell me about Daddy, Mom. Before the oil, I mean."

Her mom laughed. It was a dusty sound, rocks rattling in a dry creek bed. "I ain't supposed to talk about the oil."

"*Before* the oil, Mom. Before."

"Yeah." The couch creaked as her mother settled in a little further. "Maybe I'm supposed to tell you. You were beautiful, you know."

It was Courtney's turn to laugh. "Me?" Her boobs were too small, her butt was too big, and while she didn't have Carleton Smoot's zit farm, no one would ever mistake her skin for clear and clean.

"You're pretty now, girl, but when you were a baby...ahh." A sigh, years pressed out between chapped lips. "I was bound and determined to have you natural. Mercer, he kept saying, 'use the drugs, damn it.' His sister'd had two long, hard deliveries when he was still a boy, I guess. He didn't believe in natural childbirth. But I did."

"Mmm..." Even before Mom had gone away, there had been a long time when her mother had talked about nothing but oil and Mercer Laing. Hearing about herself was a new, or at least renewed, experience for Courtney. She didn't want to interrupt.

"So I went at it the hard way. Even Mama thought I was wrong, and she don't hold with much that ain't in the Bible. But I did it. Screamed and sweated and bit on one of Mercer's belts for seventeen hours until you came out. You took forever, but when you finally showed, you popped like a watermelon seed."

This time her mother's laugh was genuine.

"Midwife caught you and clipped you, then smiled to say you were the prettiest thing she ever did see. She put you on my chest and my God, you were a little blue-faced rat with a pointy bullet-head and covered with gray goop like some bird crap. I screamed. I don't know, I was thinking of one of those diaper-ad babies or something. Not the real thing. Nobody'd ever told me nothing about it."

Courtney's heart skipped with a cold shiver.

"Then..." Her mother stopped and drew a deep breath. "Then I looked at your squinty blue eyes and those two tiny fists and I knew that you were all the beauty in the world, and you'd come out of me. I made you and that was the greatest thing I ever did."

"And Daddy?" She had to ask.

"He laughed at my screaming, and he laughed at the midwife, then he took you in his arms and sang awhile." She sighed again. "You were the beautiful bridge to make things right between us."

Those words made Courtney's heart soar and sink at the same time, like she was two girls in one body. Mom cried then, but the tears were soft, almost gentle. A while later, Courtney heard her Grams' bedroom door snick shut.

⚘

Right before she went to sleep, Courtney read in her biology textbook:

Anadromous fish are those fish born in a freshwater stream that migrate to the ocean for their adult phase. Most salmon are anadromous. Some species populations can be trapped by changes in water flow, or perhaps impounded behind a dam and still survive. Those non-anadromous populations are considered resident. Anadromous and non-anadromous forms of the same species can have different life cycles and even different morphologies.

Morphologies. That meant what their bodies looked like. Mom had certainly come home with a different morphology. A hundred pounds different. But no one could be more impounded than Courtney was.

No, she thought. Grams and Mom had both been more impounded. The dry mountains and high deserts of eastern Oregon were a giant dam behind which all the people struggled for escape.

⚘

149

She dreamed of the salmon that night. It sat in her little study chair in front of her desk, bent at an angle that looked uncomfortable. The upside-down mouth seemed cruel somehow, and the fluttering gills were wounds on its body, stigmata for fish dying in air.

"You're supposed to be in the river," Courtney said. It smelled like the river, the river-rot in particular. She didn't remember that odor from before.

"I can go wherever there is water to hold me."

"There's no water in the house. Outside the kitchen and bathroom, I mean."

"Saltwater tears are enough for me."

Who had been crying? "I looked at Grams and Mom," she told the fish. "Really looked."

"What did you see?"

She thought about how to answer that question. "I don't know. More than I ever knew was there."

"You're growing up."

Courtney hated it when people said that. She always had. It didn't sound any better coming from a fish. "It's crummy enough being in high school. Don't patronize me."

The fish gave one of its not-shrugs. "Truth is truth. What is there for you now?"

She thought of the ocean reflecting all those summer stars, salmon swimming their long cold migration through distant seas only to finally come home again.

Why would anyone ever want to come home again?

But Mom had.

And Grams after her, when Mom got sick.

She knew then, in her heart and in her gut, something she'd never quite believed or understood. "They love me," Courtney told the fish. "They're trapped behind their dams, but they still love me."

The River Knows Its Own

✶

The next day she went over to the King-Freeze after school and asked for a job application. Courtney figured if she could save enough money in the couple more years from now until she graduated, she could follow the river down to the ocean.

Carleton Smoot's oldest brother was the day manager. He was cute in an older guy sort of way, no pimples, and he grinned at her when he handed her the greasy sheet of paper. "Come to drop some fries with the big boys, eh?"

"Keep your oil to yourself," she told him, but she smiled back at him.

She folded the paper into her pack and went down to her secret place by the river. The salmon wouldn't be there now — it had done its totem animal thing, right? But when she settled in among the bushes at the base of the cottonwood trees, the creature flopped up into the shallows.

"Ocean's cold, you know," it said.

Courtney thought of her biology textbook. "Life's a challenge for a fish. You've survived it."

"I'll never die. Not until I spawn."

"How long...?" In the middle of the question, Courtney realized she was being rude.

"No one's asked me that before," the salmon said. "I remember the biggest flood of all. More years ago than you've had days in your life. It tore mountains from their roots and pushed half the continent toward the sea."

"Missoula," said Courtney, memories stirring of a trip to a museum up in the Columbia Gorge.

"The Missoula Flood. That's what you call it now."

"What did you call it then?"

Somehow the salmon managed to smile. "Life."

Jay Lake

"Life." Courtney laughed, the honest laugh of water on rocks and wind in the trees. "Why'd you wait this long?"

The fish wiggled, a sort of silver-scaled shrug. "Life. Waiting to see tomorrow. Waiting to meet you."

Courtney imagined the march of all those years, all the history of water and Indians and Lewis and Clark flowing by while the salmon waited for her. "Maybe," she said. Then she knew she wouldn't see the fish again, the same way she knew she was going to draw her next breath. "I got to ask one last thing."

The salmon said nothing, just smiled its upside-down smile.

"Was it you that killed Grandpa Bill?"

"It was time for the river to take him home. Everybody comes home in the end."

Sometimes, Courtney thought, if they were real lucky people started out at home too. Then she waded into the water to kiss the fish before heading back to the house to fill out her job application. She thought maybe she'd practice by cooking eggs for dinner for Mom and Grams.

✞

The River Knows Its Own

THE WILLAMETTE VALLEY WOODS were filled with that old magic of childhood. His thoughts suspended somewhere between dreams and memories, Jorge walked among the bright-speckled shadows like spilled coins, stepped over mossy logs with long green fingers, scrambled down stony creek beds that could have been fortress walls a hundred generations past. Early autumn in Oregon was brisk without chill, sunny without warmth—an intermediate season, as if all the Earth were held in balance.

That was the day Jorge saw the dragon.

It rustled among the trees, moving against the wind. He glanced toward the sound expecting to see a deer. Instead there was flash of dark-veined brown, like world's largest maple leaf gone half-rotten, accompanied by a smell to match, borne on a gust of air colder than a Mt. Hood glacier.

Jorge stopped. His boots squelched as they sank ankle-deep in mud the color of fresh cow manure. He stared across the banks of mist-spotted ferns that covered the ground between the boles of the trees.

What had he really seen?

Then a raven screeched in the hawthorn branches overhead. Distracted by the noise, Jorge slipped and landed on his hands and butt in mud. He pulled himself out and tried to remember why he had stopped. Shaking the cobwebs from his mind, he continued his hike.

✣

Two days later, Jorge sat outside It's A Beautiful Pizza on SE Belmont Street nursing a tall iced chai. He hadn't felt the same since he came back from his hiking trip. After a few hours of futzing around at work that morning Venera had told him to get out, take the day, and find his damned head.

Given the shoestring their little water quality nonprofit ran on, she had been mighty generous with his time. That was typical of Venera. His boss was something of a witch chick with her purple skirts and weird silver charms, but she almost always knew what she was about. It was one the many things he really dug about her, though he'd never quite had the nerve to put a move on to match his feelings.

Old Volvos in need of valve jobs clattered past, interspersed with VW Vanagons, ancient Dodges, and all the other stereotypically unique vehicles driven by the tragically hip and hopelessly hippie types that haunted Belmont. "If you believed your own shit, you'd ride the bus," he told the traffic.

As ever, the cars didn't listen. No one listened. That was only one of the world's many problems. Getting close to Venera was one of his.

"Hey," said a woman. "Didn't you hear me?"

Jorge looked up, half hiding behind his chai cup. She was a skinny white chick with a shoe leather tan and wind-burned cheeks, muscled arms like knotted ropes, and a macramé vest that didn't show much chest. Her hair was dark brown matted dreads that almost matched the brown of her eyes. She wore a pair of faded jeans covered in ballpoint doodles that were either high art, deep social commentary or disguises for the stains.

The kind of chick Portland was full of. The kind of chick he

154

liked.

A chick he didn't know.

Thoughts of Venera blew out of his head like mist on a sunny day.

"No," Jorge said slowly. "I'm sorry. I didn't hear you."

Then she laughed. In that moment she transformed from earthy-attractive to heart-stoppingly beautiful, with no more than a few loud breaths and a flash of teeth like white corn. "That's okay, I didn't say nothing. I was just wondering if you heard me."

"Sit," said Jorge from the depths of love-struck awe. "Please." He waved his chai at the plastic chair on the other side of the tiny table.

Sit she did, and took his chai right out of his hand. After a long, slow slurp she smiled again, this time without the laugh. "I don't know how you can stand this stuff." She took another long slurp.

"Are we having the same conversation?"

She cocked her head, a brown bird on a green chair. "We could be. I didn't think you were the type."

"I'm not." He was ready to be whatever type she wanted. He wished like hell he'd worn his Guatemalan vest that morning.

"You're whatever type I want, right?"

Her words jarred. How had she known? "Ah..." he ventured.

"I can read the signs. Any girl does. Any girl that wants to make it in the world without a McHouse and three kids for shining armor." The smile again. She set the chai down on the little table. "But somebody told me about you."

Another slip of the mental gears. He reached for the cup, for something to do, and to feel the transient warmth of her hand. "Who?" he asked before taking a sip.

The chai now tasted old, stale, like rotten leaves and the smell of cold rock on the face of the mountain. Bending forward he spit it out, swallowed a curse, then wiped his hand across his lips and looked up to apologize.

No one was there. The sidewalk was empty. A crow screeched like a rusty hinge as two Volvos banged bumpers and Jorge suddenly wondered why he wasn't at work. Venera would be missing him.

✤

"Something's fucked up, man," Jorge said. He sipped on a fuzzy navel which he then set down in front of him next to some peanuts in one of those little parquet-looking salad bowls from the 1970s. Buzzing beer signs cast murky multicolored shadows across the bar top like a slow motion disco show. Silent televisions flickered through Keno, ESPN and an old Tom Cruise movie. It was the Bear Paw on a Monday night.

Clark the bartender grunted. "Something's always fucked up. Wouldn't be having this job otherwise." He drew off a pint of the latest Widmer seasonal ale for someone back at the pool tables. Clark was a huge black man, with a flaming wheel tattooed on his bald scalp, right pinkie finger missing. He wore a blue muscle shirt and those long-legged basketball shorts in red-and-blue Kansas Jayhawk colors.

"No, no, you don't get it." But Clark was gone, and for a moment that scared Jorge. Things kept disappearing, he didn't know what—or worse, who—only that they were gone.

Clark came right back, though, which eased Jorge's mind. The bartender reached for the remains of the fuzzy navel, but Jorge waved him off.

"Maybe you've had enough, friend," the bartender said.

"That ain't it."

Bar towels snapped for a moment as Clark busied himself. Then the big man chuckled. "I ain't getting out of this, am I? Tell old Clark."

"Stuff keeps disappearing."

156

"You sound like my Momma. She got the Alzheimer's. Thinks people steal her underwear at night." Clark chuckled without any humor. "While she's wearing it."

Jorge felt a cold tightness in his scalp. "I don't know, man. It's like I *am* crazy."

"Mm..."

"In the woods." He drained the last of the fuzzy navel. Leaves swirled in memory. "Muddy trail, I stopped. There was something, but I can't remember what. Like it left a hole in my head."

Clark frowned. "You fell down and hit your head? Go see a doctor."

"No, no. I mean, I wound up on my ass, but not like that. Then the next day, something happened to my chai."

"Something happened to your chai?" Clark flicked a bar towel at him. "You *do* be fucked up, friend."

"That's what I'm trying to tell you."

Then a big guy, seven feet at least, covered in hair and not much else, shambled in through the padded door and took the stool next to Jorge. That was when he *knew* he was crazy.

"Try again," rumbled the big guy in a voice like rocks falling in a canyon.

"Try what?" whispered Jorge. He glanced at Clark. The bartender was dropping onion rings in the fryer and not noticing anything. I will not forget this time, Jorge thought. He began to draw a crude sketch of the newcomer on his bar napkin.

"Hard to talk."

"Hard to fucking remember." Jorge immediately wished he hadn't said it that way. This was a time to be polite.

"Hard to be," said the Sasquatch.

And it *was* a Sasquatch. Jorge was certain. "What's hard to be?"

"Listen." One massive paw pinned his writing hand to the bar. Jorge could feel the pen barrel snap as cool ink flooded across his skin. "Things move. Things change. The stones are being called to

157

Jay Lake

dance."

He had that wrong party feeling again. "I don't know —"

The Sasquatch interrupted. "River man. Tree man. Land man. You can listen, know. The stones dance, the waters spread. The west flies."

Jorge's temper welled up. "For Christ's sake, talk some fucking sense."

Clark turned around. "What?"

Alone at the bar, Jorge looked at his ink-stained hand. This time he remembered. Some. Love, fear, a hairy monster spouting cryptic wisdom.

It didn't make a hell of a lot of sense, but it was *memory*. And there were words soaking into his skin, written in a crabbed script that looked like no alphabet he knew.

"What the hell's the matter with you?" Clark asked as he realized what the ink mess on the bar top was. "I'm cutting you off, Georgie-boy."

"It's not..." Jorge stopped. He flipped a twenty on the dry part of the bar—more than he could afford, but he didn't want Clark mad at him. Jorge had to live in this neighborhood. "I'm sorry. I told you man, I'm a little fucked up today."

Clark grunted something and made the bill disappear. Jorge was whistling when he banged his way out the padded door. Venera would help him. She was a mystic *witchy* chick. He'd never believed that shit, but this disappearing memory stuff was right up his boss's alley.

There was just one question. Who had he fallen in love with? It had been something different than his low-level hots for Venera.

Not the Sasquatch, surely.

ϙ

The River Knows Its Own

There was fire in the sky above Wye-east mtn. last night after I kilt the she-baer. I tole Whiskey Jack we shood ott to of asked them Clakkamas about the she-bear but he larfed and spit at me. We watched that fire shoot up sparks and flame and clouds whitch glowed like a Chinee lanthorn. A while after Whiskey Jack passed on to snoring I spied wings in the fire. It were a lizzard bigger than all of St. Louie I swear on my Bible. Today Whis. Jack tells me I am plumb crazy. But I am go-ing to find me them Clakkamas injuns and ask about the lizzard.

-- Journal of Oregon country frontiersman Marc Beaulieu, undated, ca. 1793-1795

☥

Jorge banged on the door of Venera's apartment. She had to be home. Monday night wasn't one of her date nights as far as he knew from office chat. Such as it was. She was very private about her life outside work.

He kept track of that dating stuff anyway. Just in case.

Light gleaming through the blinds just to his left threw thin lines on the damp concrete of the third-floor balcony. He'd never actually been inside, just picked her up for carpools to state Watershed Enhancement Board meetings and stuff. He cupped his hands to his mouth and pressed against the window. "You home?" he shouted.

The cheap aluminum frame distorted his words into a sort of industrial echo of himself.

There was no answer, but he heard thumping. Then the door was yanked open. Venera stood there wild-eyed and angry. She was African-American, head shaved, with skin darker than espresso, well over six feet and built like a mechanical pencil. Right then she wore a pair of panties a few threads away from being a thong and a torn t-shirt that was inside out and backwards.

Jay Lake

Jorge's pulse shot up and his mouth went dry.

"What the—" Venera shouted, then stopped. Her eyes narrowed as she studied Jorge. "You still ain't found your damned head, have you?" Though her voice was softer, she wasn't smiling.

An unsmiling Venera was often a bad thing.

He found his voice. "No, I haven't found it. But I know what happened." Sort of.

"And this involves me *how*?"

He showed her the markings on his right hand, words written spontaneously in ink.

"Ah." She stared at his hand a moment. "I see," she finally said. "Wait here." Then Venera slammed the door.

Jorge leaned against the jamb for a little while, trying to look like he wasn't a drug buyer waiting on a score. Voices rose and fell with the rhythms of argument somewhere inside Venera's apartment.

Oops.

It *was* date night. No wonder she'd been pissed. Now he wished he'd stopped at the Plaid and grabbed a six of microbrew or something. It was too late, though—he couldn't be gone when she next opened the door.

Besides, he really wanted to see what kind of person it took to score with her.

Ⴔ

Twenty minutes later Jorge wished he'd headed for the c-store after all. He'd gone so far as to drag out his car keys, but hadn't worked up the nerve to leave after bothering Venera. The letters on his hand were starting to look blurry—sweat?—and his memories which had seemed so clear, if confused, when leaving the bar were vanishing like a nitrous buzz.

He should go home and take a long, hot shower.

160

Then the door banged open again. Different woman this time, heavy chick not much over five feet tall with a sort of Filipina/blended-race look and Frieda Kahlo eyebrows. She had on a tattered Howard the Duck babydoll worn to translucency by too many spin cycles, and not much else—massive dark nipples showed through like a pair of bruised eyes.

That explained a lot, he realized. Why Venera never seemed to vibe off him the way he vibed off her.

"You know," the woman said, "I don't get out much." She grinned at him, nasty and irritated. "Even when I do, I don't get a lot of nookie." A pudgy finger tapped his chest. "So skinny-butt Mediterranean hunks bothering my girlfriend piss me off. Now let me see your hand."

Jorge offered his ink-stains. She grabbed him hard on the wrist like his grandmother used to do, then spread his fingers. Front, back, she flipped the hand. Back, front. She even sighted down his fingertips as if they were arrows. Or gun barrels.

He was really starting to wish he'd just gone home. This was embarrassing.

"Where?" she asked. Her expression wasn't as hard now.

"Bear Paw over on Milwaukie, near the Aladdin."

"Some guy just attack you with a biro?"

"No...it was..." Jorge glanced around. He didn't want anyone listening in. The story was too weird. He leaned forward and whispered. "Sasquatch."

"Sasquatch?" Her face went sour, like she'd eaten a bad malted milk ball. Or was talking to an idiot. "Bigfoot? Hairy pecker, about so tall?" She reached up as far as her arm would go, setting Howard's tattered cigar bobbing on her shirtfront.

"Taller, I think," he said, trying to keep his eyes on her face.

"And you're not drunk." It was a statement. "Better come in." She turned and walked into the apartment, trusting him to follow. "Hey, V, the Lansquenet's going to be pissed!"

Jay Lake

✦

A few minutes later the three of them sat around a dinette table that boasted a ridged aluminum edge and a formica top in foam green with those little boomerang thingies running in a pattern all over. The rest of the apartment was decorated to match the table — faux-Fifties Portland kitsch mixed with metrosexual modern. The table was covered in roach burns, Chinese takeout wrappers, beer bottles and, now, Jorge's forearms.

He was very tired, but Venera's girlfriend insisted on copying the smudged letters or patterns or whatever they were on his right hand. She wasn't doing what he would have done — trying to reproduce them in lines of text — but rather executing a more-than-competent life drawing of his hand and illustrating the ink stains in place.

Venera touched Jorge's chin with her long, cool fingers. That gave him a little shiver on the spine, and he found himself wishing she meant it. After a moment her fingers trailed around his face before dropping to his shoulder, then away. Already he missed their faint pressure.

"What?" Jorge asked. He felt bleary, almost drugged.

"You ain't right, Jorge, and you ain't getting any righter. Can you remember what the hairy man said to you?

He wanted to say, *touch me again, please.* Instead: "He was going on about rivers and trees and stuff. How I'd understand. Then he said..." Forgetting her fingers, Jorge reached for the words. "He said, 'The stones dance, the waters spread. The west flies.' And when he talked, I remembered other stuff."

"Yeah?"

"A dragon on the wing in the woods. A beautiful girl who wasn't there."

Venera got her smile back. That made him shiver again.

"How'd you nail down your memory of the hairy man?" asked Venera's girlfriend.

"Drew him on a napkin."

The two women exchanged a glance. "Like a Scriptor," said Venera.

Her friend nodded. "You want to summon the Five?" she asked. "He's Coloring up good. A wild Skill maybe."

Venera looked thoughtful. "I'm thinking of calling Aristides instead. Back in New York."

"I know where he is."

"Well, this is his kind of thing."

"Don't you go calling him up, girl. That man is not your friend, and he sure ain't mine. You don't want the Five, we'll work this through ourselves." Then, almost grudgingly to Jorge, "Good work, skinny butt. Not a lot folks would think to do that. Even them that should know better."

"I think he *wanted* me to remember," said Jorge, who was no longer making any sense of the conversation. His ears were cold. The tabletop rushed up to meet his face.

⚭

Jorge woke up flat on his back to a pressure on his chest that made him gasp for air. He looked up into the pendulous naked breasts of Venera's girlfriend. She was straddling his belly, eyes closed, singing.

He, on the other hand, was fully clothed. Besides the view, there didn't seem to be much in this for him. And she was *Venera's* girlfriend.

In some dreams maybe, but not this one. "Um, hey, this, uh..."

Something whacked the top of his head and Venera hissed, "Quiet, fool."

So he was quiet.

Jay Lake

The girlfriend kept singing. It was tuneless chant that didn't stick on any tempo or key, but seemed to wander like a spring breeze. Her head swung back and forth as she sang—as if she were listening, too.

After a while she grabbed his inked right hand and pressed it between her breasts. Jorge felt his face grow hot while his penis seemed to crinkle tight and small in a sort of anti-erection. Then she opened her eyes. He would have sworn they were glowing.

"Things move." Her voice was a strange, squeaky echo of the hairy man's. "Things change. The stones are dancing, the waters are spreading. The west flies."

"Why me?" he asked.

"You do watershed conservation work," said Venera, still out of his sight line though he tried to roll his eyes back far enough to find her. Her burred voice was softer than he could remember ever hearing it. "And you walk the land. You don't just stare at hydrology reports and doodle on maps like some office dork. The land *knows* you, Jorge."

The girlfriend dropped his hand and leaned so close that her breasts nudged his chin. "There's Skilled been working forty years in the Lansquenet that don't have your kind of grounding, skinny butt. You ain't gonna be popular."

"Skilled," said Jorge. Trying not to look at her tits was making him cross-eyed. "Lands-canay. Dancing stones. Whatever. Look, I came over here because Venera's witchy and this felt like witchy business." He tried to nod, indicate his unseen boss somewhere behind him. This was definitely not the evening of his fantasies. "Been hanging around you too long, V. I think I'm going to go sleep this off."

The girlfriend got up off him, moving fast and spry for such a heavy woman. "Lost that option when you bound the hairy man to your memory. Now you can't walk away."

Jorge staggered to his feet. "No, I'm going home. Slam a double

164

shot, drop a few aspirin, sleep twelve hours, it'll be like none of this ever happened."

Venera caught his eye. "I can't stop you, but that's a bad move."

He shrugged. He could start looking for another job in a couple of days. Way this was going, he'd have to. Maybe then she'd let him take her out. "I don't believe this shit anyway."

"It don't matter what you believe. The land is real with or without you."

The girlfriend finished shrugging back into her Howard the Duck top. "Next time, skinny butt, we both get naked." She winked. "More power, more fun."

Now he had an erection. Jorge stepped as quickly out the door as his dignity would allow, then trotted stiff-legged for the car. He wondered if Clark would serve him any more tonight.

All the way home, the ink on his hand itched as fiercely as any paper cut. It felt blood-warm.

✦

He rode the Filipina witch from behind, her broad sweat-slicked buttocks pressed up against his pelvis as his cock split her vagina like a pomegranate. She pushed and tossed, growling so deep he could feel the rumbling where their bodies met. The room wasn't clear to him—an enormous black space with distant, shadowy pillars—but the sheen of perspiration on her skin was cake icing.

Jorge pulled out slick and hard, ready to cornhole her. As he slid in into the rubbery fist-grip of her anus, she turned to look at him, but it was the hairy man from the bar who grinned. The sweet, salty icing on her back turned to his fuzz. Jorge didn't usually play that way, but he was too far into the sex to stop. As he pounded against the hairy man's ass he realized that his partner's back was tattooed with a map of the Willamette Valley, from the Columbia River along his shoulders—complete with a red-orange splotch at

165

the top for Mt. St. Helens—on down to Grant's Pass where Jorge continued to thrust.

Mt. Hood sat below the tattoo of Bonneville Dam on hairy man's right shoulder blade, the volcano an orange glare much brighter than St. Helens. Jorge found himself staring into an eye at the center of the mountain's tattoo, a glossy, angry eye that returned his look. The eye tracked his gaze as he bucked and thrust. The hairy man began to shake with his orgasm, an earthquake rocking the valley, until Jorge was thrown off into a screaming freefall high above the textured white mountaintops that ended tangled in his sticky sheets.

✦

Pyroclastic flows are high-speed avalanches of hot rock, gas, and ash that are formed by the collapse of lava domes or eruption columns. They can move up to 100 miles per hour and have temperatures to 1500° F. They are lethal, burning, burying, or asphyxiating all in their paths.

— United States Geological Survey Fact Sheet 060-00

✦

Morning brought a watercolor sky and that kind of Oregon rain that was basically aggressive mist. Jorge drowsed facing the window and wondering at how humid his bedroom seemed to be. His eyes and mouth felt gritty while his entire body ached as if the fall—

That thought brought him bolt awake in remembered panic. His clock was blinking, reset by some electrical failure in the night, but that much light outside meant he was late for work. And his bed...his bed...

Jorge was surrounded by half-rotted leaves, pine needles, rich loam. He was lying in it, like a man dragged from a shallow grave on the forest floor. The grit on his face was soil. His nails were stained brown with the stuff.

"Holy crap!" he shouted. Somehow Venera's girlfriend *had* gotten in here last night. The two witchy-women were fucking with him. In all the wrong ways.

He picked his way through a litter of sticks and bark to the bathroom. He would wash the dirt and grime off, get to work, and have it out with Venera. There were other jobs, damn it. Other women, for that matter. This creepy shit about breaking into his apartment was for the birds.

The bathroom was blessedly clean in a relative way, no more than the usual Portland mold and shower stall grunge. Jorge hurried his way through his morning routine, plus a couple of extra rinse cycles under the showerhead—God, he hated being filthy. There was no getting rid of the ink stains on his hand. They did seem a little faded, at least. Out of the shower he picked his way back across his bedroom to get dressed.

Ordinary clothes, he thought. *Like going to traffic court.* Don't dress to distract. Jeans and a plain green flannel shirt.

Jorge paused for a moment. Those were what he had been wearing on his last hike. When the craziness started.

He put on the clothes anyway. Kitchenette for a bottle of Odwalla organic orange juice and a blueberry Special K bar, then heading out the door with his car keys in his hand to give Venera a piece of his mind.

When he opened the door everything went wrong all over again.

⚬

Jay Lake

The man outside dressed like a wizard. Or more to the point, dressed like someone who thought he was a wizard. He was a short, fat white guy with piggy eyes that gleamed a dark blue over a salt-and-pepper goatee, with long hair to match. Half-moon glasses in silver frames lined with tiny rhinestones. A floppy hat of chocolate-colored velvet, large enough to lose a housecat in, covered with tiny charms. The wizard's brown velvet coat—complementing the hat—was a cross between a smoking jacket and a Renaissance fair costume, complete with large silver buttons worked in some ornate crest.

"Get out of my way, twinkle toes," said Jorge with his best Venera-growl.

"You need me," the wizard replied.

Jorge placed his hand flat on the wizard's broad chest. He had six inches on the overdecorated little tub. "I ain't got time for your shit."

"The Lansquenet is interested in you."

That stopped Jorge. He pulled his hand back. "Lands-cannay. That's the second time I've heard that word in the last twelve hours."

"Lans-que-net." The wizard spelled it out. Then, "Servants of the land. We, well..." He smiled modestly. "We watch over the earth, or at least our portion of it here in the Northwest."

Jorge had a bedroom full of earth at the moment. "No kidding? You must be friends with Venera and her pet sex witch."

"Ah..." The wizard tapped his lips, serious. "Did you happen to get the other woman's name?"

"No." Which had been kind of weird.

"No matter." His hand stuck out, grabbed Jorge's hand in a sweaty shake. "I am Dagobertus Magnus, Bert to my friends. A key man in the Lansquenet."

"Wizard, right?"

168

Another modest smile. "In a sense. Technically I'm an Edaphomancer. Someone whose power is, ahem, *rooted*, in the soil."

Jorge wanted to slap the idiot. "You're as crazy as they are."

"No." Bert shook his head emphatically. "Venera fancies herself a power here in the Willamette Valley, a Fluvimancer. A Locan, in the old words she prefers. Power from the rivers. But *she's* crazy. I know what I'm doing."

"Right. Look, I work for the Northwest Watershed Trust. I know from rivers. I also know Venera's a witchy bitch. Right now I got an apartment full of dirt and some real bad dreams to show for it. So you, Mr. Bert the wizard of dirt, are either going to help me get this crap swept back out of my life pronto, or you're heading right back to wing-nut central to commune with the rest of the squirrels and leave me the hell alone."

"It's the girlfriend. That one with no name. She's doing these things to you. The Lansquenet has important purposes. Her spells distract you, make you think the land is reaching out."

"I don't believe in spells," Jorge said, pushing Bert out of the way. He yanked his door shut, giving it the lift-and-twist the swollen frame required in damp weather. "I don't believe in dragons or Bigfoot or beautiful women who vanish with the wind." He stomped down the stairs, the pudgy wizard hurrying after him. At the bottom, Jorge turned to face Bert, who was a step up so that they met eye-to-eye. "I especially don't believe in an apartment full of dirt and leaves. For the love of God, this crap's enough to make me move to Los Angeles!"

"I understand your frustration," Bert said, bobbing after Jorge as he went to look for his car.

It had to be out here somewhere, Jorge thought, ignoring the wizard. He'd driven home last night. He hadn't been drunk.

"The Lansquenet can set these things to right. Venera is misguided. That other woman, a sex magician of the worst sort. Very much against all our interests. They always are. Subordinate to

169

the almighty orgasm. Don't integrate with the ebb and flow of—"

"Shut up." Jorge stood at the corner of Milwaukie and Franklin. "Where the hell is my car?"

"Oh," said Bert in a small voice. Almost a squeak.

The mist began to thicken to rain as Jorge thought about that for a moment. "Oh? 'Oh' what?"

"Did you have a little white sedan?"

"I *do* have a BMW 2002tii, yes. It's small. It's white. It's a sedan. I just don't know where it is right now."

"When I got here the city was towing off a car that had been messed up pretty badly." Bert pointed to an open spot in front of the US Bank branch across the street. Shattered glass, paint chips and odd scraps of metal and chrome littered the pavement as if there had been a collision.

Jorge walked over to the scattered junk. He thought he might have parked in front of the ATM last night. Things had been confused. And the paint did match his. Someone had thrown cat litter down over a big stain of oil and gas in the middle of the mess, and the pavement was cracked as if a heavy weight hand landed on it.

"What happened to the car?"

"Crushed by an enormous boulder. They had a big truck from Ross Island cement helping with the rock."

Crushed by a boulder? Jorge turned to stare at Bert. "You're the wizard of dirt. Did you...?"

"Soil, not stone," Bert protested. "Not my power. But can I offer you a ride to work?"

The prospect of mixing Bert with Venera was the best news Jorge had heard all morning. Wherever his car was—and he didn't believe for a minute it had been crushed by a boulder—could wait. He smiled. "Sure thing. I could use the lift."

The River Knows Its Own

✿

The QuickSand River appears to pass through the low country at the foot of those high range of mountains in a southerly direction, - The large creeks which fall into the Columbia on the stard side rise in the same range of mountain which we suppose to be Mt. Hood is S. 85E about 47 miles distant from the mouth of quick sand river. This mountain is covered with snow and in the range of mountains which we have passed through and is of a conical form but rugged...
— Journal of William Clark, November 3rd, Sunday, 1805

✿

Bert hummed as he drove. It wasn't far from Jorge's apartment to the Watershed Trust offices at the seedy end of the Hawthorne district, but the traffic was, as always in Portland, shitty. Not Seattle-shitty, thank God, but enough. The dumpy wizard drove like an old man who didn't care when he got there.

Bert had a weird old man car, too, a slightly miniaturized version of an early-1960's tail-finned cruiser. It sported a faded two-tone paint job that had probably once been yellow and white but had averaged towards some union of flyspecked meringue over the years. The inside smelled like, well, dirt.

"Do a lot of gardening?" Jorge asked as he flipped through the owner's manual. *Dear Sir*, it advised him. Did women never buy these cars? The driver in the picture on the cover was a chick in a hat like his grandmother might have worn. He checked the date — 1959.

This booklet has been prepared to introduce you to your new Simca Vedette so that you can get to know quickly your new car and enjoy all the good things in motoring it provides.

What language had that been translated from? No normal person would have written it that way. He vaguely recalled that

171

Jay Lake

Simcas were French.

"Soil," said Bert in an expansive, hearty tone as if he were launching into a lecture, "is one of the true miracles of life. There are more bacteria in a single handful of healthy soil than there are human beings alive in the world today. Less than one percent of the *species* of soil bacteria have been formally described and classified. And then there are the nematodes. By the land, let me tell you..."

And a lecture it was. Jorge read on, ignoring the man.

Naturally, the first things you will want to know are the locations of the various controls and instruments. We have therefore placed all information covering these and other driving essentials...

✦

They stopped right in front of the head shop over which the Watershed Trust offices were located. The building was a run-down Victorian house with a poorly-executed mural of unicorns and rainbows splashed across the walls. The Simca's brakes squealed and the dirt smell was chased out of the car by a hot oil reek.

"Nice thing about being Skilled," said Bert. "We almost always find parking."

Jorge put the manual back in the glove box and tried to disentangle himself from the Medieval seat belt someone had retrofitted the car with—the owner's manual certainly hadn't mentioned them. "Skilled. Venera used that word. That's what you New Age types are calling crystal woo-woo this year, I guess."

Bert slammed his door, walked around the car and opened Jorge's door. He reached in to flip the seat belt aside. "We've been calling it that for generations. Regardless of what you believe."

It was the first time Jorge had been moved to take the wizard seriously. "I'm sorry. I just believe so little of this." He climbed out. "Well, none, actually."

172

"It doesn't matter what you believe," Bert said mildly. "You're the one with the apartment full of dirt and the boulder on your car."

And some really strange dreams, Jorge told himself. It had to be a trick. All of it. *Had* to be.

He led Bert around the side of the head shop to the rickety outside stairs. Up close the crappy paint job was more visible but less obvious. You really had to have some distance to appreciate the artist's ineptness.

As they reached the door, Bert touched Jorge's elbow. "Are you inviting me inside?"

"Inviting?"

"It's important."

Jorge felt a little chill. He still thought the whole business was stupid, but the wizard of dirt clearly took it seriously.

Was there a reason not to invite him in? Venera would...what?

Irritation flooded him, making his face hot. To hell with her. She and eyebrow-girl should have been a lot more forthcoming last night. "Yes. I invite you inside."

Bert smiled. "Thank you."

Jorge pushed the door open. The little bell jingled.

"Hey, skinny butt," said Venera's girlfriend. She was leaning against Jorge's desk in the front part of the office. She gave Jorge a big wink, then licked her finger and touched her hip. "Next time concentrate a little more, *batang lalaki*. You might come to a better end."

She *knew*. She'd been in his dreams. Did that explain the dirt in his bedroom? "How did you —"

Then the little bell on the door rang so hard it popped off its mounting and rolled between Jorge's feet. The wizard of dirt stood beside him. "Well, if it isn't the Fricatrice," said Bert.

Venera's girlfriend's face shut down like sunset on the high desert. She was suddenly hard, looking a lot more dangerous than a woman in a Maggie Simpson t-shirt and Bermuda shorts had any business being. Her eyes stayed on Bert while she jerked her chin at Jorge. "What's the matter with you, skinny butt? You don't got enough trouble, you got to borrow him?"

Jorge felt a cold certainty that he'd made a bad mistake. Words leapt in hot defense to his tongue anyway. "He's no worse than you or Venera. At least he answers my questions."

"We did too, 'til you stopped listening." She shut Jorge out then, as if he'd never been there, focusing on the wizard. "You, dirt boy, get out. This isn't your locus."

"I was invited," Bert said mildly.

"And now you're disinvited." Venera stood in the open door of her office. She was decidedly not smiling.

Jorge's heart sank.

"We're not enemies, Dagobertus Magnus, not yet," Venera continued, "but we're years past when we were last friends. This man is my charge and charter."

"The Lansquenet knows Jorge now. His name is carried on wing and whisper, through root and tunnel, by spring and seep. He has slipped your charge, Fluvimancer."

"I believe the word you are looking for is Locan."

Bert smoothed the sleeves of his velvet coat. "Some of us stay in step with the times. Your opposition to the will of Lansquenet has been troublesome for a while, but I'm afraid you've finally crossed the line, my dear *Locan*."

"Whoever Brought your Five has a lot to answer for, *Éarling*."

"I believe the word you are looking for is Edaphomancer."

They stared at one another until Jorge thought the air would crackle. He didn't understand the underlying argument, but both Venera and Bert were angry about him.

"You know," he said, "I don't give a damn about your Lansquenet. I don't even know what a Locan is. But I can damn well tell when people are talking over my head. I've got a truckload of dirt in my apartment, my car is missing, and I'm two days behind in polling water districts. You guys want to fight, go fight." His voice started pitching higher. "You guys want to help me, help me. Otherwise, *shut the hell up*! Or I'm done with this. My ass will be out of here and to hell with all of you."

"You can't," the Fricatrice said to Jorge. The staring contest between Venera and Bert continued unabated. "The land won't let you."

"Fuck the land!"

Her smile was hard and toothy. "Didn't you try that last night?"

Bert touched Jorge's elbow. "Very well. I'll find you later, Jorge. The Lansquenet will make all this worth your while. We can show you your power."

Then he was gone, the door rattling shut behind him as the fire sprinklers in the office went off and the taps on the sink by the coffee maker burst free atop twin fountains of water.

⊕

Venera had chased them out of the Watershed Trust offices with an incoherent screech of rage as soon as the flooding had started. Soggy and irritated, Jorge grabbed a chair in a Salvadoran place down the street. He sat down opposite the Fricatrice. Their table was ridiculously tiny, not much bigger than a waitress' tray, hammered out of old sheet metal.

There was such as thing as taking hip too far.

"*Dos pupusas, por favor*," the Fricatrice said to the waitress who hovered nearby. The other woman wore a peasant's linen blouse and had a nose fresh off a Mesoamerican idol. "*Y un poco de café. También, un agua del hielo para mi amigo aqui.*"

Jorge watched the waitress head back into the kitchen, then glanced out the window, looking up Hawthorne toward the office. "What was all that?"

"I assume you don't mean the *pupusas*."

175

"No."

The Fricatrice sighed. "Well, my friend, the land has awakened to you."

Jorge felt a rush of pressure in his temples, an almost literal boiling over. The logical part of him recognized the fear of strangeness and the bed full of soil. The thought didn't hold back his words. "That's exactly the kind of New Age crap you guys fed me last night, and look where it got me." He slapped the little table, toppling the tiny ceramic cube of sugar packets. "Don't *tell* me that *shit*."

"What do you want me to say? You saw a dragon, a pretty girl, a hairy man. I didn't do those things to you."

"But you were there, last night."

"You mean late, in your sleep?" She smiled again, softer this time. "In a manner of speaking, yes. You might call it magic, but that's not really what it was."

"Yeah, I know. Skill." He managed to make the word an insult, but she didn't blink. "And the dirt in my bed this morning?"

"You drove me from your dream, invited the land in my place. Like I said, the land awakened to you. It left its calling card."

"And I suppose the land dropped a boulder on my car."

"Unless you think that twit Bert did it."

"He's the wizard of dirt, not rocks."

"Right, as far as it goes. And damned good the Trust offices were on the second floor, where Dagobertus Magnus couldn't be properly grounded. You'd best believe Venera did that on purpose."

"Why did the pipes break?"

"Venera was trying to drive him away. She really is a Locan, a water wizard. Bert pulled a sucker move when he just stepped away from her pressure. She must have been angry, to lose control like that."

"At him or at me?"

"You guess."

His ice water and coffee arrived while Jorge was thinking that over. The Fricatrice made a nasty sludge of hers with six or eight sugar packets and most of the little clay pot of cream. He kept his black, but chose to let it cool, enjoying the sharp scent of the roasted beans.

"It all comes back to what I saw in the woods," he said.

"The land is...the land. It's not a thinking being, not like you or me, but it has a mind. Purposes. A sense of self-preservation. The land is holistic. Venera concerns herself with the waters. Dagobert is one with the soil. You may be something else. Someone who can see the land's intent."

"As a dragon in the trees?"

She sipped at her sludge. "Why would the land send a stone to your car? Think in simple terms."

"To keep me from driving away, I guess. That's the most basic answer."

"Right. It wants you around for something."

He decided to keep pretending this was real. "The pretty girl the other day. The one I fell in love with in a moment. Like it wanted to bind me here."

"Good. Why?"

He remembered the map tattooed on the Sasquatch's back. "I saw Mt. Hood as a glaring eye. Orange, like fire."

Another sip. "Something is coming."

"I don't know what, though."

"I don't know, either. But the land sent the dragon to you for a reason."

"Did Venera know this...land thing about me?" He couldn't figure out how he felt about that. It bothered him to think that his feelings for her might have been manipulated by that Skill crap, too. "Is that why she hired me, kept me around?"

The Fricatrice just smiled over her coffee sludge.

177

Jay Lake

✦

In 1862, the Oregon Steam Navigation acquired both of the portage tramways (north and south sides of the Columbia River) in the present-day Cascade Locks area. The Oregon Pony remained in operation on the Oregon side of the river while OSN reconstructed and improved the portage railroad on the north side of the river. The portage railroad on the north side of the river was incorporated as the Cascades Railroad Company in Washington Territory as a subsidiary of Oregon Steam Navigation. It was six miles long, built to a track gauge of five feet, and was built from the start to standards that would allow for operation with steam locomotives.

— A History of the Oregon Steam Navigation Company,

by Glenn Laubaugh of the National Railway Historical Society

✦

Later they went looking for Jorge's car. The Fricatrice — he still didn't know her name, but figured that her anonymity was one of those Skill things — didn't have a car either, but she had a bus pass and she wasn't afraid to use it.

"Busses are a great place for Skilling," she told him as the number 14 rumbled fitfully toward downtown and the Portland Police Bureau. "Every kind of energy you could want, all in one place. Sexual desperation, drug addiction, ghosts — you name it."

"Ghosts." As if. On the other hand, there was all that dirt in his bed. Were ghosts any more unlikely? He squirmed in the plastic seat. "On the bus. What would a ghost want on a bus?"

"A bus is a place, skinny butt." She glanced at him with that leering smile. "A locus. Locii can be important in Skill. And to ghosts. Those poor bastards need places. Most places don't move around. Busses do. Ergo, ghosts on the bus."

Jorge studied the bus's interior. Signs overhead advised him not

178

to eat, to keep his music private, where to convert his life experience to college credits. Two Mexican guys at the back chatted quietly about women and work. A wall-eyed black kid bobbed his head to some private music without the apparent benefit of headphones. A pair of women dressed for the office — coming back from an early lunch, maybe at this hour? — sat not quite touching, ignoring each other and everyone else on the bus.

"I don't know, man. It's just a way to get around."

"And you know what else? Skill is just a way to get by. Some people speak Italian, some people juggle, some people got Skill."

"Juggling doesn't attract so many weirdoes."

⊕

All he learned at the Police Bureau was that his car had been impounded as inoperable, and he owed them $345. Irritated but unsurprised, Jorge thanked the public information officer and left without paying. He and the Fricatrice wound up walking down by the Willamette in Tom McCall Waterfront Park. The park was a pleasant stretch of greensward a couple of blocks wide separating the Old Town district of Portland from the river proper. It was a fine example of no-profit urban planning from that long lost era when people thought their tax dollars ought to be spent on the public good instead of refunded. Later infusions of krusties, homeless and the just plain strange hadn't succeeded in robbing the park of its charm.

Jorge studied the Willamette with a professional eye. The river's color shifted between olive green and muddy brown depending on the light. Topsoil runoff upstream, agricultural waste, dumping from the shipping in port. And Portland had a serious problem with sewage overflow mixing with storm water runoff. The city was fixing it. Slowly.

It made Jorge sad to see what so many people had done to the water.

"Can't eat the fish," he said.

"Rivers are bound, land man." The Fricatrice took his hand, held it as they walked.

Friend, he wondered, or guard. Guardian, maybe. Still, the warmth of her grip was comforting. It made him think of Venera. Like the three of them were a chain.

She continued her thought. "White men brought the first rails in all those years ago, tied the Columbia and the Willamette both down with ribbons of steel. Then the dams later on. Nothing but prisons for the river's spirit. Steamboats were more honest than locks and railways. At least they worked with the river, not against it."

He thought about the map on the Sasquatch's back, looked around the grassy park. "There's no steel right here."

"Redevelopment is all. Rail used to run on this side too. Still does, north and south of this break. The river, it has rail chains. Animals can't get to the water, rising mist has to cross cold iron."

"Look, maybe I can believe this land thing and maybe I can't. But why are railroads bad? People live on the land, we need railroads to live. Stuff has to get to stores, whatever. Otherwise we'd all still be sleeping with our cows in little huts. Railroads have got to be better than highways."

It was a discussion that ran endlessly at the Watershed Trust, and every other environmentalist movement that didn't fall in the absolutist camp of Earth First. Use versus conservation. People could be as passionate about this as about capital punishment or abortion.

She squeezed his hand. "You'd fit right in at a Lansquenet gathering, skinny butt. They've been arguing this point for well over a century."

"Jorge. My name is Jorge. Not 'skinny butt.'"

"Jorge." Another squeeze. His groin got that warm tickle. "All you had to do was ask. Jorge the land man. You could have been Brought to Skill, you know. That's part of what the land can see in you. You ever see Colors? Like, auras on things?"

"Auras." He snorted. "No. And I don't need no Skill Bringing. I like being me."

He wondered if that was true. Early thirties, single, lots of time in the Oregon wilderness, socially progressive job, dated—and sometimes fucked—socially progressive woman. If they weren't strict vegan, and he met all the other criteria which were important that week. It had been the right shampoo in his bathroom for one chick. No animal testing here, dude. But where was it all going? He had a good time, mostly

Until the last few days.

"The land doesn't care what you like," she said. "It doesn't think of you as an individual. The land is everywhere, everything. That's why the Lansquenet is in a twist about you. They're the servants of the land. They've been at it for generations. Doing good sometimes, mostly just debating themselves to death. And here you come along, some random normal as the focus of everything they've worked for."

"Are the Lansquenet all Skilled?"

"Just about. Along with a few very dedicated normals. But the Lansquenet are dangerous to the rest of us. They don't play by the Skilled rules."

"Which are...?"

Another squeeze. He had a quick flash of his sweaty sex dream of the night before. She was taking him there again, this time in the flesh. It would be like fucking Venera at one remove. How weird that was, he didn't know.

"Only one way to learn those rules, Jorge the land man."

That was when he heard the dragon scream.

Jorge dropped the Fricatrice's hand, spun with his arms out, already wondering what he thought he was doing. She shouted something he couldn't make out as two burly kids on skateboards ran him down — no, grabbed him.

He kicked, trying to fight the leather-clad krusties, but his thin strength was no match for their muscles. Not to mention the lassitude which settled over him almost immediately.

The Fricatrice ran after him only to be assaulted by a cloud of pigeons. Jorge tried to screech blue murder, but the same inertia which had overcome his abortive struggle against his captors seemed to have settled on his tongue.

No one was watching anyway except the ragged-winged dragon soaring high over the Burnside Bridge as the krusties bundled Jorge into the back of a faded yellow Simca Vedette.

☥

They tied that big old river
They dammed up that big old water
Mississippi of the West
They put you to the test
And made you into something you're not

There's farmers up upon them highlands
There's loggers on wooded mountainsides
Waiting for that power
Waiting by the hour
Them poor folks been waiting all their lives

I hear the engines moaning
I see them barge boats straining
Columbia's she's in hock
Chained to dock and lock
Only her old spirit is complaining
— "Columbia River Blues," Abednego "Bargepole" Adams, 1940

The River Knows Its Own

✥

Jorge lay slumped in the back of Bert's Simca as the car jerked through stop and go traffic, made some turns, rumbled across one of Portland's drawbridge decks, then eventually settled into the smooth rhythm of highway driving. Maybe Interstate 84, but face down and essentially paralyzed, he couldn't lift himself to look out the windows and check. His body still wouldn't respond. It was as if he had been shot with one of those Mutual of Omaha Wild Kingdom tranquilizer guns.

"Relax." It was Bert the wizard of dirt up front, of course. "As if you weren't already. Heh heh. I apologize for the inconvenience, but the Lansquenet requires your presence. That dreadful woman was drawing you further into her libidinous spell. Trust me, this is for your own good."

Trust, thought Jorge, would be easier to come by if he hadn't been dumped in the back of a car.

"Some of us think you are Skilled, and playing dumb. For myself, I believe that you are a terribly lucky normal, perhaps a wild Skill. Or some odd project of Venera the Fluvimancer and her dreadful Fricatrice. In any of those cases, you are a significant challenge to many in the Lansquenet. I consider myself more open-minded, but that of course comes with being so, ahem, earthy."

Bert chuckled at his own wit and rambled on about nematodes for a while. Jorge studied the carpet fibers and tried to decide if the dragon he'd seen soaring overhead had really been there. And why it had looked so ragged.

That part worried him.

That fact that he was worried told Jorge he believed in the land.

Maybe he always had and never knew it before.

✛

Lack of muscle control apparently did nothing to keep Jorge from feeling all the aches and pains of his cramping body. Bert nattered on for what felt like hours until the Simca exited the highway and dipped long and slow to the right. They went through a series of tight, careful turns. Old man driving in an old man car. Jorge prayed to God the trip was almost over. Even if he was going to be manhandled by more krusties, it had to be an improvement over the floor of the Simca.

Plus he had to pee real bad.

Bert stopped for a murmured conversation—security? Why couldn't the guard see him?—then on again, winding back and forth some more, across the buzzing metal of a bridge deck, the clack of rails.

The car finally ground to a halt with a familiar squeal-and-reek. The back doors opened immediately and people pushed and pulled at Jorge to drag him out of the back seat. They were having such a hard time moving him that he figured the Lansquenet were not kidnapping pros.

"Just unbind him, then," said a testy voice, an older woman. Much older.

After that he was out of the car and up with someone's hands cradling his armpits to face a small crowd. It was like a New Age retreat. They were all dressed as outré as Bert the dirt wizard. Flowing skirts in earthy colors, beaded vests, veils, all manner of amethysts and moonstones and silver charms.

With that thought Jorge found his tongue. "The Lansquenet, I presume?" He didn't bother to hold the nasty out of his voice.

"Keep a civil tongue in your head, young man!" That was the testy old woman again, a tiny thing with a pair of metal crutches. She was wrapped in scarlet silk and wearing an improbably feathered hat.

"Make your God damned invitations more civil next time," Jorge growled.

"Enough," said Bert. "We should repair to our meeting." He grabbed Jorge's elbow, whispering, "Come on, or things might become unpleasant."

Jorge looked around as they walked across an open parking lot. The rain had cleared during his involuntary car ride and afternoon sunlight flooded the scene. There was a scattered assortment of vehicles, most of them as self-consciously odd as Bert's Simca. The lot was on a bluff, with cottonwood trees and sugar elms nearby, and a 1970's-modern building ahead with some landscaping in front of it. There was water on both sides of the lot, and a hell of a lot of industrial concrete.

They were somewhere on the Columbia. After a moment he recognized the layout of powerhouses, shipping lock and islands — it was Bonneville Dam, the lowest dam on the river and a flagship project of the WPA years. That meant this had to be the Bradford Island Visitors' Center.

Then the whole crowd clattered through the lobby of a little interpretive museum with cheery waves to the docent and small bills casually slipped into the donation box. They banged through a blue fire door into a concrete stairwell decorated with paintings of leaping salmon and headed downward accompanied by the swish of silk and the ringing of dozens of tiny bells.

The last thing he saw as Bert pushed him into the stairwell was a view of the river to the west, the ragged dragon circling over the mist-wreathed bluffs on the south side like an errant shadow.

☥

Jorge realized that whatever the Lansquenet had in mind for him, only he could do something about it. The Fricatrice was far behind in Portland, and Venera...well, he wasn't sure about Venera,

185

except for her mounting anger. And he was under no illusions regarding the Lansquenet—they might look like a gaggle of half-stoned old hippies, but these people could control his muscles and bend his mind at a whim.

And they were mad at him. He'd screwed up whatever game they were playing with the land and their self-appointed stewardship over it.

He wondered if his sightings of the dragon had been a good thing or a bad thing. How the hell did this Skill thing work? Did he just somehow start thinking, *here, dragon, dragon, dragon*, and hope for rescue?

If it was that simple, everyone would be doing it.

After the kindness of a brief pit stop in a restroom at the bottom of the stairs, Bert marched Jorge into a largish room finished out in slightly dated museum-kitsch. Sunlit doors exited at both ends of the room. Carpeted floors, large glass cases with models of fish in them, blue directional signage painted over the concrete walls, posters with fish identification information, and a set of varnished backless benches arranged before a pair of windows behind which there was...water.

And fish.

They were in the fish counting room. And there were lots of fish. Squirming, swimming, thrashing against a turbulent current the color of old tea. Salmon, shad, lampreys, all in a boiling silver mass against the windows.

Jorge stared. In September the salmon run was trailing off. It was way late for shad. Lamprey were rare at any time.

The land was reaching out to him. He could feel a slow wave of cold-blooded intent through the windows. Something between panic and anger.

Then the Lansquenet swirled around him. Fingers brushed against his cheek, touched his hair, plucked at his clothes. It was like being mobbed by the Gray Panthers.

That was when Jorge realized what was odd about the Lansquenet. They were all old. Bert was the youngest, given Jorge's not very precise impression of the others, and even Bert had to be in his fifties. Venera was exactly the same age as Jorge—thirty-three—and he'd bet the Fricatrice was still in her twenties.

That had to mean something. Where did the younger Skilled go to serve the land? People of his generation and the kids coming up after cared passionately about the environment. The Skilled among them would be naturals for the Lansquenet.

On the other hand, there was certainly a near-violent opposition between Venera and Bert.

Bert tugged Jorge around the perimeter of the room to stand in front of a smaller door which stood ajar very close to one of the fish windows. Inside was a video set up and a metal-faced board of switches sort of like an old-fashioned mechanical calculator, all facing another fish window.

The fish counter's station. And no doubt the Lansquenet had sent the fish counter out for coffee with a side of amnesia. Or maybe arsenic.

Jorge grinned in spite of himself.

The old woman in scarlet stood in front of the fish windows with her hands pressed together like a Buddhist at prayer, crutches propped against her elbows. She closed her eyes, began to hum, and quickly the chatter of Lansquenet died down. Someone rang a bell—silver, no doubt—and the old woman's humming reached a crescendo.

"Honor to the earth that is mother to us all," she intoned.

"Honor to the earth," echoed the Lansquenet.

Jorge took advantage of their moment of ritual to count heads.

"Honor to the air that lends us life with every breath."

"Honor to the air."

Twelve, fourteen...

"Honor to the water that fills our veins and slakes our thirst."

"Honor to the water."

Twenty-seven, twenty-eight. Plus the old woman in red, Bert, and himself.

"Honor to the fire that is in our bellies and in our souls."

"Honor to the fire."

She opened her eyes and stared at Jorge. He was surprised to see that her irises were almost as orange as the eye on the Sasquatch's back in his dreams.

Dreams.

Was that his way out?

"This gathering of the Lansquenet is now in session. I am Edith, a Pyretic of the witch line of Joanna and as senior-most I name myself speaker of the gathering."

"Honor to you, Edith," said the Lansquenet, their response more ragged than the tight timing and cadence of the opening ritual.

This was nothing like the aggressively casual way Venera and the Fricatrice seemed to approach their magic.

No, he thought. *Skill.* Call it what it was for them.

Jorge wondered if he did have Skill. Was Skill really like Italian? Or juggling? The Fricatrice had suggested it was just another talent, after all.

"Our Great Unbinding is near its end," Edith said. Jorge was startled at the venom in her voice. "A project we have worked toward for two generations. And those...children...in the city claim to have found a new favorite of the land. As if any Landesmann could arise now in the Northwest from outside our ranks. The Lansquenet is all."

"The Lansquenet is all," repeated the audience.

That echo was starting to creep him out pretty badly. At least he was beginning to understand the reluctance of the younger Skilled to join the Lansquenet. He was torn between a sense of their silliness and fear of their seriousness.

"You!" Edith pointed at Jorge. "Why do you set yourself in opposition to us?"

"Me? Your boy Bert sought me out. I've got nothing to do with opposing the Lansquenet."

"You have set yourself up as a false Landesmann."

"I don't even know what the hell a Landesmann *is*."

"You claim to have called the land to you. You claim to have seen it in dreams. You claim the land has followed you, spoken to you, become one with you."

His night-dream of the Fricatrice and the Sasquatch had definitely been a "becoming one with" kind of experience, but Jorge wasn't about to discuss that with Edith. "I don't claim anything here. All I know is I've been kidnapped and brought against my will."

"Easy, Jorge," said Bert, still standing beside him. "Those are strong words. We're you're friends. Edith's just doing *pro forma* business."

"*Pro forma* my left foot, Dagobert," said Edith. "This little punk isn't going to interfere with the Great Unbinding. Not on my watch."

"And what is the Great Unbinding?" asked Jorge. Behind him the fish counting windows rattled slightly. He felt a chill, like he had that day in the woods, and his mouth tasted of old leaves and cold stone.

This was close to the heart of whatever crisis had sent the land to him in the first place, he realized.

"Nothing that concerns you any further, young man."

Could these nuts make Mt. Hood erupt? That would explain the orange eye in the Sasquatch's back, and his warning about the dancing stones. But he couldn't even begin to imagine why they would do such a thing. Mt. St. Helens was a sufficiently recent memory here in the Pacific Northwest to keep anyone from having fond illusions about the restorative powers of volcanic eruptions.

The river. That was why they were here, in the fish counting room. "You want to free the waters," he whispered. The dancing stones would be the dam collapsing.

Bert jabbed Jorge in the ribs with his fingers. "Shut up, boy. Don't ask for trouble."

"So you do have a head on those pretty shoulders," Edith said. "Water is the blood of the land. That blood is bound by steel and concrete, which we must overcome. You raise yourself as a false Landesmann in opposition to our work, claiming power over earth and air, water and fire."

"You're not listening to me!" Jorge shouted. "I'm not opposing anybody in anything." Now he *was* lying. The thought of these nuts blowing the Bonneville Dam horrified him. But he couldn't fix that right now. Not yet. He had to get out of there, alive and with his memories intact. "I can't help it if something came to me. I don't know what it was. I don't want to know."

Don't deny the land, whispered a voice in his head. The dragon? The Fricatrice?

He heeded it. "Maybe it was the land," he continued. "I've seen miracles of water and earth this very day. But this has nothing to do with the Lansquenet. If it is the land, the land chose me."

"Lies." Edith literally waved Jorge off. She was flushing to match her fiery silk wrap. "Self-serving piffle. The Lansquenet are the servants of the land. If it sought a true Landesmann, it would have reached among our worthy Edaphomancers and Fluvimancers and Aeolians and Pyretics."

The members of the Lansquenet murmured as Bert's grip on his arm tightened to the point of pain. Hard gazes turned on Jorge. He saw his death in pursed lavender lips, long glossy fingernails, swept back graying hair, the pulled-tight crows feet of angry eyes. It was like being cursed by every grandparent he'd ever met.

And so this comes down to jealousy, he realized.

Edith placed her palms together again. "I call upon the will of the Lansquenet in this matter."

How was he going to get out of this? Jorge had no doubt of these peoples' menace towards him. Bert wouldn't meet his eye now. The crowd of Skilled were talking amongst themselves in the indistinct muttering voice of a mob, angry cadences rising and falling.

Landesmann. Power over earth and air, water and fire. Which meant...dirt in his bed and rocks on his car.

But he'd been distracted, almost in a dream state when he saw the dragon. The same for the girl. And asleep and truly dreaming when the Sasquatch came and the dirt happened.

The soil in his bed proved the Skill-magic was real.

The voices of the Lansquenet were trailing off. Agreement was being reached. To his right, the fish squirmed against their windows, their presence a cold pressure against his mind.

I have to dream, Jorge thought. The land comes when it wants to, as dragon, woman or Sasquatch; but I can only call it to me in my dreams.

How the hell was he going to dream on demand?

He could pick a fight, right here, but they might just as well kill him as knock him unconscious. He couldn't make a break through the room and out the doors—and how the hell were there doors down this many flights of stairs?

The bell rang again. Edith looked far too satisfied with herself for Jorge's peace of mind.

"I'll speak for you," said Bert quietly.

Right, Jorge thought. *Dreams. Now.* He urgently imagined the ragged dragon swooping down from the cliffs along the south bank, skimming from mist to sunshine like a falling leaf to rescue him.

The fish swirled against the glass like fingers tapping on a windowpane.

Fish. Fish don't dream, but I do.

Just as Edith began to pronounce judgment, Jorge threw his

elbow hard into Bert's ribs, following up with a punch that slid past the dirt wizard's jaw but clobbered him in the ear. Then Jorge stepped backward into the fish counter's station and slammed the door.

It had a deadbolt lock, which he threw. He dragged the desk with the video equipment in front of the door.

There was a tall, narrow window next to the door, partially obscured by a fish poster. He could see Edith hammering on the glass with one metal crutch, so he grabbed a couple of other posters that were hanging in the tiny office and crammed them into the metal-framed space of the window.

"Screw you, fire-woman!" Jorge shouted.

Then he turned to face the fish.

They mobbed this window now, thicker than ever, a solid wall of scales, fins and colors. What he had thought at first glance to be silver was a mass of glinting hues, from red-bodied sockeye salmon to the rainbow sheen of the steelhead.

Jorge tugged the counter's chair right up to the glass and sat down, leaning his head against the window. The cold pressure was the hand of the river on his forehead, like a mother checking a fevered child. Fish flickered in front of him.

"Send me some dreams, guys," Jorge whispered as the pounding began.

He pushed his thoughts outward toward the fish, following that pressure they had been placing on him. It was like counting sheep. One by one, his thoughts left, each carried away by a single fleeing fish, until he slipped into unconsciousness even as the door behind him hummed and smoked with the anger of the wizards of the Lansquenet.

✢

The River Knows Its Own

Scars left by the powerful current mark the high narrow walls of the [Columbia River] Gorge to this day. It is evidence that the water got deeper and deeper. As water filled the narrow channel, the depth reached more than a thousand feet. The flow accelerated to 90 miles an hour, gathering an increasing payload of debris. The Gorge contained most of the raging water — an overwhelming torrent aimed directly at what is now Portland.
  — David Hulse of the University of Oregon in
  Ice Age Flood: Catastrophic Transformation of the West,
  Oregon Public Broadcasting

⚤

The ragged dragon circled over the three islands in the Columbia, stiff with the scent of damp firs and forest mold. Watching over its shoulder, Jorge could see the narrow lines of concrete stretching from bank to island to island to bank like the garden paths of a drunken industrial giant. Water upstream glittered placid behind the great walls, while downstream it boiled from the spillways and powerhouses. The islands and dams themselves were a complex arrangement of cranes and railroad tracks and vast metal gates, power lines strung between them on towers painted orange and white, the whole thing tinker toys for the giant's child.

He shifted his attention to the dragon itself. Its wings were a vast, mottled patchwork of autumn leaves and narrow veins of wood, an airplane built by woodland spirits. The body was little more substantial, a prickly collection of twigs and pine needles like a giant thatch ant nest.

In a way, it was a giant maple leaf in flight. Jorge clung to the dragon's wooden spine with hairy hands that seemed familiar, though they were not his own in waking life.

Down, he told the dragon.

His gaze slid toward the parking lot of the visitors' center out on Bradford Island in the middle of the river. A familiar faded yellow car sat near the front doors, surrounded by faux-gypsy redwood camper shells and pre-Jerry Garcia VW bus-pickup hybrids.

There.

As the dragon circled closer, Jorge tried to figure out where the fish windows were. He quickly realized that the building was four or five stories tall, the front which faced the parking lot actually being the top of the building. From the other side, the structure descended with the slope of the bluff that was the center of Bradford Island until it footed in a little maze of walkways, landscaping, and the narrow, churning channel of a fish ladder.

The other side of the building.

The dragon swooped lower, creaking like a forest in the wind. A walkway bridged a lower one that seemed to lead to the bottom level of the visitors' center. The dragon spilled air from its wings to come to a shuddering landing on the bridge. It extended its neck downward and peered into the double glass doors where the lower walkway met the building.

A pale face pressed against the doors from the inside for a moment, then vanished with a shriek.

Jorge smiled with satisfaction, and jumped from the dragon to shamble onward in rescue of himself. On the ground, he realized how huge he was. The map tattooed on his back itched, up by his shoulder the hardest.

He burst through the doors without opening them first, howling and venting his musk in the spray of glass splinters.

◈

Jorge's head snapped back as he jolted awake. For a moment he felt witless. The fish were gone, leaving only tea-colored water behind. The counting station reeked of electrical smoke and incense.

Outside, people were shouting.

There was no other way out except through that room.

He somehow felt overly short and thin as he pushed the table back from the door, as if he'd returned to childhood. The door handle was too hot to touch, so he grabbed one of the fish posters from the narrow window and wrapped his hand in it.

Out in the fish counting room there was chaos. The varnished benches were overturned as people surged back and forth. The Sasquatch from Clark's bar—and in fairness, from his dream—roared an incoherent challenge as it shambled through the room. Most of the Lansquenet were either panicked or awestruck. A swirl of red caught his eye as Edith fled by the south doors all the way across the room, followed by Bert, his brown velvet coat flapping.

And if Bigfoot was in here, the dragon must be outside the north doors.

Jorge pushed through the crowd as hard as he would have moshed at the Aladdin. These old dudes might have made the scene at Woodstock, but they'd never done smashmouth punk. And no one had the concentration for Skill-magic at this moment.

As he made his way toward the dragon, Jorge could have sworn the Sasquatch winked at him. Then he was out the shattered doors in sunlight, staring into a vast pale eye the texture and color of a queen ant's abdomen.

This is it, he thought. This is where the dreams and the magic and the frou-frou New Age Skill bullshit become real.

Not the dirt in his bed.

Not the boulder on his car.

This dragon of leaf and wood and insect parts, that he could mount and fly to chase down Edith and Bert before they did something truly regrettable to Bonneville Dam.

Do you believe? he asked himself.

He patted the dragon's mossy muzzle just below the eye. It reeked of the land, forests and fields and cold, hard mountain rock—much ranker than the gentle pine scent of his dream. "Did you come for me, girl?" It was a she, he realized. Was all the land female?

Not the Sasquatch, certainly.

The dragon's head dipped a little further, nearly pulling her off balance from her perch on the walkway above. Jorge grabbed the neck, which despite seeming so fragile took his weight easily, then hoisted himself up to sit above her shoulders, just before the roots of her wings.

She leapt upward, flapping hard to make air, spiraling away from the visitors' center and the roadways surrounding it. Jorge clung to her rough-textured neck in a spot where all her materials seemed to come together in one leathery skin and watched for the flash of red that was Edith's silk.

He'd never spot Bert the dirt wizard from up here.

As they rose higher, he glanced for the parking lot. The yellow Simca was still there. Then he saw the color he was looking for. Edith and Bert were by the north side of the first powerhouse, the dam section linking Bradford Island with Robins Island where the navigation lock was.

"There they are!" Jorge shouted.

The dragon wheeled and dove. Swooping toward the powerhouse, his gut finally felt the reality of being in the air, essentially unrestrained. He felt a moment of eye-watering panic tinged with vertigo before that was overtaken in turn by the realization that the dragon was diving right into the north wall of the powerhouse.

There were three tall metal doors there, each large enough to pass turbine sections or generator housings. Jorge prayed the dragon was going for one of those instead of the solid concrete of wall.

And go for them it did, Jorge screaming his lungs out as the dragon exploded against the central door in a cloud of dust, dirt, sticks and leaves. The door ripped open with a boom like a giant's footfall as Jorge was thrown inward, riding a wave of forest debris to tumble flat on a concrete floor surrounded by interpretive museum signage.

The dust settled as klaxons began to wail. Venera stood up from behind a picture of the dam being built. "What the hell took you so long, Jorge?" She was smiling.

His heart jumped in his chest. "Oh, God." He wanted to kiss her, but there wasn't time. "Edith," he gasped. "Bert." The roiling dirt made him cough.

She cocked her head, nodding down to the powerhouse floor.

Jorge pulled himself to his feet and looked.

They were on an observation balcony at one end of a room that had to be a thousand feet long, and at least ten stories high. Generator housings receded into the distance like a series of mechanical wedding cakes, while a partially-assembled turbine awaited more blades on the floor beneath them. The hub of the turbine was about the size of his lamented car.

The walls and floors were tiled in ocher-and-brown geometric patterns, ornamentation from an age when people built even industrial facilities to please the eye. The safety orange of the overhead gantry cranes was a jarring contrast, as was the red Corps of Engineers logo painted on the nearest generator housing.

"Damn it," he said, recovering his breath. "They must be out on the generator floor already. Now what?"

Venera's smile grew toothy. "This is a dam powerhouse, Jorge. We're standing *on top* of the Columbia River. Fire-woman and earth-boy down there are about to learn not to fuck with a Locan over running water."

In that moment, he knew his love for her was real, not just a crush or a Skill charm. And he thought he could see a spark in her eyes, too. Grinning he asked, "Can I watch?"

"Count on it, Landesmann."

When she leapt over the rail, he followed her without even looking first.

✦

They scurried around the downstream curve of the second generator housing. Equipment carts stood nearby, and their sightlines were obscured by cabling and pillars. Everything smelled of machine oil and the tight, crispy tingle of lots and lots of electricity. Doors boomed open to the distant shouts of security guards. Jorge reflected that you could hide a boatload of old hippies in a place this big and complex.

Venera placed a hand flat on the generator housing. The great slab of metal hummed slightly. Jorge could feel a vibration through the floor. "How are you going to—"

"Shh." She waved him to silence and bowed her head for a moment. Then, "The water tells me. It doesn't like Pyretics. Natural opposition."

"Is that why she wants to blow the dam?"

"Water is power, Jorge." Her fingers brushed his, sending a spark of static between them. "Now come on."

They sidled on around the housing, keeping as close as the cabling and support struts would allow. Venera pointed at the next housing.

Judging by the echoes the shouting security guards seemed to be getting closer.

Jorge scurried after Venera as she dodged across the open space between the generator housings. She did not pause this time, but kept racing around the curve toward the upstream side, fingers trailing against the metal.

The hum from this turbine sounded different to Jorge, as if it were spinning harder. Was she calling the water? He tried to feel the force of the land in his mind, the water flowing as its blood, but outside of his dreams, Jorge had little control.

Love or no love, he would have felt better if the Fricatrice had been around for this little showdown. Strength in numbers.

Venera stopped suddenly. "Get your lousy asses out here, *now*," she shouted. "No more warnings."

A brilliant snake of flame came arcing around the generator housing. Venera ducked it without losing her contact with the housing, while Jorge simply hit the floor. It splashed against the posts behind him supporting the service catwalk that reached the tops of the generator housings. Sparks spit where it hit—a power connection cut?

"Hey, Landesmann." Venera's voice was distant, as if she concentrated hard.

The turbine was definitely whining hard now, the concrete floor thrumming.

"What?"

"Keep them off me another minute or so. And if I can't get the genie back in the bottle, you'll have to ask the land to do it."

"I don't know—"

Then a shambling man-mound of sticks and leaves and soil came around the curve of the housing.

A sending from Bert. Made from the remains of Jorge's ragged dragon. There wasn't anyplace else to get that much organic matter from down in here.

It was like pissing in a church. "God damned dirt wizard!" Jorge shouted.

He sprinted past Venera and charged into the man-mound shoulder first. It was like running into a tree. Jorge bounced off, his arm in agony.

Jay Lake

The man-mound reached for him with a large, indistinctly formed fist.

Jorge backed up, banging into some copper piping stacked against one of the pillars supporting the catwalk overhead, perhaps waiting to be installed as a water line. He snagged an eight-foot length and used it to stab at the man-mound.

Keep it at bay, keep it at bay, he though. At bay was fine for a moment or two. How to kill it?

The concrete floor was vibrating now as smoke poured out of the generator housing. Another flame snake shot toward them, but it became diffused by the smoke.

Jorge stabbed again and backed toward the pillar that the first shot had hit.

Bert's sending still followed him.

"You were a dragon," he told it. "Spirit of the land. Look at you now. Bert's made you a mockery of yourself."

The man-mound took another swipe at him.

Jorge could hear sparks spitting overhead. He prayed he wasn't about to bump into a hot line. A quick glance upward showed a slagged junction box.

Aha. Good. Do this just right, he might live long enough to see what Venera was going to do next.

The shambling thing took one step closer and Jorge leaped. He jabbed the back end of the copper pipe into the slagged junction box, feeling a harsh buzz in his palms as he made contact, then spread his hands and fell away, thinking: don't ground yourself, idiot.

The far end of the pipe drooped toward the concrete, spitting sparks, as the man-mound grabbed at it. Power from the junction box grounded through the man-mound. Flares arced all over its body to erupt in bursts of flame as the leaves and wood burned off.

Jorge ran around the other side of the generator housing without waiting to see more. Bert's sending was occupied, and there wasn't any more soil handy to make another—he hoped to God—but he had to distract Edith from shooting more flame snakes, at least until Venera finished her Skilling.

He caught up with Edith and Bert standing over a glowing box. Edith turned to him and shouted, "Aristides will—" just as the arc of the generator housing closest to them burst open with a torrent of Columbia River water, thick with fish.

Somehow, Venera had reversed the turbine and called the water *up*.

It was like a liquid bomb going off. Bert was caught full force by the water jet and smashed backward into the upstream wall of the powerhouse, pulped by the pressure along with dozens of salmon and steelhead. More fish shot out at angles to fall into the glowing box and buffet Edith like giant silver fists. A whole new set of alarms began going off overhead, barely audible over the roar of the river.

Jorge could have cheered. Venera had succeeded. The Lansquenet's spell had been disrupted. But now the genie definitely needed to go back into the bottle, fast. Already the rushing water was tearing at the adjacent sections of the generator housing, and flames shot up out of the top.

Jorge grabbed a wildly thrashing male sockeye, bright red. The fish took a bad bite of his left hand. He held it close to his temple, trying to think in cool, crisp, simple fish-dreams. "Back," he told the water. *Help me, ragged dragon.* "Back." *Help me, Sasquatch.* "Back." The pretty girl drinking his chai smiled, and for a moment the fish was not so cold.

The roar of the water abated then, dying quickly. When Jorge opened his eyes Edith was nowhere in sight. He dropped the sockeye and pushed through the mass of wriggling fish to find Venera curled up on the ground, fingers still on the generator housing. She seemed smaller, wrinkled like a used condom.

Discarded.

I am the Landesmann, he thought. I can bring my love up out of this place.

But there were men with drawn guns and bullhorns on the catwalk overhead, and he had nowhere to go. He scooped up Venera anyway and ran for one of the service doorways leading out to the downstream face of the powerhouse. Bullets whanged off the concrete but missed him as he plunged through the door.

Outside was a roadway with inspection ladders leading upward and downward across the face of the dam. A helicopter clattered overhead, and a whole new family of sirens screamed out here. He just kept running, across the roadway, and leapt into the high space above the lower reaches of the Columbia.

As he fell, still holding tight to Venera, Jorge could see the fish below him parting like hands to admit him to the river's depths.

⊕

He came up sputtering for air like every drowning man who'd ever lived. The water was September cold. Power lines marched in the distance upstream, but no one was shooting at him.

Where was Venera?

Jorge splashed around, looking. She wasn't with him. She wasn't nearby. He struck toward shore. Maybe he could spot her from a rock.

"Hey," said the pretty woman in the birchbark canoe. She was dressed differently today, in buckskins to match her boat.

"Venera," he said, grabbing the side for support. Where had this girl come from? She'd done it to him again. "My..." He didn't know what she was. "Thin black woman, a Locan. She's out here somewhere."

"No. She's not. The waters have claimed her." That laugh, the one that pierced his heart all over again. "The river knows its own."

Though it pained his heart, Jorge had to believe her. He was the

Landesmann, she was the land.

The girl helped him into the canoe, smiling like she kept all the secrets of the world. A little while later, they landed on a tree-topped gravel bar. She slipped out of her buckskins and offered him some of those secrets, but he refused, miserable for Venera. She smiled and held him to her breast a while and sang river songs until he slept.

When he awoke near sundown with her earthy scents still on him, the land-girl was gone, but her canoe remained. He paddled his way through the evening fog back to Portland, thinking hard without reaching any conclusions.

✦

Jorge didn't know what else to do, so he went back to work the next day. His body ached terribly, and getting dressed was a hassle with all the dirt scattered around his apartment, but the long walk from his neighborhood to the Watershed Trust office seemed to work out the worst of the kinks.

The office was a mess, of course, from the sprinkler incident the day before. The sight of the wreckage made him want to kneel down and weep for Venera, but he could imagine what she'd say about *that*. He had to act as if she was coming back.

So instead he tried to do some actual work. Venera had cleaned up the worst of the flood, and somehow his computer had been spared, though there was already mold growing on the monitor.

Jorge logged into oregonlive.com to see what was what. He hadn't even tried the radio at home. An aborted terrorist attack at Bonneville Dam was all over the headlines. One generator had been badly damaged in the incident, but far worse consequences averted. Apparently a quick-thinking group of senior citizens had spotted some radical environmentalists on the prowl and alerted security. There was mention of a single unidentified casualty. He wondered what had become of Edith.

"That Lansquenet," Jorge told his monitor mold, "always one step ahead."

Later as he was spreading out files to dry, the Fricatrice turned up with two cups of Salvadoran coffee—hers sugar sludge, Jorge's black with a sharp odor that cut right through his fatigue. She was wearing a Trixie t-shirt today, from the old Speed Racer cartoon, and a pair of bicycle pants several sizes too small for her. She gave him a big, sloppy kiss, as if they were old lovers. "You did the right thing, Landesmann."

He asked the one question that was on his heart. "What about Venera?"

"The river knows its own. Maybe she'll be back. She's tough."

"Not tough enough." He brushed the warm sting from his eyes, but he realized the Fricatrice didn't look sad at all. He figured she understood more about all this than he did. Maybe Venera was coming back.

After he regained his composure, Jorge said, "I never could figure it out, you know."

"¿Que?"

"Coming down the river last night, I couldn't figure why the Lansquenet wanted to blow the dam. I mean, I understand about the river being chained by steel rails and concrete dams. But they have to live here, too. We're all part of the land, us people with our cities and everything."

"Water is power, *batang lalaki*."

"I know, but why release it?"

She slurped on her sludge, took some time answering. "They got a...vision...for the land. To return it to what it was. Maybe they're not even wrong. I don't know. But as for the river...anybody can feel the power of impounded water. Why do you think there are so many stories of lake monsters? It ain't like there's really dinosaurs swimming around down there with the frog shit. Water holds the memory of what has passed through it, and what it has passed through. Water holds secrets. Water holds death in its murky bonds."

"Like ghosts on the bus. Water is a place. A locus, you said."

She winked. "Exactly. A place that's everywhere and nowhere, always moving. Now maybe you understand what it means to be a Locan like Venera. People who don't have elemental Skills, they think it's fire that's hard, always changing, always calling. Pyretics, they got it easy. Throw a few tantrums, get on with life. Water's the toughest master."

"So why release it?"

"Think of all the power they'd have. There would be a flood, a tiny little Missoula, the symbol of the scouring the Lansquenet would bring to the northwest. Restoring the land. And then the Skill power the flood would give them. Spells to move mountains. Or erase cities." She slurped again. "But they made one big mistake in their thinking—the land is always changing. People are just another part of the change. You think Kennewick Man didn't pee in the river or fish for salmon? Erasing man's hand from the land is like trying to put Mount St. Helens back together."

"Yeah." Something else bothered him, a loose thread. "And Aristides?"

The Fricatrice stared over the plastic lid of her coffee cup for a moment. "Where you hear that name?"

"You and Venera, that first night. Then Edith the Pyretic started to say something about him when Venera blew the generator housing."

"Forget him. He's a different kind of problem. Lots of people think he's their friend, they're all wrong. There isn't a side he hasn't played. You ever hear from him, you run the other way. Then maybe you call me for help."

Jorge smiled. "How would I do that?"

"In your dreams, baby."

After a moment, he realized she wasn't kidding. "I see."

"No. You don't. But you will. Good-bye, Landesmann." She stood, gave him another sloppy kiss, and walked out.

✦

Bringing It On Yourself

YOU REMEMBER THOSE FUNNY little lecture desks back at Taipei American School when you were in the sixth grade? The ones with the skinny Formica writing surface attached to the right hand side, so all the lefties had to crab over further than usual to take notes.

The desks they threw at you.

So one day when Mr. Smithson was out of the room, Lance Prather started shoving you. You backed into the corner as everyone else laughed or just ignored you. You were a geeky kid, nose in a book, never knew what was going on, didn't drink or screw like most of the rest of the class, and you always blew the curve on tests. This was back when progressive ideas first leaked into education, along with disco and sideburns. Grade curving worked great unless there was kid in the class like you who actually *paid some fucking attention*, thank you.

There's Lance, twenty pounds and four inches on you with an Air Force sergeant of a dad who whips his son with a belt every time he brings home a D on a quiz, which Lance blames entirely and exclusively on you. He's working up to a dermatologist's wet dream of a face, and his complexion will probably be scaring women and children before he turns twenty. He doesn't blame that on you exactly, but you're a more convenient target than oily skin, bad hygiene or the crappy food his mom burns on the stove every night at home. Plus you're skinny, slow, and too damned smart.

207

Jay Lake

So *slap*. Big, fast hands against your chest. *Slam*. A shoulder into your shoulder.

"What's the matter, Edwards? Can't take it?" He has that big leer, garlic breath and yellow teeth, but somehow all the good looking girls still find him cool and attractive when they can't even remember your name. *Shove*. "Stand up like a man you little prick!"

Then it's just you and Lance in the corner of the room, and some easel or map stand or something is pressing into your back as you slide to the floor and he's laughing, and behind him Tommy Thornton is laughing and Kevin Boudreaux starts to snicker and even some of the kids who don't give you shit are smiling, because it is funny when the blush and the blood and slide-down-the-gutter embarrassment belongs to anybody but them, and besides, laughing keeps Lance's attention away from them.

No one's ever going to stand up *for* you. Not if they don't want to suffer your fate.

The laughter isn't 'ha ha ha' *All In the Family* laugh track laughing either. This is a whole choir of laughs, from Lance's fuck-you bray to Emily Milton's sweet giggle. If hymns were funny, these kids would have been stars. Lance the conductor, you the sheet music, every last one of the bastards another laughing voice in the chorus.

Then Lance realizes he's run out of places to push you. Smitty's still gone from the room, no one's coming to find out why sixth graders are laughing—the sweet innocence of childhood echoing down the halls is a rare enough sound without disturbing it—so like a clown juggling scarves, then plates, then chainsaws, Lance needs a different act.

He grabs one of those little study desks, hefts it like he's pumping iron, mugs for the class, then heaves it at you. One the legs connects with your forehead, a painful punch of the clock, then it falls right in front of you, an addled aluminum and Formica insect tipped over to starve.

Tommy, Lance's perpetual second and me-too man, jumps out of his desk, grabs it, and tosses it at you as well. This one scares you more, but hurts you less. Then Kevin hurls another one, trapping you in a cage of study.

Smitty walks in just as the last of the desks has been added to the pile, a semicircle of laughing kids the moat guarding your wall. "What the hell's going on here!?"

All the kids shuffle and snort, swallowing giggles.

He stares at the pile, finds you in the middle. "Jim, get out of there."

You're stifling sobs. Being piled with furniture is bad enough. If you let tears slip here, now, in front of Lance and Tommy and Kevin and Emily, that *will* be the end of you. So you don't have any words to spare for Mr. Smithson, because if you open your mouth a torrent would erupt, and you might not stop once you'd started.

He kneels down. Smitty is tall, red-headed, with a John Brown beard and a late sixties intensity of purpose. "What happened?" he says, his voice almost a whisper.

You're still wallowing, but even if you had your head back, you wouldn't breathe a word. There's lots worse misery than being tripped in the hall during class change or having locker doors slammed into you—that's just life in sixth grade. Ratting out Lance to Smitty right now would buy you a whole new ration of shit.

Answered only by your silence, Smitty stands and sighs. The moment of outreach is over. "Lance, Tommy, get those desks off him. Edwards, if you can't tell me how this happened, you go to the office and explain yourself there."

Once again, you brought it on yourself. What did you say to antagonize them, all you have to do is stand up to them and they'll leave you alone—all those stupid lies adults tell victimized kids to make themselves feel better about doing nothing to stop the bullying.

Jay Lake

✦

Summer is looming, as it does every year. Though in Taiwan it's not much different from the other seasons. You're not any happier about life in school, but you've had your fellow outcasts to eat lunch with, to warm benches with during P.E., to compete with for who can check the most books out of the school library before the semester ends. Then the school year does end and you trade the misery of sixth grade for the misery of being home—a much better misery because you suffer it in splendid isolation and no one tells you that you read too much or that you're too damned smart.

Then Dad enrolls you in the summer activities program at school.

"Christ, what the hell were you thinking?" you yell over the amah's strange notion of an omelet, eggs and tofu and those tough, skinny Chinese mushrooms.

"Don't use those words with me, James." Dad's got his mad on—something at work, some negotiation with the Chinese government he's already fighting out in his head. He's got no time for you, for this.

Same as it ever was.

"I'm not going."

"James." This in his you'll-be-sorry-if-you-don't-shut-up-and-mind-me voice.

You've spent most of your life being sorry. Why break the streak now?

You shut up anyway. You're driven to school the next Monday. You're let off with a cheery wave, as if it's all okay now that you're back in the place that is the vortex of your misfortune the other nine months of the year.

But when you get to the summer session, there's a teacher you don't know running it, and he's okay. He hasn't written you off yet. A couple of your fellow outcasts are there, so there's someone to talk to. Lance and his buddies aren't there—they wouldn't be caught dead on campus during the summer. They'd rather be out stuffing firecrackers down the throats of frogs, or getting drunk under the footbridges in the park, or getting head off Emily Milton and her friends.

Which leaves you nearly safe for the first few days, until the session kids shake out into the normal hierarchy of monkey see, monkey hit.

Only *this* time you're not at the bottom of the shit chute.

Maybe it's the couple of inches you grew in the spring. Maybe you've been slapped around so much you finally learned to keep your mouth shut once in a while. Maybe it's the birthday you just had. Maybe God is sending you a message.

There's this Chinese kid in the class. Taiwan Chinese, not an ABC—American-born Chinese. He's a skinny toothpick, with knobby knees and a face like a plate. His hair's cut mental-institution short, and he's got ears sticking out like a second pair of hands. He doesn't speak any English, and he shows up wearing a Chinese school uniform, which is basically blue Mickey Mouse short pants with suspenders over a white cotton shirt.

The dictionary definition of 'uncool' just had someone else's picture pasted into it over yours.

God, are you grateful. It's enough to make you fall down on your knees and pray to the empty sky.

The same old shit starts up. This time, you get to giggle when someone pisses in his Coke can when he's not looking. It's a familiar taste, but now *you're* in on the joke. The sneakered foot tripping him on the way to the bathroom turns out to be pretty funny, too.

It's not like you're cool, but you're part of the pack for the first God damned time in your life and it feels *good*.

Except you know why his eyes are red.

You know why he keeps wiping his nose and having trouble breathing.

211

Jay Lake

You know why he looks scared all the time.

If you had any fucking guts, any fucking integrity, you'd go put your arm around him, say *ni hao ma* and *wo shuo yi din din guo yu* and actually learn his Chinese name.

But that would put you right back in the shit barrel with this funny looking, strange acting, permanently and dangerously unpopular kid. And you just can't do it.

It keeps you awake nights, thinking about how it is when he goes home. Somewhere out there in Taipei, there's a pair of parents that are proud of their kid for sticking it out with the Americans. Somewhere out there in Taipei, there's a kid crying into his pillow, wondering how to make it stop.

You know how to stop it. Just walk over, stand with him, and take his lumps with yours. Exactly what no one else ever did for you. Ever will do for you.

Are you better than them? Better than Lance or Tommy or Kevin or Emily? Better than Smitty or Dad?

Aren't you? Don't you know, in your bones and in your broken heart?

It's just so good to be on the inside, one of the guys. You can't let go of that feeling, that tiny breath of cool. That glimpse of belonging.

It'll be okay.

The beginning of the second week, it's a hot day, dusty and dry with the sun in the sky like a penny on a stove. You're all outside playing dodge ball, which is pretty much gym teacher sadism at its most refined—especially when the teacher's off doing paperwork or something. Only somehow the ball keeps slamming into the Chinese kid, and no one will let him out of the circle. He runs back and forth.

Pop. The ball catches him in the small of the back. He starts to snivel.

There's a ringing noise as it bounces off his head, the sound a basketball makes on concrete. He's crying now.

Then the ball comes to you. "Go for it, Edwards," says the summer session's Lance Prather stand-in. Less cool, but keeping the seat warm till the big guy comes back in the fall with his dick sucked down to glassy-clean and pot smoke leaking out his ears.

You're standing there with the ball in your hands. This is it. The Chinese kid stops running, stares at you, tears on his reddened cheeks.

He knows. It's like he's inside your head. He knows you know. He knows you've been there. He knows you're the only one who could save him now.

The ball is hot against your palms.

Put it down. Walk into the circle. Stand by him.

Do the right thing. Do what you've prayed for someone else to do since you first darkened a schoolhouse door. Stand up to the shit of the world.

You want to do it.

You want to.

You want.

Laughing, you cock your arms back and let fly.

✿

How old are you now? Pushing forty? Disco's dead, buried and back from the grave under the name of karaoke. There haven't been any Air Force kids in Taiwan for decades, not since the Phantoms stopped flying back and forth over the South China Sea on their way to napalm somebody else's miserable kid in the name of democracy.

What have you accomplished? Married, divorced, married again, tried to raise a kid of your own, mostly done the right thing. You pad your expense report once in a while, run red lights late at night — nothing serious.

But if God came down from Heaven with all the host behind Him, with a flaming sword in one hand and a time machine in the other, there's one thing you'd ask Him if you could do over.

When He finished laughing and gave you the time machine, you'd go back to that hot Chinese summer of your youth, step into that circle, put your arms around that big-eared kid, and tell your younger self to go to hell.

Then maybe you could sleep well.

☥

Of Stone Castles and Vainglorious Time

IN THE VAINGLORY OF HER youth, she'd asked him for a castle as the price of her hand. Flush on railroad money and other more obscure profits from Reconstruction, Colonel Striker set men to work. Eloise Hammond took the rising towers as surety and they wed on Midsummer's Day, 1884 on a mountainside just outside Powder Springs, West Virginia, amid the wooden derricks and ramshackle scaffolds of her growing fancy.

φ

"Missus Striker?"

Eloise turned from examining her hat in the mirror. The hat had come from Paris by way of Boston, and would set any woman in the state to envy. It was fashionably tiny, covered in black lace and pansies of velvet beaded with jet. She was quite proud of it. "Yes?"

The young man looked to be one of the workmen, perhaps from the crew in the North Gallery. His ragged homespun shirt and rough leather shoes were so clean they shone. He obviously hadn't been outside with the stonemasons.

He smiled, displaying teeth like mother-of-pearl chips while his violet eyes—the same rare color as her own—flashed below neatly trimmed pale bangs. Eloise felt her bosom heave, and the familiar, loosening warmth in her female parts. She tried to count the days until the Colonel came home from his trip to Baltimore.

"Begging your pardon, ma'am, but this is for the memory of times past." He took her right hand in his, turned it over to slip her a tiny box. His hands were uncommonly smooth, as soft as Eloise's own. A sharp spark of sexual excitement caught in her throat.

To hide her confusion at his presumption and the rising blush warming her cheeks, Eloise looked down at the box. It was covered in a gold-threaded red silk. She shifted her hips a bit—both easing and feeding the itch in her loins—and opened the gift.

Inside was a silver locket engraved with her initials, "EHS." She pulled the locket out by its chain and looked up at the workman, her smile dawning with the charm she knew no man could resist.

He was gone, as suddenly as he had appeared, leaving not even an echo of his steps on the parquet floor.

Declining the indignity of pursuit, Eloise opened the locket. There was a picture of a young girl inside, crisp as a daguerreotype but painted in the colors of life. Pale-haired and pale-eyed, the child looked familiar, but Eloise could not place her.

⚛

The happy couple soon had a son, Ephraim Hammond Striker. As strong as Eloise was, it was still a hard confinement and a harder birth. The Pittsburgh doctors said she would have no more children, but Colonel Striker proudly said that Ephraim was more than sufficient to his ambitions. Mother and child joined the Colonel on some of his trips, and when they could not accompany him, he raced home at first opportunity. The couple's open displays of loving affection and their mismatched years would have made them the scandal of the town, save for the Colonel's money.

Two years later the Colonel was shot and killed by persons unknown while out riding on the mountainside. His head was blown off, and his wallet and his cavalry pistol taken. Eloise could identify her beloved only by his clothing. She was left with his child, his fortune and her appetites, which like the summer sun would seem to never cool. Her grief and his money finished the castle, which she named Striker Manor.

As he grew, Ephraim reminded Eloise so much of her lost Colonel that she came to dread the very sight of their son. She bribed the stationmaster in Powder Springs to put Ephraim on a Children's Aid Society orphan train to Kansas, in order to lose him so completely she could not call him back in a moment of weakness. In a final spasm of maternal regret, she gave the boy the stranger's locket by which to remember her.

Eloise vowed never to marry again. In consolation for her lost love, she set herself to a life of pleasurable idylls. More than three decades of Pullman cars brought her young men from Columbus and Pittsburgh, sometimes New York or Boston, and once even a dapper and acrobatic gentleman from faraway Italy.

☥

In the fall of her forty-second year Eloise was forced to dismiss yet another young woman, returned to Powder Springs for lax morals.

"I cannot abide a maid who interferes with my male companions," she wrote in a letter to her local attorney. "Because of her I have had to send Jack F. back to Cincinnati as well. This much vexes me as I have no young men waiting in the wings, as it were. Please hire me a replacement for Cora Jane, preferably a young woman who can keep her legs crossed. The usual terms will apply."

She signed with her typical flourish, then folded the note into an envelope which she sealed and blotted. Eloise laid it atop a Jules Verne novel and pressed the service button to ring her driver, Patrick.

A young man with striking violet eyes and pale hair stepped into her study instead. He wore black evening dress, just like

Patrick and her other male staff, but Eloise did not recognize him. She slipped her hands into the pockets of her quilted silk dressing gown and smiled at him. The derringer fit perfectly into the palm of her right hand.

"Hello," Eloise said in her best come-to-mother voice. "You're not one of my regular staff."

"Madame Striker," he said. The voice was familiar, an echo of something long forgotten. "My apologies for disturbing you."

"Yes?" His voice, his eyes, this young man stirred her loins, better than many of her new boys had in the last few years. Wishing she *had* sent for him, Eloise wondered where he had come from, how he had gotten this far into Striker Manor. She silently cocked the derringer.

"This is for who you are today," he said, setting a silk box on her writing desk.

It was covered with a familiar gold-threaded red. Eloise ignored it. "Did I meet you...no, it would have been your father, here, perhaps twenty years ago? Who are you?"

"Not my father." The young man smiled his perfect mother-of-pearl smile. "But someone very close to me."

"And you *are*?"

At that moment, Patrick stepped into the doorway, his movement catching her eye. "Madame rang?"

"Enough," she said. Men had sought her money, in many ways. Eloise waved her free hand. "Patrick, please remove this gentleman."

Patrick glanced around the room, an uneasy expression flickering across his face. "Whom does Madame wish me to remove?"

The young man with the violet eyes was gone like mountain snow on a spring morning. Eloise found that she was unsurprised. Ignoring Patrick, Eloise uncocked the derringer, then opened the silk box.

Inside, in a silver frame, was a portrait, perhaps five inches tall. It was Eloise as she looked that very day, right down to the green ribbon in her hair. Like her long-gone locket, it was a beautifully rendered painting, brushstrokes so fine she could not see them, again as if it were a color daguerreotype.

How had the young man done it, she wondered? He had arrived, made the picture in a moment, and gone again like so much dust. She stared into the distant places of her memory, wondering if the answer lay with the lost locket.

"Is Madame well?" Patrick finally asked.

✦

After October of 1929, the trains no longer brought young men for Eloise, and the servants had to be dismissed. Harder, older men from around the county made the climb up the mountain to Striker Manor. Some brought wagons or trucks loaded with salt and flour, firewood and wine, returning loaded with Dutch paintings, German furniture, British chinaware and Persian carpets. Others brought only cash, to buy a few hours of her time. Eloise past sixty looked half her age, and was more woman than any of them had ever met.

Eventually, as times grew leaner and she grew older, even these gentleman callers trailed off to nothing more than the occasional grocery delivery, C.O.D. Only her books she kept—Rimbaud and Lovecraft, Darwin and Wells, patient, quiet lovers for her twilight years.

✦

Eloise sat among her books in what had been the servant's kitchen and rubbed horse liniment into her knees and ankles. Tearing the wainscoting out of the Gun Room had given her a new round of aches, but she had no other firewood on hand. For want of funds, the oil furnaces had been shut down for years, as had the electric lights.

She still wore her quilted silk dressing gown, patched as it was with calico and gingham scrap. The derringer never left her pocket, although she only used it to scare off the youths who clambered in the shattered library windows to whoop through the halls of a moonlit night. She wished she'd learned to shoot a rifle. Then at least she could have rabbit stew from time to time.

"Eloise," he whispered from the doorway of the lower stairs, a voice so familiar that for one heart-stopping moment, she thought it was the Colonel speaking.

Then Eloise came to her senses and cocked the derringer. "I always knew you'd be back. Bad things happen in threes."

"So do the good." Pale hair, violet eyes, gleaming teeth, he walked slowly toward her, young as ever, a mockery of her hard-lived years. He wore dark wool slacks and a finely woven shirt of a cut she'd never seen, pale as a spider web to match his hair. He carried an enormous red silk box, the size of a card table. "I have something for you, an image of times to come."

"I've lost my youth, my beauty, and my money," she said with a short laugh. Even now he could make her feel that old twitch in her loins. "What is left to come for me?"

He laid the box down on the ground in front of her. "That would be up to you. I bring choices, bargains for you. Your medical heritage is invaluable. The patterns of your body can help us live a very long time, perhaps forever."

"So here you are, to buy my body like a thousand others?" Eloise tugged at her robe. "Surely these breasts are too withered for a young man like yourself."

"That's not how you are wanted. Tests, rather, and the pursuit of medical science."

"Why now?" she asked, tears standing in her eyes. "Why not in the bloom of my youth, or the vigor of my middle age?"

He smiled, sad and beautiful. "I had to wait until your circumstances were sufficiently reduced to ready you for my appeal." He extended his hands, a child reaching for a mother's embrace. "Step into the future with me. An endlessly glorious life awaits you as mother of a mighty race of men."

Eloise did not answer. She knew without looking what was in the box. The young man was a pendulum weight on the chain of her life, swinging from extremes of youth to extremes of age. When she was a young woman, he had brought a picture of her girlhood. In middle age, he had brought a picture of her that very day. Now there was another of those color portraits in the large box, of her in her coffin perhaps. Like Mr. Wells' Time Traveler among the Eloi, the young man had come from outside the world, somewhere else in time or space, to offer this unholy bargain, with her portraits laid in evidence of his power.

"If you can go forward, I can go back," Eloise said, thinking of her lost Colonel. "But no one lives forever, young man." She shot him in the chest. He buckled, falling backward into a sitting position against a pile of encyclopedias with an astonished expression. "No one should even try." The second barrel of the derringer fired, catching him in the face.

"You weren't supposed to..." he whispered through bubbling blood, then sighed himself to a surprised death.

Eloise put the latest silk box unopened into the fireplace with the shattered wainscoting. Then she searched the young man with a practiced efficiency that came from undressing generations of young men.

Eloise found her locket, the one he had given her fifty years earlier, on a chain around the young man's neck. In his pants pocket she found a little brushed silver box with numbered Bakelite buttons and radium dials. It had a knob which when turned showed the passing of years. "So you *are* of science, and not the devil," Eloise whispered to him.

Jay Lake

In death, the young man who might once have been her son looked very much like her Colonel had that terrible day, save for the clothes and a lack of large caliber shot through the head from a cavalry pistol. Those two wants could be remedied, she thought, with the aid of his time machine. Eloise kissed the young man's bloody, cooling lips, then cast the locket into the fire where the boxed portrait was burning merrily. She took his silver box and tried her hand at puzzling out the precise function of the buttons.

After a while, Eloise hefted the corpse into her wheelbarrow and left the dark, chilly halls of her castle for the old riding trails on the mountainside, in search of her vainglorious youth and her beloved Colonel.

✦

Partitioned

SALVATION STRUGGLED IN John's throat, a fish caught on a line the length of time itself. God had given him money, and he had his rights. Three cans of hairspray and a Mars bar, no one could say different—that and some righteous malt liquor already whispering its secrets to him. The good Lord was coming to Seattle, and John aimed to catch the last bus to Glory. He just needed to bring someone with him, another soul to be his ticket home.

Lady at the register, something in her eyes. Was she one of God's people too? John's lips strained at the good news, words like feathers in his mouth.

"Seventeen dollars even, sir," she said. Her lips were as red as her store apron, her hair as gray as his memories.

He dug deep in his jeans for the two grubby tens God had sent him that morning. The words rushed out, not the right ones but close, dross pouring from his lips when he'd meant to spit gold. "You going to Seattle?" John asked, handing her the bills.

There. He'd done it. Reached out for her immortal soul, offered a hand up Jacob's ladder. Would she be the one? He'd never get to Heaven by himself.

The cashier stared at him for a moment, eyes fishbowl-wide behind her glasses. "Excuse me?" she finally said.

Her betrayal stung like soap in his eyes, the feathers in his mouth turning to dust. He wanted to howl, spit mud, tear his hair.

Jay Lake

Another soul lost. He couldn't be alone in Glory, just him and God. It wasn't permitted. "You will be partitioned," John shouted. *Cut off from the promise of salvation.* "You are anathema!"

Lips tight, eyes frightened, she gave him his thirty dimes. God always made sure he got dimes. John took his salvation with him and stumbled out to the parking lot. Seattle was a long way yet, but God was patient. John would find another soul to get him into heaven.

✟

Hunting Angels

A SMALL HOST OF THE angels of the Lord—about half a dozen—gathered around Johnnie on the lower deck of the Steel Bridge where the railroad ran. Johnnie sometimes slept there tucked in among the girders, his head inches from the wheels of the long-haul freights. Right now his head was inches from the angels' chrome-winged motorcycle boots. Their hard, tattooed faces and knife-edged black pinions should have intimidated anyone.

"What?" Johnnie snarled as he scratched at his needle scabs. They always itched in the morning.

The boss angel had his arms folded on his chest, tattooed dragons writhing across the muscles. Literally. "Hello, birthday boy."

Johnnie spat down between the gaps in the bridge girders. "Is that today? Fuck you very much."

"I see. Don't know when you were born." The angel leaned forward, bracing hands on leather-clad thighs. "Know *where* you were born, asshole?"

"Hell if care."

The angels laughed.

"No, not *there*," said the leader.

Johnnie'd had enough. "What kind of fucking stupid-ass angels are you, need me to tell you anything?" This wouldn't be the first beating he'd ever took.

225

Jay Lake

"The kind of fucking angels," the big angel said in a mincing, sing-song voice, "that fucking *know*. I just want to see if you know, birthday boy."

"Kiss my ass!" Johnnie rolled backward, dropped through a gap in the ironwork, and dove into the Willamette River sixty feet below.

The water crashed into Johnnie like a bus before swallowing him down. His lungs felt flattened, air driven out by the river's enormous slap. He swam through a cloud of bubbles and stinging pain generated by his impact. *Crap*, he thought, he'd lost another sleeping bag.

Johnnie broke the surface midriver to find the boss angel standing on the water right in front of him. The angel leaned down and attempted a smile. "Let's start over. Hi, Johnnie. My name's Zeb. We need to talk."

✟

They sat under the western embankment of the Steel Bridge amid a rubble of greasy sleeping bags, shattered wine bottles and dog turds. The krusties who'd camped there had split fast when Zeb's host swooped down from the bridge like angry ravens.

Johnnie had just watched the angels' flight with a hunger for the freedom of the air. When they landed, he shook his head to blink away the dust in his eyes. "Somewhere in Texas," Johnnie said, as if they had never been interrupted.

"Lockhart," said one of the other angels.

Zeb glared back over his wing.

"Could be." Johnnie snorted, swallowing bitter laughter. "What the fuck is it to you?"

Zeb placed a hand on Johnnie's wrist. It was like being touched by a river, or the night sky, or an entire mountain. The only place Johnnie had ever found that feeling was when he jumped—off bridges, off grain elevators, off the harbor cranes. During the fall he was free. Scared the hell out of the other krusties, too, which kept them off his ass.

"Ever meet your Daddy?" the angel asked.

Johnnie stared at Zeb's hand. Lacquered black nails, silver rings with skulls and crosses on them, weird letters tattooed across the knuckles. "No. Sometimes I don't think Momma did either."

"That's because you're one of us, boy," Zeb whispered. "And we never forget our own. You're a man now, sixteen. Can't be alone in the world without our blessing."

"Ain't never going to die," said another angel. "You're forever young, whatever age you want to be."

"Shut up, Mike," Zeb said. "I'm handling this."

"Everybody dies," said Johnnie. "Who the fuck cares? You gonna look bad in Heaven if I catch a bullet?"

"We look out for own. Even half-breeds." Zeb's eyes glowed like fires on a distant cliff. "How would you die? If you could?"

"*You* know," said Johnnie, nodding at Zeb's wings. "Falling. I'd fall forever if I could."

"Flying," said Zeb. "Not falling. Your soul remembers Daddy's wings."

"Don't got no wings. Not like you."

Zeb reached over his own shoulder as if to draw a sword and broke off one of his pinions. Johnnie could see the angel's blood leaking from his fingers as Zeb held the knife-edged feather. It was almost a yard long, and looked as if it had been wrought from iron.

"I can't give you wings. But I can give you powers of air and light. You'll never fly, not like us, but you could fall forever and never die. It's your birthright and my gift to give in place of your Daddy. You ready for it, boy?"

Johnnie watched the blood drip into the scuffed, dusty earth at their feet. Pale shoots of green sprang from the soil at the touch of each drop. He looked away from the new growth. Like his Daddy had turned away from Momma, before Johnnie was born. Zeb's offer might even be true, but he wouldn't touch it. Johnnie never took nothing off nobody he couldn't smash or grab for himself.

"If God gave a shit, He'd have sent my Daddy back to me. I'm nobody's boy now, Zeb-angel. Not yours. Not God's. Never will be. Thanks, but no fucking thanks."

He stood, turned his back, and walked away. He knew Zeb wouldn't let it rest but he couldn't give in.

Zeb didn't disappoint Johnnie. It was like being cut right down the spine with the biggest straight razor in the world. Johnnie collapsed onto a dirty sleeping bag, a couple of old condoms and a cigarette pack crushed beneath his face.

The jagged edges of the feather sliced into Johnnie's back over and over, tugging at his skin like a rough-nailed hand. Zeb breathed in his ear. "You're going to live forever, *nephew*. Should have taken it the easy way. We were ordered to do this nice, but you won't do nice. So I'm making this hurt. Maybe you'll learn something."

"Good," Johnnie grunted through the blood pooling from his bitten tongue. If they hurt him, the power belonged to the pain, not to him.

"Good?" Zeb's breath burned the side of his face, the angel's weight growing to something large and terrible. The ground around Johnnie glowed with Zeb's anger as the angel carved into the skin of Johnnie's back. "I'll show you *good*. A special gift, just from me to you, half-breed. The only way you'll feed your power is one life at a time. You have to take someone with you when you jump. And everyone that dies, a little piece of you will die with them. But you'll never die enough. Not enough to get to Heaven. Enjoy eternity alone, fuckwit."

For the first time in more than a decade, Johnnie cried. He sobbed around the blood and pain, crying for a Daddy he'd never seen.

✚

The krusties came slinking back and found Johnnie lying stunned on one of their sleeping bags. They kicked the living shit out of him, then threw him into the river.

Johnnie bobbed in the cold water for a while watching the darkness come. Gulls and ravens circled overhead, dirty little angels searching for scraps. Like Zeb had searched him out in the river.

"Hey, God," Johnnie said to the night air. "If You're listening, I'm coming. I'll find a way to climb to Heaven and hunt down every one of Your fucking angels. And when I find my Daddy, I'm dragging his sorry ass in front of You. We'll see who judges who."

✚

The next day, Johnnie bumped into one of the krusties who had beaten him, hustling change along Naito Parkway near the Fire Department building. "Kid Marco," Johnnie said. "We gotta talk." He had one hand on the krusty's elbow. "Come on up to my doss. I'm gonna teach you how to jump."

"Hey, Johnnie," Kid Marco laughed, fear on his face. "No hard feelings, right?"

Johnnie just smiled as they walked.

There was a raven perched on the bridge girders about eye level, watching the two of them pick their way along the railroad tracks. Its wings reminded Johnnie of Zeb's. He grabbed it off the girder in one swift move, breaking the bird's neck with a flick of his wrist while hanging on to Kid Marco's elbow with his other hand.

Johnnie stuffed that broken-necked raven in Kid Marco's screaming mouth before they jumped off the bridge together.

He did it over and over, starting with the rest of the krusties from the bridge camp. It wasn't as good as the angels he hunted in his dreams, but no matter how far he fell, Johnnie had no wings to spread and fly to Heaven.

✚

The Algebra of Heaven

ONE MORNING CEDRIC FOUND a small object perched on the glistening, porcelain perfection of his apartment's bathroom sink. When he had wiped the sink down for the last time before retiring the night before, there had been soap in the dish, his toothbrush in its plastic holder, and nothing else.

Nothing.

He wiped his fingers on the hand towel. He then took a deep breath and picked the thing up, pinching it carefully between thumb and forefinger to minimize contact.

The offending object was narrow, roundish in cross section, and a little less than an inch long. It had an organic sort of shape. The color was organic, too, pale beige with darker brown mottling.

Cedric realized he held a finger bone. He shrieked, dropping it into the bathroom sink where it rattled and danced about.

"Darn!" he told the mirror. Now he would have to bleach the sink before he could use it. He fetched his dirty tongs from their plastic bag under the kitchen sink and transferred the bone to another bag. He sealed that bag inside a second, larger bag, then set to work cleaning the entire bathroom.

You could never be too sure.

He didn't ask himself where the bone had come from. Some questions did not bear answering.

✦

Late to work, he stayed late to make up and missed the correct bus home. The regular driver on the next bus, the 6:17, was a filthy lady whom Cedric avoided whenever possible. The nasty woman grinned as Cedric waved her off the stop, and Cedric was forced to wait for the 6:32. *That* bus was almost two minutes off schedule. It smelled like homeless people and their dogs, and someone had been eating onions.

By the time he got home, Cedric's pulse was elevated, he'd developed a migraine, and worst of all, there was gum on his left shoe. If he'd had a cat, he would have kicked it.

"Darn, darn, darn," Cedric muttered as he scraped his shoe clean in the little foyer that served him as a mud room. He couldn't step into the rest of his apartment until he put his shoes away. He couldn't take his headache pills until he was in the apartment. He couldn't—

Then Cedric noticed a pale sliver peeking out of the top of his Wellingtons. He dropped the gum knife, which rattled on the floor, making a scuff he'd have to buff out of the tile later. He took his second-best scarf from the hat rack, wrapped his hand in it, and carefully tipped the boot toward himself.

Inside was another bone. This one was long and thin, knobbed at the end, the same mottled beige as the finger bone had been.

Cedric shrieked again, then clapped his hands over his mouth. That action pressed fuzzy wool against his lips and teeth—for he had forgotten the scarf—while the boot toppled free. The bone fell out and spun on the tile floor as Cedric dropped the scarf to spit little threads and fibers out, his frustration overflowing in hot tears.

"Damn you," he whispered to the bone when he'd gotten control of his breath. Mother would be so ashamed. Cedric's chest shuddered like a washing machine. He was already required to scrub himself with bleach and lye, thanks to the horrid bus, so he grabbed the still-spinning bone in his bare hand and marched it into the kitchen.

His gummy shoe would still be waiting for him later. Cedric felt a reckless sense of wild abandon, as if he'd become a hippie or something.

There were two more bones on the kitchen floor—ribs, it seemed—and a small pile of teeth on the counter. Cedric completely lost control of himself. He raced in circles about the kitchen, swinging the long bone in his hand like a club, trying to smash the ribs and scatter the teeth. "Get out," he shouted, "get out of my home, you freaks!"

The bones danced away from him, ribs skittering like mice before a broom while the teeth clattered and chattered up and down the counter. Every time Cedric swung the long bone, the ribs would slip away in a new direction. The cupboard below the kitchen sink popped open and the captured finger bone shot out, followed by a flood of its fellows—knuckles, patellae, feet. The apartment kitchen quickly became a swirling blizzard of bone, rattling like maracas as they flew around Cedric until the long bone danced away from his hand and he collapsed crying onto the little throw rug with the kittens on it that Mother had hooked for him long ago.

✦

"Filthy, filthy, filthy," Cedric whispered. His face was buried in his folded arms, as it had been for the better part of an hour. He ignored the occasional thumps and clunks that came from outside his safe place.

It wasn't very safe, unfortunately.

"Filthy, filthy, filthy."

When he was a boy, Mother had stripped Cedric naked every day when he come home from school, picking the lice from his head—later on his underarms and groin as well—and scrubbing his entire body clean while he stood in the footbath in the kitchen with the plastic sheeting spread around.

"Bad, bad, bad."

She'd taught him over and over about all the things that could go wrong with his body, reading from health magazines and newspapers and the Bible.

"Wrong, wrong, wrong."

She'd watched over him while he slept, turning the sheet back every few minutes to make sure he didn't touch himself at night, taking naps during the day so she could always be there for him when he was home.

"Life is a vale of filth and sin," was one of her favorite sayings. Cedric had never been sure about the sin, but the filth was self-evident.

And now the bones had come to him. A plague from the Lord, or some final warning of Mother's, though she'd passed on years ago.

Cedric's thoughts were interrupted by a puckering sound, the seal breaking as the refrigerator door opened, followed by the click and hum of the compressor.

Why would bones need the refrigerator?

He shifted his arms, peeking out a little.

The kitchen floor was horribly scuffed, and bottles of household cleanser had tumbled out of the cabinet under the sink. Untidy. The bones were untidy. Cedric shifted his trembling arms, scanning, trying to see without being seen.

It reminded him of playing hidey-body under the sheets with Mother. Despite the filth and fear, he smiled at the memory.

The vegetable drawer squeaked open. He'd polished and lubricated that slider dozens of times, never to his satisfaction.

Why would bones need vegetables?

Cedric lifted his head and looked.

The bones were a body now, a skeleton with strips of thin tissue dangling like ribbons on a gift box. It stood facing away from him, leaning into the refrigerator, making crunching noises.

He would have to find another home, Cedric realized. This apartment would never be clean enough again. The anger in that thought gave him the nerve to speak. "Excuse me," he said with almost no quaver in his voice.

The skeleton turned to face Cedric. Pale blue sparks gleamed in the dark eye sockets, and it was eating a stalk of his celery. Or at least chewing it. Cedric was fairly sure skeletons did not need to eat. Somehow, it was less frightening as a skeleton than as a loose collection of animated bones.

His visitor nodded, still crunching on the celery.

Cedric took that as an invitation to go on. "Would you please leave? You're dirty, and you make me nervous."

The skeleton shrugged, which produced a curious ripple that echoed down its ribs and even to its waggling pelvis. Cedric saw that the strips of tissue were moving, growing, finding each other like little worms dancing in dark soil.

Skin. "You're eating to make more of you."

This time the skeleton nodded.

"And when you're done?"

His visitor shrugged again and returned its attention to the fridge. That was when Cedric realized there were too many bones on the back. The extras stuck out, long and thin and crazy-shaped.

Wings.

It was a bone angel.

Cedric got to his knees and backed slowly out of the kitchen. Maybe some time in the bathroom, giving himself a good scrub with the wire brushes, would be enough for the skeleton to go away. Then he could pack the things that were still clean enough to be salvaged and set about the laborious process of finding a new place to live.

✝

Cedric lay soaking in the clawfoot tub enjoying the familiar stinging pain of his skin. Almost his entire body was underwater, only his face and toes in the cold air. That way he couldn't hear the rattles and thumps of the skeleton making its way through the kitchen.

Though he tried not to, Cedric kept thinking about wings.

"Angels are just devils in disguise," Mother had always said. "Beauty tempts a man to sin just as much as evil does."

The bone angel had been many things, he realized, but beautiful was not among them.

The tub rang, startling him into sitting up as he opened his eyes to see the angel standing over him. The skeleton must have kicked the tub wall.

Only the bone angel wasn't a skeleton any more.

His hands flew to his crotch, sending sprays of water onto the bathroom walls and across her bare thighs.

Everything about her was bare, in fact.

Cedric stared at his hands, trying to cover himself without touching himself. He felt a mortifying stiffness down there, just from the barest *glimpse* of her...her...

Of her chest and groin, he thought. Those were the words Mother had made him use.

Mother would be so angry to see him like this. Every day when she scrubbed him, she would slap him, well, *there*, if he stiffened. His high school years had been difficult that way on a daily basis. He wasn't supposed to be stiff. That was another temptation to sin and filth.

"Well?" said the angel.

"Well what?" Cedric asked the water. He realized he could see her reflected there, thin as a leather belt, skin tight over her bones. Her... chests... were tiny, dangling down like little bags, with large dark… circles… on their centers. A darker triangle gleamed below.

He had to slap himself in his own groin and look away from even the reflection.

She reached down, grabbed Cedric's shoulder with hard, bony fingers, and dragged him bodily to his feet. The raw, wounded skin he had scrubbed with the wire brushes burned beneath her grip. She was so *strong*. Just like Mother had been, when he was young.

Despite himself, Cedric smiled.

The angel leaned in close to him, so they were nose to nose. Even with Cedric standing in the tub, she was taller than he. He could see the arch of her wings stretching up behind her, though they were wrapped with skin like a bat's, rather than feathers — translucent skin, papery and pale as Mother's had been during her last year in that nasty, filthy hospital. The angel's face was drawn thin over her bones, and that blue spark still burned in her black-on-black eyes. Her lips were black, too, as was the hair on her head.

He couldn't decide if she was beautiful or terrible.

"There's nothing else to eat here," the angel said, her voice a hiss. Her breath smelled slightly stale, like the inside of an old closet, but much to his surprise it wasn't unpleasant. "Except you," she added. Her free hand slapped his away from his groin, then she grabbed there, right where he was stiff. "You want it the easy way, you want it the hard way, or you want it hard *and* easy at the same time?"

"Te… tem… temptation," Cedric stammered.

"You bet your sweet ass," she said, then kissed him so hard his lips bruised.

☥

They played hidey-body for hours, her always on top because of the wings. It was much better than any of his games with Mother. She licked his raw brush-scraped skin, sometimes cutting him first with her long, dark nails so the blood ran more freely. The pain was an old friend, but the tingling pleasure of her saliva was something new to Cedric. She let him kiss her chests, and even gnaw them until she bled, which he told her made them twinsies. She put her knees around his ears and made him burrow and chew and lick until his chest burst for breath and his gums stung from the curly, wiry hairs jammed in among his teeth. The moist, meaty smell of her made him want to sing. But the best was when she took his groin into hers. The angel clamped him tight inside her, tighter than Mother's fingers ever had when she was picking lice, but the deep warmth of her was like nothing in his world.

The longer they played hidey-body, the richer her skin became. Though still pale, she had a little bit of color, and the bones had more flesh over them. Her chests puffed out a little, the marks of his teeth healing over so fast he just had to make more. Her face widened a little, and her lips became full and smiling. Most magical of all, her wings were shot through with ropy veins that pulsed dark blue as the wings spread and cracked like flags in the wind.

Cedric felt drained, weak, thin and pale. Eventually he was reduced to laying flat, gasping, as she crawled back and forth across him, her wings brushing first the ceiling, then his face.

Finally she stopped, cradled him in her arms, let him rest his lips upon one of the dark nubs of her chest.

"Thank you," the angel whispered to him. "For making me whole. My work here has just begun."

Cedric pulled his mouth away for a moment, reluctantly. He had something important to tell the angel. "Mother was wrong."

Just saying the words he'd never even dared think in his life gave him a chill. Once he started shivering, Cedric realized he couldn't stop.

The angel kissed the top of his head. Hanks of Cedric's hair settled on his shoulders, scattered on her chest. "No, your mother was right," she said. "Temptation is sweet, but it is still temptation."

"Now what?" Cedric's breath had grown thin in his chest.

"When an angel comes into the world, someone else must give up to make room." She reached down to take his hand. "It is the algebra of Heaven, which the affairs of the soul must balance." The angel snapped off Cedric's left pinkie finger.

It didn't hurt, much.

She showed him the bone, then like a party clown with a child's carefully-hoarded quarter, made it disappear.

"Will I be clean enough for God?" he asked her.

The angel took him to her breast again without answering, and began to pick away at his body. After a while, when there was much less of Cedric left, she said, "Do not fear. I have scrubbed you to the bone."

"Mother would be proud," he tried to say, but her nipple swallowed his words.

The last thing Cedric heard was the beating of leathery wings, which sounded just like the click of Mother's heels as she came to the door to welcome him home.

☥

Hayflick Limit, 12 Miles

SUSAN AND I WERE CRUISING down some two-lane blacktop in back country Oregon when we shot past a highway sign that made me slam on the brakes. The old Eldorado ragtop shimmied to a stop in the chilly shade of some Doug firs, spitting gravel like an irritated cat.

"Wha'?" she asked, waking up.

"Wait." I dropped the lever in reverse and let five hundred cubic inches of pure Detroit power idle me backward through the last hundred yards of my life.

The sign said what I thought it had said. 'HAYFLICK LIMIT, 12 MILES.' "Since when?" I asked.

"Sounds like it might be a cute town," she said, waking up. She scratched at the diamond stud in her nose. "I need a pit stop."

"Pit, pit." Hayflick Limit? That was something else entirely, from biology. The end of life as a cell knew it.

After a few moments of steaming the damp, cool air, Susan hopped back over the door. I pulled a u turn. Might as well head back to Crooked Finger and points north. I saw no need to head into a town called death.

A few minutes back up the road, I slammed on the brakes again.

'HAYFLICK LIMIT, 10 MILES.'

"Spooky," Susan said in a voice that suggested anything but, then tugged her knit caftan across her shoulders and rested her eyes.

I glanced around. Were the trees getting any older?

Straining on the clutch, I nudged the car in gear and crept down the road a little slower.

The top was up.

When had I put the top up?

'HAYFLICK LIMIT, 7 MILES.'

This time, I didn't bother to stop. I had to pee, but whatever this was, it was coming up soon. Susan had found glasses somewhere. Her hair was different, not as black as I remembered it. I clung to the wheel, staring out at the drooping trees. The bastards were changing on me, dying.

'HAYFLICK LIMIT, 3 MILES.'

The wheels were thumping as if all four tires had gone flat, and the engine sounded like hell. The roof was gone again, but I'd be damned if I could remember ever buying a car this small. It was like driving a motorized cart. My hands ached, and if I hadn't known what it was going to say, I couldn't have read that last sign.

'WELCOME TO HAYFLICK LIMIT.'

The cart and I stopped together. I still held the reins, but nothing pulled us now. Susan sighed once, then went quiet. There was nothing but bare rocks around me now. The trees and ground cover were as bare as the bones of my hand.

I staggered out to clutch at the shiny metal signpost. There was a light shining there, but I wouldn't look up without Susan.

"Hon?" I said.

Even the wind had died.

After a while, I crawled back up the road. Away from Susan, away from the cart, away from the rocks. When my legs become too stubby to propel me any further, I lay there and screamed until someone took me home.

✦

The Black Back-Lands

THEY SAY THE SILENT PEOPLE can hear you talking in your dreams. I guess that's 'cause the Silent People only speak in dreams, so's they listen real good there too. Kind of like the dead, maybe. But I always been told to keep my mouth shut when dreaming comes upon me, for fear of giving away too much of myself and being sewn into some woodspocket and carried ever more through the fir shadows and pine bays while my body starved and fevered.

Our little town ain't much, but it's what we got. We're up on a hill east of the greater stoneways, which is good on account of safety from bears and cats-of-the-mountain and landless, lordless raidermen that prowl the fields. But it means someone's set to walk up and down a lot with buckets. That gives me good legs, better for running when I need to, and shoulders I can stack wood on. Not much to talk to, though, just beetles and bones and the horizon that rises and falls beneath my chin with each step.

The worst is how them bones whisper to me. I know they ain't the Silent People, and they're Old Dead, no harm to us and ours, just complaining about the way things used to be. But still they whisper and call my name and ask me to open the gate leading to the Black Back-Lands and beyond so they can find their way into the next world.

"No and no," I tell them, like I been taught, "no and never more. Away spook, begone shade, bother someone else's day."

Jay Lake

It don't never impress them much, but I think maybe they just want to be talked to, attended to some. I can understand that.

One day, coming up hill under a double bucket on the number three yoke for the millerman, I was setting my mind to wander-wondering. My feet knew the way of course, so I was thinking on the Old Dead in life. If their whispers was to be believed, they had carts and chests of clothes and magic wells within their walls. I 'magined myself walking among their proud, bright houses, admiring their clothes and the flowers around their doors, when one of the Silent People stepped onto the path.

Now you got to know the Silent People are as real as your fist. That is to say, they're always there, but you can't see them unless you close things up just right. I must've been calling in my dream-of-daylight, and this one heard me. It was small, maybe to my lowest rib, and furred as a good bear-robe, with a smile big enough to split its head in two like a muskmelon beneath an axe.

A three-fingered hand was held up as if to stop me—which it did—and in my head the doors slammed on the bright houses. The Silent Person frowned as the dogs within my 'magination howled and scrabbled to get away. There were two suns in my sky now, one warming my neck and the other casting shadows behind my eyes.

I felt the number three yoke slide away with a crash and burble that meant a beating later at the least, but the whispers of the Old Dead were like thunder now.

"The gate..."

"...open the gate..."

"...make it open..."

"...see the black sun..."

"...sun shining on the black..."

"...Black Back-Lands."

Then the Silent Person handed me a pumpkin and a knife. Inside my head, or on the path, I could not tell, both was real now. I looked at that big orange ball and someone had drawn my face upon it with a sharp tip so fine it was like looking at my own skin. My eyes opened and stared out at me, the colored parts black as the gate of any land.

"Open..." whispered the Old Dead in angry chorus. The Silent Person tugged at my knife hand, making little motions. Its touch was summer wind, the walk of a wasp upon my sweating neck, mold settling on old meat.

I looked at the knife. The tip was busted off, the blade spotted with rust or blood. I could see both sides, from the pumpkin eyes and from my own. Water from the spilled buckets chilled my feet, while the cicadas in the trees shrilled a clicky-winged call to life. What did I smell? Blood?

"Black Back-Lands," they whispered.

The place no one ever went. The country behind the eyes, beneath the heart, the hills ever in shadow. Where life maybe had gone on without fire and plague and the breaking of the stoneways.

"Just a boy," I said quietly. "Got no maps, me. No servant to the missing or the dead, neither. Millerman's master enough, thank you."

I handed the knife back to the Silent Person, but it was gone. I turned to set the blade among the bones lining the path, but they were shrubs in flower, bright with bees and butterflies.

Still, there was a pumpkin in my hand and I was hungry. It bled when I cut it, but the pulp was sweet and hot. The seeds tasted like iron. As I chewed, my jaw squealed loud as the rusted hinges of an ancient gate, and shadow cloaked my shoulders.

✷

Apologizing to the Concrete

EVERYBODY HAS A STORY. The junkie kid who tried to rob the bar half a block from my house. The hotshot customer who drew down on him. The woman in the street outside. Even the stray bullet that took her in the temple. Especially the stain in the sidewalk.

All I was doing was walking to the post office. I'm the only one without a story.

⊕

The sky was clear and pale, a perfectly glazed ceramic lid over the world. Mount Hood loomed purple-white in the eastern distance while crows grumbled from the rooftops. About three in the afternoon, I locked the front door of my ageing Victorian, trotted down the steps, and paused at the curb to watch for a break in traffic.

The heavy wooden door on O'Reilly's Bear Claw slammed open with a bang. I glanced over just as I heard a thin crack. I guess everyone's used to the echoing thunder of movie bullets. In real life, the gunshot sounded like a small firecracker. In real life, a short, frumpy woman with gray hair collapsed onto the sidewalk half a block to my left.

⊕

Jay Lake

The stain on the sidewalk wouldn't go away. The City of Portland sent a crew around with chemicals and high-pressure hoses. Then the bar hired a couple of guys who sandblasted and bleached the concrete. After that didn't work, I went out every day around three o'clock with baking soda and a scrub brush. I got yelled at some, but I stuck with it.

✟

There are ethics in church and there are ethics in the boardroom. People who will hold the door for you during the dinner rush at Jake's will cut you dead in traffic. The only ethics that count are the ones that you find in the moment.

And in that moment, my ethics failed me. Blood and bone sprayed, a fluid pink arc hanging in the sunlight. Her plastic raincoat glittered. Her right foot missed its step and she toppled. Someone screamed. I don't think it was me. By then, I was running away.

I'm one of the good guys—a lifetime of principled opposition to firearms. A strong, liberal voting record. Women should control their bodies and religion doesn't belong in the textbook or the statehouse.

Too bad I didn't stand up for my beliefs.

No more Mr. Good Guy.

✟

A week later I bought a drum of trichloroethylene, hip waders and long rubber gloves. The stain on the sidewalk remained no matter how much I scrubbed it. After a while the cops cited me for environmental violations.

✟

I took the *Oregonian*, just so I could follow the story. Somehow the crisp, slightly greasy newsprint made it real in a way that Web sites couldn't.

The junkie was a street kid, fifteen. He'd already vanished into the juvenile justice system. Some Assistant D.A. wanted to nail the would-be hero for carrying a firearm without a permit. The papers had a field day over vigilante justice. The defense was looking for a mystery witness, a man who had been standing nearby when the shooting happened. I went to the arraignment hearing, sat in the gallery. Nobody knew my name.

☦

The stain on the sidewalk continued to accuse me. People stepped around it as if the victim still lay there. They knew what I knew, even if I was the only one who could see it clearly. I tried to buy explosives, to destroy that segment of sidewalk, but no one would sell them to me without a permit.

☦

The victim finally got a funeral, after being held down at the Multnomah County Medical Examiner's office for almost a month. I brought a big bouquet of lilies. No one showed up at Riverview Cemetery but me, two people from the M.E.'s office, and the Episcopalian minister who gave the service. Miss Helen Graham had no surviving relatives, and apparently no friends. An anonymous donor had paid for the burial costs. No one asked me any questions.

On the way home, the car radio said the charges had been dropped against the shooter. I guessed Miss Weeks wasn't beautiful, or important, or wealthy, enough to matter. The D.A. said the mystery witness might have helped solidify the case.

✿

If I had a time machine, I'd go back to that moment, run to her aid. Maybe grab her arm and ask directions to the post office, delay her for a few seconds so the bullet would part empty air.

I had to settle for a hammer and chisel. The cops came to talk to me around 3:30 one afternoon, when I had gotten "I'M SOR" hacked into the concrete of the sidewalk. They were pretty nice about arresting me.

✿

Stories ramble onward. The kid's in juvie. The shooter's free. Miss Weeks has all the peace and quiet she'll ever need. The bullet's in a labeled baggie somewhere in a Multnomah County evidence room.

Me, I still don't have a story. I just drink Mad Dog under the east abutment of the Ross Island Bridge. Every afternoon around three I push my shopping cart over to the Bear Claw and whisper apologies to the stain in the sidewalk until someone makes me leave.

✿

Changing the Game

DRIVING ONE-HANDED. Sodium-vapor street lamps flicker, yellow-orange San Francisco night punctuated by dim stars and distant brake lights. The car smells of your perfume, a gentle scent I'm too dim to identify, but it's something like rainwater in the Texas spring of my younger days.

"I feel like I've been dealt the right hand at the wrong time." It was as close as I could come to saying what I was feeling at that moment.

Your fingers squeezed mine. That was as close as you could come.

The tires hummed, the pavement clicked, the world turned beneath me. There are moments in life when I can feel every atom straining at its bonds, where time slows to its fintesimal detail, and I am in that place halfway to forever.

Then your grip loosed, but did not drop away.

I took the turn one-handed, swinging dangerously wide but unwilling to let go of you. No one around, not even cops at this hour. Not even homeless guys.

Just us. Just the night. *Paradise Lost* by the dashboard lights.

I could have wept, but I didn't.

✤

251

Later at your house there was an outbreak of avoidance. Elliptical conversations that went somewhere else. I was hung on my hormones, you were hung on good judgment.

Or at least common sense.

But sleep came in separate beds, then morning came way too soon. Dogs barked outside, San Francisco woke up, and I dragged myself through the shower and my luggage, heading home to Elaine and Ariadne, to a parent-teacher meeting and all the impedimenta of middle-aged, married life.

I saw you on the stairs at the last, smiling through the slats of the banister, wrapped in an orange sarong.

Your fingers said good-bye, a little wiggle.

There were no more words.

φ

Where did it start?

Fourteen years ago in the Mongolian valleys, underneath a pale sun in the cool Central Asian summer sky. That's a country of tiny flowers and long, long horizons, makes Montana look busy-crowded as Hong Kong. You can breathe air so fresh it might have just left God's lungs, eat the most atrocious food known to man, and walk your nights away under a billion brilliant stars.

That's where I met Elaine, on that trip. Her hair was long, dark and beautiful. She had a quick smile and one of those predatory Mediterranean noses that could make her look like a falcon at rest. She was happy to be there with a pack of half-nutty late-twenty-somethings, though she had fourteen years on us. Dave had brought her, hoping to find that elusive click with her somewhere on the long flight over the Pacific, in the shops of Nathan Road in Hong Kong, at Peking duck in a side street in Beijing, or in a fire-warmed yurt holding off the Central Asian summer chill.

He hasn't talked to me since. Fourteen years.

Me, I've never made a damned decision in my life. Drifted into college, into career, into marriage and out of it again, over the ocean to Mongolia, into Elaine.

I'm not good at signals. Never have been, though I can read yours now, it seems.

Couldn't read Elaine's, either, until she took matters — and me — into her own hands.

After that was romance, dating, a short slide into marriage and time together. Me in marketing, her in, well, marriage. What Elaine wanted was not to work, to be with someone she liked and loved, to have a simpler life filled with more complex things.

There's good money in marketing, or at least there was before the tech bubble burst.

I was fine. She took care of me, I paid the bills. So we didn't hug so much. So she dodged sex.

It was okay.

Life was easy.

Life didn't stay easy. We decided to have a kid. Miscarried twice. Went bankrupt over a bad real estate deal back in Massachusetts. Adopted Ariadne. All the things that happen to people.

Eleven years, babe, eleven years of marriage, up and down. Six years of Ariadne, up, down, upside-down and sideways. Kids will do that. I know you know that, what with your own daughter.

How do you build a marriage? With love. Patience. Time and tact.

How do you build love? With practice.

But the hormones can leach away, to be replaced by the paired fossils of habit and affection. Fire can't burn an entire lifetime. Look at anyone's parents. Old, comfortable, separate beds and support hose and doctor's appointments.

Who burns bright forever?

Who gets to try?

253

Jay Lake

✦

Where did it end?

Leaving your place with my head in a whirl and my heart in a knot. Car to the airport, hassle through the check-in lines and the chirpy smiles of the Alaska Airlines counter girls, the headache reek of jet fuel in the back of an MD-80—"no, sir, that smell is normal," *like hell, lady, I fly a couple dozen times a year and never smell Jet A inside the fuselage* –shitty bathrooms in-flight with sticky floors while the easy endless clouds stretch outside the window, Heaven at thirty thousand feet, a storm-tossed sea afoam without tides or traps.

I could climb those clouds and dive into them, sometimes, I think watching the airplane's shadow flicker over them.

What would it take for me to come back to you right then, I wondered? Just to turn back at the airport, catch the next flight south, never go home.

With no words between us, no understanding save some form of mild regret, with the sense that we shouldn't have gone even the little distance we did between us, I still began to make a decision.

The first damned decision I've ever made in my life, for truth.

✦

You were there in San Francisco, at the big art show with the trade press and all the heavy names, some with entourages, others moody and alone in snakeskin tuxedos or whalebone corsets revealing their tattoos. That was where the trouble in my heart happened, though not where it started. We'd been at a dozen conferences, art shows, retreats together over the past few years, you and I. Ever since I'd first hit the circuit.

Not alone together, mind you, not the pressure of hand on hand in the street-lit night. Together in crowds, rather, until we knew

254

each other well enough to hug in bars, to crack smutty jokes at our mutual expense, to share a single chair when possible—and sometimes when not even needful. Together enough to see each other's agendas, each other's ambitions, each other's moves.

You tell me that the reason women like me is that I give them my full attention.

Elaine says I don't pay enough attention.

You tell me I'm funny.

Elaine tells me to stop clowning around.

You like me.

Elaine finds me exasperating.

You see where my art is going, what it can be.

Elaine doesn't have time to look at it.

The art which burns inside me, the brightness, the holy fire, is in your eyes.

At home I set off the smoke detectors in my wife's soul.

✟

Patience. Time and tact. Marriage is a settling in together, two plants in one pot. With Elaine and me, that pot includes a wild, leggy sprig bolting toward the sun.

But plants don't stand up one day and wander off in search of a distant glint. Plants stay put, play the game they were dealt in to, offer leaves and seeds and fruit and grow to fill their pots.

The lives of plants don't catch fire.

✟

"Jim, can you do something with Ariadne Saturday? I've got to finish up those festival projects over at the school."

"Sure. Hey kid, want to go to the zoo?"

"Daddy! Can Tyler come, too?"

Jay Lake

"We'll have to ask his Mummy and Daddy."

✛

"Jim, it's my Mom...Gary says she's had a heart attack."
"When do we leave?"
"She's already dead. My God, she's dead."
"Okay, sweetie. Okay, I'll call work then get the luggage out."

✛

"Jim..."
She looks terrible coming out of surgery. They've wrapped her, a mummy without the preliminary funerary rites, and there's a smile on her face which would shatter anyone.
"You're okay, sweetie."
"The baby's gone."
"I know."
"The baby's gone."

✛

We got married to a jazz band and a French dinner, in a little restaurant back in Massachusetts. She was happy, I was dazed, everyone had a good time.

We never did have sex on our honeymoon.

✛

We had our first date in Hong Kong, dinner down in Tsim Tsa Hsui, then a late night in a big old park until we were locked in and had to climb a wall to get out. Some kissing, some giggling.

256

✤

Maybe the end was built into the beginning. Maybe all things carry the seeds of their own completion within their secret hearts, like girl-children born with full ovaries, so that each mother has also carried her grandchildren to some kind of term. What did I ever decide? To follow a crush? To walk in beauty's shadow a while?

To be cared for. It seemed good, then. Before the holy fire entered my life and set me to blazing.

✤

So here's my decision: whether or not to change the game. Do I follow the flame, or put it out? I'm not leaving my wife for you or anyone. I'm not leaving for any reasons except my own.

But I'd never had room in my heart for someone else before. One at a time. That's always been my rule. It's the way I'm wired. To do anything different would be like asking my heart to beat backwards.

My heart must have left Elaine while I was looking in some other direction.

How the hell did that happen?

Where did it start?

I think I was staring into the holy fire when I saw you.

✤

Ariadne was a year old when we adopted her. Elaine and I flew to China, on an airplane full of tourists and businessmen and foreign exchange students, along with my sister, my mother, my step-mother and my mother-in-law.

Adoption is a deliberate act, fraught with social workers, judges, smiling coordinators and a great deal of cash. No one ever adopts on a whim. The paperwork alone can fill the trunk of your car. The subjects of a criminal investigation don't get as much scrutiny as prospective parents going through that mill.

Everything gets notarized. Then all the notarizations get certified by the Texas Secretary of State. Then all the certified, notarized documents get translated into Chinese. Then all the certified, notarized, translated documents get authenticated by the Chinese consulate in Houston.

Even my birth certificate was six pages long by then.

How much does it take to have a family?

Everything, that's all. And us and our everything flew across the dark Pacific, leaving on Ariadne's first birthday, going to meet a child of our hearts for the first time. A whirlwind of Hong Kong, Beijing, tourist busses and the obligatory trip to the Great Wall, eating duck in the markets and buying silk in the shops, then off to Nan Chang and our future.

The kids were due one afternoon, on a bus from Nan Feng. No, we couldn't go there. There was flooding. Cholera. Bandits. Whispers, nods, silent hours in the carpeted hallways of a hotel inhabited mostly by expatriate Ford employees and bewildered German businessmen.

The nannies finally spilled from the elevator in a scattering of bright polyester shirts and nervous, I-don't-speak-English smiles, each with a tiny child in their arms. At one year and four days, Ariadne was the oldest of the group. Our daughter was worried, with a smoldering intensity I never would have believed in a child of that age.

And so began the grand adventure of parenthood and family, which for most people is ushered in by a hour of passion, months of swelling, and a day of pain. Our pregnancy was paperwork, our delivery the bell of an elevator.

But our child was our child. Intense, staring, smelling of the vinegar someone had used to purge the lice from her hair, wearing every piece of clothing that was hers in this world. Hungry. She will go through life hungry, this child, hungry as a girl, hungry as a woman, and always angry because her hunger can never be filled.

✦

Wrap a life around a child. Draw a paycheck. Move to Oregon. Buy a bigger house. Decorate. Plant a garden. Go to work. Fight with kid over all the things parents and children fight over. Live in beauty, an eleven thousand foot volcano out the front porch, topped in glaciers and mist, roses and rhododendrons in the yard. Rooms on rooms in the old Victorian, doors behind doors, high ceilings and tiny bathrooms and a city designed for the way people ought to live.

What's not to love about that life? What's not to love about that child?

What's not to love?

Enter the holy fire, stage left. Enter the burning flame of art, a lifetime hobby, a Sunday afternoon's amusement, suddenly blossoming into holocaust.

And the holy fire brings its own priestesses, its own muses, its own desires and demands and demarcations. The roses will shrivel, the high-ceilinged rooms fall to hushed dust, the cats will cry their thirst while I retreat to the basement and ply my newfound trade, wondering how I fell into this comfortable life and how I can leap out of it now.

Then you, with your silences and your hand in mine and your easy familiarity with all the people and places and issues of my unfolding life, come and show me that a creative life can be a partnership.

Why'd you do that to me?

✦

Home one day, not long after tripping over you. Not long after facing the fire. Not long after realizing that it was art or family, family or art, but something had to give and be given up.

Wherever you wind up in my life—and, lover, partner, distant memory—you have been the catalyst. Holding hands in the sodium-vapor lights is one thing. Burning down a marriage is something else entirely.

Elaine was outside, doing something with roses. I could hear the snip of her shears through the window. Her friend Lynette was in the kitchen, looking sour.

"Hey." I kind of liked Lynette. She was cute, English, always had a funny-testy relationship with me, but her divorce was making her weird. She left her husband for another woman who chickened out on the deal. After going nuclear on a restraining order—purely for the sake of her pride, rather than any real or reasonably imagined danger from her pediatrician husband—there won't be any returning to the way things used to be in her life.

"Hey yourself, buster."

Her kid with the unpronounceable Welsh name was crawling around on the kitchen tile. I leaned down to say hi, drew tears. Typical.

"Something wrong?" I asked, once that crisis was settled.

"You've got a lot to answer for."

Lynette didn't know the half of it. Even though I was the one preparing to leave, reflex took over. "What are you talking about."

"That trip to San Francisco. You had an affair. Elaine's just sick about it."

It just slipped out of me: "No, I didn't have an affair. But I could have."

"You *bastard*."

Which was rich, coming from her. I shrugged. "I didn't."

"She knows something's wrong. What are you going to tell her? When?"

Now, I thought. It's over and she doesn't know. But she must, or Lynette wouldn't be in my kitchen, doing Elaine's dirty work.

We stared at each other as the sound of pruning shears clicked over and over again outside the kitchen window, the reek of bruised roses an echo of your perfume.

☦

But I hadn't told, not yet. I hadn't said. I hadn't jumped off the cliff, drank the Kool-Aid, slammed into the brick wall.

All I needed to do was open my mouth.

All I needed to do was say what had been in my mind in the weeks since the San Francisco show.

All I needed to do was tell Elaine that I was following the holy fire, that I wanted to be with you, not her, that I wanted to close the door on eleven years of marriage and our only daughter in a few sentences, that I wanted to set fire to all our lives in the name of art and a little hand-holding in the sodium-vapor light of a warm San Francisco night.

If I didn't open my mouth, if I slowed down and made nice, if I backed out of the weeks of surly silence, evening absences over wine with friends, long letters unsent to you, if I let all that drop, could I mend things?

Certainly.

Elaine was terrified of being alone, being poor, raising Ariadne by herself.

What was I terrified of?

Moving forward. Making a damned decision for the first time in my life, reshaping my existence in the name of a dream and for the hope of a woman.

What was I terrified of?

All the endless, lifelong consequences of burning down my life, cutting my child's household in half, inciting my wife to

261

desperation and depression.

What was I terrified of?

The same happy life, sinking quietly into contented age. It would easy enough to let go of the art and leave peacefully. The scars would heal.

If I hadn't tripped over you, I might never have found my own reasons without some of yours in my hand.

Liar.

But I didn't know if they were good enough.

Leave. Stay.

Follow the holy fire. Pour water on the ashes.

Set fire to Elaine's life, and Ariadne's. Or douse my own.

Right hand at the wrong time, I'd told you. Fold the hand, or change the game.

My call.

☦

"Well, buster?" said Lynette. Proxy for my wife, whose shears were snipping slower and slower.

The baby fussed a little as one of those moments of fintesimal time settled on me. Whatever I said here and now, I had to follow those words up now, and for the rest of my days.

"I..." The words swam in my mouth, fish working against the running tide of my life. "I'm moving out."

Lynette gasped. Even the baby was silent. Everything was silent for a moment. "You never--" she began, then stopped.

"That's right," I said. "I never."

I went outside to break a decade's worth of promises. The yard was littered with rose blossoms, each cane cropped down to pale, bleeding stub, color carpeting my feet in tide of rainbow tears. Elaine's shears lay in her hat along with her gloves, just below the kitchen window.

The River Knows Its Own

"Sweetie?" I said.

Somewhere nearby, Ariadne burst into tears.

I hope like hell you answer the phone when I call.

About the Author

Jay Lake lives and works in Portland, Oregon, within sight of an 11,000 foot volcano. He is the author of over two hundred short stories, four collections, and a chapbook, along with novels from Tor Books, Night Shade Books and Fairwood Press

In 2004, Jay won the John W. Campbell Award for Best New Writer. He has also been a Hugo nominee for his short fiction and a three-time World Fantasy Award nominee for his editing.

Jay maintains a Web site at *http://www.jlake.com/* and a blog at *http://jaylake.livejournal.com/*

Other Works by Jay Lake

Trial of Flowers

Night Shade Books

(*http://www.nightshadebooks.com*)

A decadent urban fantasy in the tradition of K.J. Bishop's *The Etched City*, China Mieville's *Perdido Street Station* and Jeff Vandermeer's *City of Saints and Madmen*.

Rocket Science

Fairwood Press

(*http://www.fairwoodpress.com*)

Vernon Dunham's friend Floyd Bellamy has returned to Augusta, Kansas after serving in World War II, but he hasn't come back empty-handed: he's stolen a super-secret aircraft right from under the Germans. Vernon doesn't think it's your ordinary run-of-the-mill aircraft. For one thing, it's been buried under the Arctic ice for hundreds of years. When it actually starts talking to him, he realizes it doesn't belong in Kansas — or anywhere on Earth.

The problem is, a lot of folks know about the ship and are out to get it, including the Nazis, the U.S. Army — and that's just for starters. Vernon has to figure out how to communicate with the ship and unravel its secrets before everyone catches up with him. If he ends up dead, and the ship falls into the wrong hands, it won't take a rocket scientist to predict the fate of humanity.

Mainspring

TOR Books

(*http://www.tor.com*)

Set on a clockwork Earth, Mainspring combines familiar elements of quest fantasy and steampunk science fiction with an innovative world – Ringworld for fantasy readers.

Greetings From Lake Wu

Wheatland Press

(*http://www.wheatlandpress.com*)

The first short fiction collection. Illustrations by Hugo Award-winning artist Frank Wu.

American Sorrows

Wheatland Press

(*http://www.wheatlandpress.com*)

Four novellas, including the Hugo-nominated "Into the Gardens of Sweet Night."

Available from these fine independent booksellers:

Borderlands Books

866 Valencia St.

San Francisco, CA 94110

http://www.borderlands-books.com

Ziesing Books

POB 76

Shingletown, CA 96088

http://www.ziesingbooks.com

DreamHaven Books

912 W. Lake St.

Minneapolis, MN 55408

http://www.dreamhavenbooks.com

CPSIA information can be obtained at www.ICGtesting.com
Printed in the USA
BVOW01s0212020614

355141BV00001B/36/P

9 780975 590393